The Independent Bookworm

ABOUT THE BOOK

In 2002 ADR, the jewel of the southern empire is the city of Cryssigens, where life is an unending carnival of display, while intrigue brews beneath the surface. Nobles, guilds and House Cups scheme with and against each other, even in the best of times. But civil war stripped the city of its Overlord, and now factions emerge daring all in a bid to succeed to the throne.

One of the leading lights of Cryssigensian society is W'starrah Altieri, the Lavender Lady, high-ranking priestess of the sect of Argens Stargazer; while others see only her dazzling beauty her eyes are filled with foreknowledge of the future. She willingly risks life and reputation to save her city, but juggling visions, rivals, suitors and the occasional assassin pushes the real world further from her grasp. Who could expect that in the midst of this she would meet the promised love of her life, or foresee that he too is doomed?

"Perilous Embraces" is the third book in the Shards of Light saga set in the Lands of Hope. It is highly recommended that you read "The Ring and the Flag" and "Fencing Reputation" first.

ABOUT THE AUTHOR

Will Hahn has been in love with heroic tales since age four, when his father read him the Lays of Ancient Rome and the Tales of King Arthur. He taught Ancient-Medieval History for years, but the line between this world and others has always been thin. The far reaches of fantasy, like the distant past, still bring him face to face with people like us, who have choices to make.

Will has written about the Lands of Hope since his college days (which by now are also part of ancient history). He chronicled the adventures of Solmn Judgement dilligently in two tomes of over 1000 pages each (it's now being published as an eBook series and in print) and his Shards of Light series, a sword and sorcery story. He also chronicled stand alone stories like "The Plane of Dreams" or "Three Minutes to Midnight." More of Will's tales of Hope are available at several online retailers.

Find out more on his website: www.WilliamLHahn.com

PERILOUS EMBRACES

Shards of Light
Volume III

William L. Hahn

Perilous Embraces, Shards of Light III
published by the Independent Bookworm, USA und D
this book is also available as eBook at various retailers

If you find typos or formatting problems in the book, please contact
the publisher (www.IndependentBookworm.de).

printed On-Demand Publishing LLC, 100 Enterprise Way, Suite A200,
Scotts Valley, CA 95066, USA, www.createspace.com

ISBN-13 978-3-95681-096-1

Find more information on the publisher's website:
http://www.IndependentBookworm.de

For Dorie,
The most beautiful woman in the kingdom
And my future.

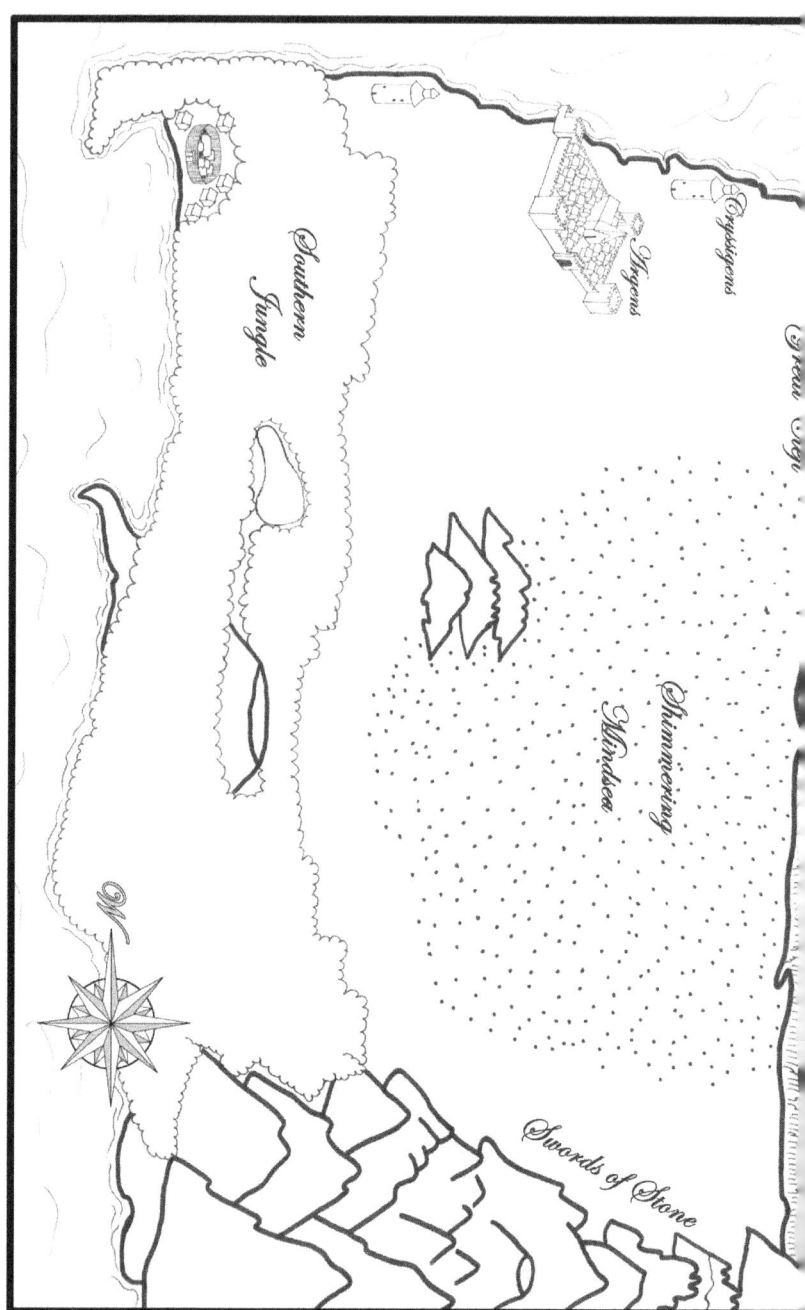

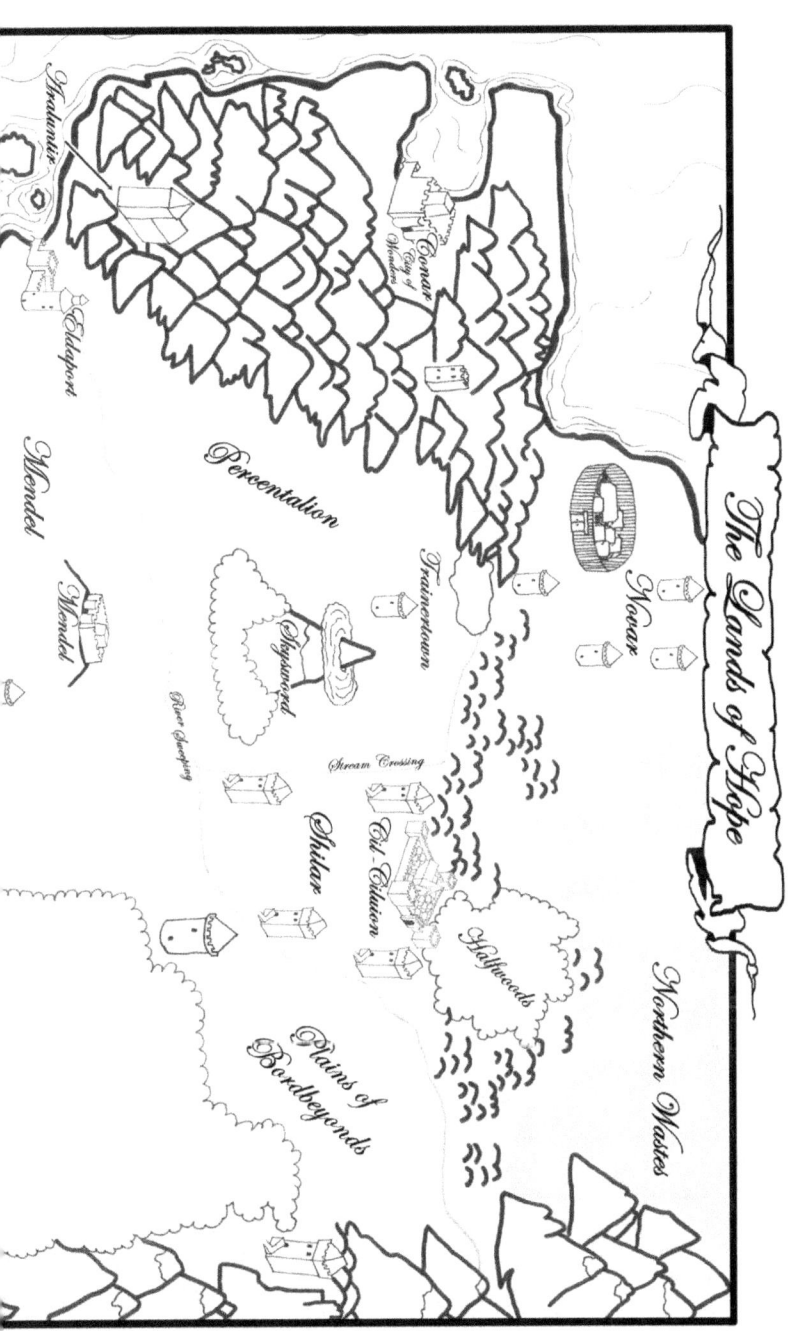

Cast of Characters in Order of Appearance

Perilous Embraces is set in the North Mark of the Argensian Empire, settled by Elves centuries ago and still dominated by that race. Every character is Elven unless otherwise noted.

W'starrah Altieri	also called Heaven's Eye, Myster, High Priestess, "Star", and Lavender Lady, prophetess and famed beauty of Cryssigens, Purple House leader
Chaktha	human, W'starrah's Nubian bodyguard
Welles	jeweler commissioned by W'starrah
Ellesmera	also called Elle, W'starrah's estranged daughter who has left the city
Myster Tanar'h	High Heart of the Stargazer church in Cryssigens, rival to W'starrah
Devout Teretheny	monk of Sinter
Curate Ekaterinye	also called Kat, Stargazer preacher, school-teacher, and W'starrah's friend
Et'run	young knight and devotee of the Red House, leads the city cavalry in battle
Vosur	Curate and Preacher of the Cryssian temple
Myster Cruryn	leader of the Cryssian temple
Minstrel Tambouri Shai	beautiful singer in Cryssigens
Cup Carnad Mias	head of Red House in Cryssigens
Captain Justin Thyme	Argensian officer on a mission to prevent war
Patriarch Z'kammet Hammer	leader of the church of Argens Hope-forger in Cryssigens
Emperor Yula	dwarf, also called the First or Usurper, ruler of the Argensian Empire
Fire Grip Gaspar Heugen	virtual regent and leading member of the Blue House in Cryssigens
Overlord D'stagnon Kreel	former Mark of the North, slain by Yula in 2001 ADR

Overlord Kreelon Kreel	son of Kreel, died soon after
Baron Pa'u Breret'n	Baron of Cesmir, allied to the Red House
Baron Soln Ge'para	Baron of Gaden, allied to the Blue House
Dekentar M'nesa Zetee	noble-son enrolled in the Imperial Army
Baron (of Blood) Voev T'yr	Baron of Tralmachia
Jal'i	Stargazer guard loyal to Tanar'h
Tamess	Stargazer guard loyal to Tanar'h
Eline	first wife of Tanar'h
Bereshutha	second wife of Tanar'h
May'stra	third wife of Tanar'h, baker for the temple
Qellen	armorer
Guildsman Farnh'y	glassblower partial to the Red House
Guildsman Trothfer	glassblower partial to the Red House
Sanhim	human, Bedou-uu tribesman, Guard of Devout Teretheny, taller
Elehar	human, Bedou-uu tribesman, Guard of Devout Teretheny, shorter
Oshuwen	mage working with Welles
Aumir'y	also called Mirry, noblewoman and friend of W'starrah, married to J'seff'n
J'seff'n	nobleman and friend of W'starrah, married to Aumir'y
Highforge Mart'l'n Ecclese	historic leader who crafted the Brow of the Ecclesiast
Myster Kama	human, also called Exemplar, Telholian preacher formerly with the Candidates
Step-Marchess Citari Kreel	widow of former Mark Kreel
Morinack	halfling, the Emperor's Hand and former member of the Candidates

PERILOUS EMBRACES

The Empire of Argens 2002 ADR

Every step of the way home from the arena to your temple is strewn with chaos. People mill in the streets, telling each other of the coronation delayed, as if they all hadn't been there. They voice fear and guesses, worry aloud about doom, shout their arguments, and call to passing leaders for guidance. You love it. The other clerics huddle in their coaches with doors slammed tight, but you draw the litter-curtains fully back. Clamor washes the ears, a soothing bath. When people need you, it feeds the fire within.

The Stargazer entourage around you babbles with the crowd, everyone asking questions and no one waiting for a reply. Remember them all, these are good questions. Half the temple contingent has splintered off by the time the outer grounds come in view—away to confer with their allies in the guilds, with captains in the City Guards and curates among the rival temples. Astor's luck to them, there will be no answers there. Lack of confidence was never your problem: I gave you that.

The citizen-mob clogs all corners and cross-streets right to the outer temple walls—some grumbling, many shouting, but most choosing to celebrate anyway. They've got the right idea, and you smile on them without speaking as they toast and salute you. You know what W'starrah Altieri's smile is worth, to folks worried about the future. Let them drink if they choose, laugh if they can; let them continue to believe that all will be well, now their leaders' delicately balanced plan lies in ruins.

The vote for a new Mark has been put off, by the ancient formula and against all expectation. Just two months, amid all that lies before us? Might as well try to build another Cryssigens with your bare hands in ten weeks' time. Still, what an entrance the Emperor's man made. He is the stooge, you have been told, the cocksure, set-up nobleman sent to flush the empire's enemies from cover. But at first he did not act the part. There was something honest, honorable about this captain, steel beneath the sneer. You think of him, and the monster he rode in on; your inner flame banks even higher.

Within the temple grounds, a receiving line has formed on the lane leading to your tower; guilders and priests eager to confer, to petition, and some just to see. They arrange themselves, each knowing their rank, with the highest nearer the door. The litter could pass by any or all, but Chaktha knows your preferences without having to hear. He stops the bearers and hands you down to start among the least, as the faraway prelates cluck with impatience.

With your feet on the path, your head barely reaches his ebon chest.

"Here already?" you protest, and the waiting crowd laughs, watching your every move as always. The men gaze with desire and awe, the women with a more studied attention. Tonight, as you decide how to save this city's future, they will crowd the inns and speak knowingly of a smile from the Stargazer high priestess, the scent of jasmine and the reassurance you left behind. And this is as it should be—let them remember, and hope they have a part to play. They do; though you cannot see it all yet, you believe in the vision as firmly as ever. With that smile, scent, and warm words you share it.

"Guilder Evann, so wonderful that you should attend on me." The happy weaver is dazzled as always, and stutters his habitual offer of assistance. You nod and smile to him, thanking without accepting—the man wears too much Green to be taken up without cause. Later, perhaps, if you need the votes.

"Priestess," a jeweler greets you with a bow and your heart flutters a bit, for with this little genius you had business.

"My dear Welles, thank you for coming."

"My task is done, lady," he replies with a proud smile, opening the empty box to indicate the gem has been crafted and set. "It works," He claims with pride, then amends, "Ahm, works well with the décor, I mean."

You place one hand on his Orange tunic in thanks, your purple sleeve draping there in a strong contrast, then slip a silver token into his palm. His eyes go wide as walnuts at this gift—his commission was paid in advance—and your delighted laughter pleases him nearly as well. With a silver token of the Stargazers, a citizen may visit and take company with any of the lesser preachers. Inspiring talk, his future read if he wishes, and then of course pleasure, if he dares. Three months' worth of commissions for a jeweler in the silver token.

Welles bows again, as you continue up the line. The others fume by the door. Let them tsk—another quarter-hour subtracted by this delay will not mean the ruin of any plan worth making.

After all, what's to be done, in two months or two decades? Negotiate the trickiest alliance of the past four hundred years, save the city and choose the next ruler of the North Mark. The quick vote, the compromise leading to war, was doomed when the Emperor's man landed atop the arena table. Now every faction will fall back to their coverts and plot, none with the needed majority of votes. No person in the Lands could hope to succeed. And you have no one else to blame but yourself.

Except it was never up to you, the thought comes as you thank and smile and work your way toward home. Argens will guide as he always has, and just thinking about the obstacles The First will overcome sets your middle kindling again. It's the same fire that has always driven you, an eternal flame heating your core and feeding on your being.

You recall the day Argens first spoke to you, just eleven years old but your vision saved that sailor's life and probably all his crew with him. He was so grateful, good man, just to have the prophecy. The other priests were angry at first, but then feared to interrupt the Son of the Sun as he spoke through the living child before them.

After that, you grew up in less than a year: a tower of your own by age twelve. Fame settles so easily when it's earned.

The clamor of your clients fades away and you're eleven again—younger than Ellesmera, dear thing—standing there in the main chamber with a circle of elders pulled back around you. Declaiming his message, your voice not sounding your own, the words forgotten until a scribe showed you later. Just a sailor—not the captain or mate, one crewman of an enormous galleon, who thought to stop and ask before setting sail. All the high priests—there stands Tanar'h among them, looking so strong and virile, impatient to start the service, yet watching you with wonder and disbelief as you utter the prophecy. And the storm that evening, so strong it broke pieces of the Cryss Cliff into the sea...

"So good of you to find the time," he said—no wait, those were not Tanar'h's words that day. The self-same man, speaking now, he cuts the string and drops you back into the present. You are grown, you stand at the door of your tower-home; Chaktha's looming frame by your side as ever. Behind you the broken remnants of the receiving line scatter to other haunts, well satisfied with whatever it was you said to them.

"Has everyone gone so soon?" you protest, while the setting sun winks warmth through the jasmine branches outside the portal. Only Tanar'h is the same, his face and form as manly and urgent as it was then, the ageless elf who led this temple for three decades. Until you. He stands now beside a tall guest in brown robes, official temple business that may not wait in courtyards. He will enter your tower, he must. But only the lower chamber, tonight; you smile engagingly at him knowing he must mask his deepest desire in the presence of others.

One full breath—worth the time just to see him fidget—and you carry the savor of those sunset-tinged blossoms while gesturing your impatient rival and his cloaked companion within. Chaktha closes the thick mahogany door behind you, his glare at Tanar'h neither missed nor minded.

"I thank you, High Heart, for your patience," you say, motioning to seats which neither man takes. The bottom chamber is beautifully appointed with cushions, hangings, and wine that you pour generously.

14

Everything here, down to the vintage, blends red with blue to your satisfaction. No need to hide your House Color here, within your own home.

Tanar'h yields to his guest, who silently refuses the offered wine, before taking a cup for himself. "You have ever walked your own path, Heaven's Eye," he says tightly, "refusing to take appointments as the other curates here. Soon, your day will be filled with gapers and droolers from dawn to dusk." He manages to keep his eyes above your chest, and you return the courtesy. But there's nothing unattractive about his intense, punching eyes; standing a step closer to you with his back partly to the guest, you can feel his desire emanating from steel shoulders and tensed knuckles. It seems a shame, or even a dishonor, to tease him as you do. Part of you isn't teasing—coupling with Tanar'h would be the joy of a year, at least.

"I can only serve as my vision guides me. Every suppliant deserves a personal hearing, and the time is now, for each of them. A preacher may make exception only for the token." And not for silver tokens, nor gold as you both well know.

Tanar'h nearly snarls at this, but masters himself enough to recall his business.

"I am privileged to introduce our guest, the Devout Teretheny, from Sinter. Devout, the Heaven's Eye of Cryssigens, W'starrah Altieri."

Sensing his ascetic training, you curtsy deeply with a hand near your sternum to mask the view most would desire. The tall, spare man is robed from top to toe in dusty brown, but now pulls down the face-cloth to reveal an angular, wind-dried face as he bows in turn. When he rises, you catch just a glimpse of something jewel-bright on his neck, tightly clasped and ornate. That seems irregular, but his words deny you the chance to concentrate.

"A privilege, sister." His voice is dry and sharp like a Mindsea wind. "I am told your preaching is among the best in the city, and am eager to hear you declaim your faith before the many. Indeed, this is the most honest faith, the sort a man would not conceal from anyone." You smile but don't reply, taken aback by the fire that burns in him. At the arena, you had hardly noticed—

15

Tanar'h presses on. "You saw another public declaration of sorts today, I understand." Only then you realize, he was not in attendance during the abortive voting.

"You knew?"

He smiles. "You are not the only seer among us, W'starrah. I had—indications, let us say, that today would be for nothing."

You are impressed, and toast him to cover it. Tanar'h's faith has always been sincere, but you never knew him to glimpse the future. Now, about something so important—you may have to reconsider his suit.

But before he can continue, the monk speaks.

"Each man—each of us, should aspire to waste no more time and effort, when the next chance to save this Mark could be its last." The Devout's tone is driven; he compliments you by inclusion and commands your obedience in the same breath. There is fire in him, without question, more even than in Tanar'h, but a strange, alien heat. You cannot remember a time someone simply speaking had made you afraid. Should you join his unknown cause, or seek an excuse to flee the room?

"The Emperor's man," you manage to sound casual, "probably saved us from a war today." A few strides to one side, letting your roaming gaze and loose walk speak of nonchalance, as you gauge their reaction. Neither man likes the truth of it—so typical, to value independence over peace. The neat plan, to elect that fop of a Cliff Grip and likely be in arms before the end of the Dolphin, was now overturned. That boy could never win a vote of a truly loyal majority; the consensus he'd have taken was born of compromise. You doubt he would have lived out the decade, even had the rebellion succeeded. And your contacts in Argens assure you, it could not.

"The lad would have united us," Tanar'h insists a bit crossly, "giving us time to weld the guilds, the Houses and the people to him more firmly. You could have helped us, W'starrah, these past days, more than you did."

You shrug and move back to more familiar ground, fencing with your rival. "Et'run lacks any grace or moderation, Tanar'h. Let him command his cavalry, eager guard dog is the job for him. We're well rid of his suit, I think. Let us spend time in prayer to the Stargazer, that he might reveal—"

"All is revealed," Teretheny interrupts heavily, "to those marked with heaven's favor." In two strides, he closes the distance and stands now with his long nose practically in your hair. You meet his eyes and there is a whirl in his pupils like a sandstorm, all movement, no hesitation. The monk is trying to search you somehow, and his abrupt intrusion is not merely corporeal. The fire within licks and tangles with another flame, fed by less wholesome fuel.

You step back, strangling a curse at the sign of weakness, and throw out a laugh to cover. "If you ask me the future of the Mark, dear Devout, I must confess that Argens has hardly been so specific with me yet."

"Not who, then when?" he persists, and you can hardly believe his abrupt, uncouth behavior. Surely, a rural anchorite with no manners would act this way. But there is more here.

"When? Before the ides of the Dragon, assuredly, when the second vote is due. In eight of the next ten weeks, perhaps six. By then all will see the matter decided." A half-lie, the best you can do under pressure. It seems oddly to satisfy the ascetic and he returns his hands to his sleeves.

Tanar'h lets out a breath, obviously also surprised and you sense almost afraid—for you? His guest must be a chore indeed. "At all events, let us settle the preaching-order for the weeks ahead, and what message we will give—"

"I must retire to my quarters now," Teretheny interrupts again, like a human would. Tanar'h, perturbed but obedient, snaps off in mid-sentence and bows his acquiescence.

"Take the inner corridor," you invite them, opening the door next to the stairs circling up, "it leads straight back to the main chapel and dormitories. Then too," you can't resist adding, "you can avoid any petitioners outside."

The monk strides through without another word or backwards glance; he acts oddly accustomed to command for an ascetic. Tanar'h pauses a moment, to gaze intently at you and once at the stairs. How often has he been here and not seen the bedroom, poor man. You feel real empathy as he turns away, tinged with amusement and a slight aftertaste of regret as you close the door. Such a splendid frame, and his passion for you is authentic.

"Star!" the lovely voice wafts down, "Star, right away, hurry!" Poor Kat, you think ascending the wooden stair to your personal quarters. So wise, but like most others even in this temple, lacking the comfort Argens sends to you. It must be awful, to always feel that time is short.

The ebonwood treads are thick and quiet, and after seven steps the reception room is out of sight. You are a child again, barely conscious and being carried here for the first time: you hear the preachers murmur, amazed at your gift of prophecy. The last Heaven's Eye had died years previously, and none replaced her; a sign, they whispered thinking you could not hear them.

You spot the light line of a nail-scratch and smile to gaze again on it. More than a decade ago, only you and Elle's father know what day that came to be there, and the remarkable manner how. Dear child, conceived in love if you can give her no other gift. His death brought more pain than Argens had led you to believe. But he was not the love of your life, still to come.

You see again a future day when armored men will fight on these treads, hot blood spilled on black wood, the sound of your lover shouting commands. He is the one Argens has promised will come, your life's love—but whether he is attacking this tower or defending, you cannot see through the press of bodies, the flickering shadows of things on fire. His face is blocked by helm and shadow, only his voice comes through to you, as always. A voice to give orders, from a mind that has obeyed them. A strangely familiar voice, one you heard before perhaps, outside the visions. The preachers whisper of your gift, your dead husband laughs and pulls you close—steel clashes and fires burn around you as well as within.

Kat brings you home. She always does.

"Star! Will you stand around all night?" There she is, mock-angry with her delicate hand on the rail and the light of your upper chambers framing a tiny face beneath a corona of angelic, snowy hair. No matter how far your spirit roams, the teacher brings you back to class. It is the night of the Dolphin-Ides, 2002 ADR. You laugh and run up the last steps to hug her tight, like a sister long unseen. Her embrace restores you—men so seldom dare to touch, poor things, and it is harder for them to do correctly.

"My dear, so many to speak with, I am sorry, what remains ahead of us?" Only she can tell you the schedule, the tasks to do before they all sleep, dear creatures. Nothing stays in your head, except glimpses of the future and past. Together you pass into the sitting room.

"I have already made arrangements, some of your clients who *urgently* wish to speak with you tomorrow," Kat says, scanning some notes. "They send their apologies not to attend on you now—no doubt visiting other allies first, trying to drum up votes and bring you their schemes. I heard about the scene in the arena—a *monster*, what a fright! And it landed on *top* of you, everyone says."

You laugh, "Hardly that. Several steps away, I should guess. Besides, I think perhaps the rider was the more dangerous of the two. You should have seen him, Kat, facing down Et'run in front of us all."

You recall again the Argensian Captain's voice and something stirs the embers deep within. You catch sight of an answering glint in the belt of the life-size statue to Argens; there is the buckle-gem Welles set for you, such an unusual stone. Larger than your palm, beautifully faceted and bright orange—the jeweler's choice of course! But clearer than quartz; where did he—

"Preacher Altieri!" Kat has been speaking about appointments and you, ungrateful woman, were again paying no attention. "Tomorrow, perhaps can wait, but you have an *imminent* meeting with Carnad *Mias* in *moments*!" Her tiny frame so wrought with worry; you have to laugh, and to hug her again until she joins you.

"I have not forgotten him, my dear."

"Far from it, and I worry," Kat is too polite to voice her fears, but you know. She suspects you will fall for the Red House Cup, who desires you, and she must continue to believe that.

"But before he arrives," Kat rushes on past her bitten lower lip, "you must hear the news from the cloth guilds, and the Cryss temple. *He* will know it, and you cannot afford to let him take—to give him any *advantage*." She returns to her notes as she reads out names and positions, things to know in advance before negotiating with one of the wealthiest men alive. Useful things, to those who don't already see the future.

Kat is priceless and you love that attention to detail marking the teacher, she who instructed you before your rise to full rank. Perhaps she taught Tanar'h as well. Today you could not get dressed without her, would forget to eat. But her age shows, and the Stargazers cannot afford to hold her up to public position—no matter how beautiful she still is, she will support and inform and remain who she has always been, whatever those sparse wrinkles may show.

You can see her face in concentration as she reads from her notes. She hopes that politics is all you talk about, and that trickling tear means she doubts such hopes will be realized. How you wish you could hold her, and let her know that Mias is not fated for your heart. Playing this double-sided game brings misery to many, you realize. But Argens commands—a fire burns and you must stand at its center.

"The tanners have made known their willingness to work with you—the usual compensations—but the vote goes to Et'run unless you say. The barrelmakers are simply *desperate* for more pine, they appeal to everyone—" Your eye drifts back to the gem, and the temptation to know whether it works becomes too great. Behind her back you slip into the inner bedroom and push the door closed, blocking the sound.

The breeze through the open window guides you to the rear corner, where stands a small statuette, in imitation of the one outside. With a tingle of fear you lay your hand on it and the voice of your friend comes through clearly.

"Curate Vosur from the Cryssian temple—seems a *lad* to me—carried word that they wish the privilege of your company, and he emphasized in an *official* capacity. As if they could wield the clout to win a token for you! But it seems clear the old man Cruryn wishes to feel you out—in an *official* capacity of course…"

It works! Now, if only you can engage your scheme, pull Mias and his closest circle into the outer room for a meeting or two. Of course, it will all have to look like a party, and some of your acolytes will probably need to answer a handful of silver tokens before it's all done. Your reputation is already a ruin with the conservative set in the city, but that cannot be helped. The information Mias shares, while you gracefully retire here to "freshen up", could be the key to unlocking this conspiracy. The halfling in Argens, the Emperor's companion, will be pleased, not that you care a bit what he wants. But when he sought an agent to serve as contact for the secret man they were sending, you volunteered to serve the turn. Now you can keep an eye in all directions, and whatever Argens brings you will be in the center when the flame of destiny breaks free.

Her voice continues, "The *singer* Tambouri Shai was here, with a stone she says comes from this Feldspar fellow you wanted to speak with. I left it in your jewel-box." You flip open the lid and there it is, a small mottled-red-brown gem lying next to the plain iron ax-symbol ring the Emperor's halfling gave you. You feel the gem's flat bottom with a number on it and the inner fire stokes again. Should the Stealthic come, you must persuade him to find the Brow. With it, you can certainly sway men like Mias, Hammer and Heugen. Whomever Argens has chosen—and why not you?

"Star!" the voice calls out in frustration loud enough to be heard through the door. "How long have you been ignoring me?"

You glide back in all smiles. "Not to worry, mother Dove. Cruryn wishes to feel me, in some way, I heard you." Her jaw drops open and you both laugh-- she thinking you must have had a vision, and you because she's not far wrong. "Remember to reward the bard, dear Kat, her contact will prove very useful."

"You have always been too much the Ferret, Heaven's Eye," she scolds, "always drawn to bright and dangerous things, too curious, too impatient to sit still and *listen*." She draws you to a seat with mock-force, and you comply.

"Say the Salamander, rather, dear teacher," you throw arms out and lean back luxuriantly. "Bathing in the flame."

"Aye, all unhurt and heedless of harm to those around you." Kat's face flinches, afraid she has said too much. No person you know would insist on her own feelings so little, and you love her for that dedication.

"The Ferret then, if it will please you," you say to soothe her. "But then are you the Bear, always wanting food? Hardly big enough! And you never eat, my dear, though you do feed me." You lay eyes for the first time on the silver tray with a few slices of fruit and cheese, and sample it to please her.

She blushes to be cast in the role of one of her beloved animal tales—perhaps if you curl up on her lap she will recite a few. "The Woodsman rather," she demurs "who brought such a wild thing out of wildness and supplied the honey-cake." She rather likes her own conclusion. You pretend to search the tray in vain for the promised sweetbread, and Kat slaps you in exasperation.

The knock on the stairway door brings you both around. Kat gasps, "He did not even wait to be escorted." She looks at you in shock, and your eagerness shows her the wrong purpose. You are glad, that the Red House Cup takes such liberties, for it means he has hopes of you, and his tongue will be looser.

"Kat, you must trust me," you say in low tones as you urge her to the door. "I do what I must, to serve the Stargazer." Rude, to put it so plainly, but time is short and Kat will always forgive you. She fears nothing, or very little, for your body—you both know well how to take care of yourselves. But your heart—sweet thing, she believes you could be led wrong in love.

She opens, and her red tunic pales by comparison to the crimson barrage adorning the Red House master. Carnad Mias matches her curtsy with a bow and says "Preacher Ekataryinye, good even." After that, he has eyes only for you, and enters looking hungry enough to eat the silver tray. One last glimpse of her worried, elegant face, and the door closes leaving you alone with him.

He moves toward you at once, smoothly and without hurry; when he takes your hand his bow shows respect, his fingers press with delight. And in his eyes—Carnad Mias devours you in an unflinching gaze, always holding your pupils with his, yet dancing with a clear memory of the rest of you.

"Would it be reckless of me to say that I have honestly looked forward to this?" He purrs with joy as if a carnal liaison was already decided, or else that a mere political negotiation with you could feel as good as sex. "As soon as our meeting with the Hopeforger went awry, I knew, you and I would need to—consult again. And Argens burn me, W'starrah, I rejoiced."

"Our meeting with Hammer, and the Fire Grip!" you exclaim in honest recollection. "Was that only last night, it seems a week ago." The Patriarch, Z'kammet Hammer and his fiasco of a summit, no sooner failed than his temple nearly burned down. And you with Kat, not quite slain by assassins as you escaped, saved by Chaktha and a mysterious stranger.

"Two nights previous, milady," Mias corrects with a cocked brow, questioning whether the Stargazer high priestess knows the days of the month. You gesture him to a chair, bring a goblet and sit on the couch nearby, where his sight line is unobstructed.

Mias remains at ease as if this were his thousandth visit; the wealth on the walls, crystal lanterns, the gem-studded statue of Argens behind you, none of it draws his gaze for an instant. He gives you his full attention, with the faultless intensity of an ageless noble. He is older than you—how many years, who can say?

"Now that farce in the arena is over," he says between drinks, "we must determine the next true Mark of Cryssigens, you and I." The exaggeration is a compliment, and from any other person alive it would make for a weak joke. But to Carnad Mias, master of the Red House, the impossible deed is merely a risky gamble.

"Great Cup of Red, Argens will do the choosing," you smile and sip, and his nod is immediate and insincere.

"Of course. And he will tell us first."

The ruby wealth on his fingers, around his neck; the pomade in his solid-oak hair, his jutting jaw, the thickness of his frame all speak to power made flesh. Even his tight-pressed midriff—not so great yet on any other man you would call it a bulge—he nearly bandies it like a weapon. He sits with his spine far back in the chair and shoulders closer to you, occluding his waist a bit so that he looks nearly svelte.

"But, a farce milord Red? You don't mean to say, you knew?"

Mias smiles paternally—first your rival Tanar'h, and now a guild-boss. Has everyone suddenly become a seer?

"Et'run is a boy, barely forty," the Red Cup continues, "He wouldn't have lasted a year. I say the Emperor's man did us a favor breaking up the vote."

"Where did the Yula the First acquire monstrous steeds to outfit his captains?"

"Who can say?" Mias shrugs aggressively, flexing his arms in a way you must notice. "His predecessor had endless wealth, and everyone

23

knows adventurers are spendthrifts in love with treasure. A gryphon to ride would be well within the grasp of that usurping dwarf."

"Now his minion is here, and another vote will be cast," you respond, as something tickles your nerves about this conversation. "The reckoning becomes more complicated. If this captain rallies much support—"

"The reverse, I assure you!" Mias is openly contemptuous as he interrupts. "My dear, find out who this sneering noble jackass favors and I guarantee, that candidate will not reign. His will be the kiss of death—politically, I mean."

He looks out the window a moment; you hear the distant sound of someone below, Mias' guards, trying to engage Chaktha in conversation by the outer door. "No," Mias resumes, "we need only to discern who Hammer wants, and then assemble a coalition to overcome it. I know the Hopeforgers have influence with the Cryssian temple, but they may not be solid."

You nod and think of Kat's message—*bless her!* While he continues you refill his goblet. What a surprise, he's drinking red.

"Of course, the Blue will side with Hammer, and between them are nearly four votes in ten. Among the guilds, though, I am the stronger; no need for boasting, W'starrah, you know this to be true."

You nod again, never a man who wasn't thrilled by his woman's agreement. "But not complete, Cup of Red; my temple, of course, will seek consensus and respect the individual conscience."

"Which is to say, the Stargazer vote will scatter like chaff in a windstorm!" Mias is fully engaged now. "I come here not for your political clout, dear matchless woman, though I'm sure it is substantial. Bring what votes you can," he still assumes your agreement, without naming his candidate, "but give me a greater gift," he pauses to allow the double-meaning to sink in, "and let me gather a harvest of votes to our cause."

He looks you in the eye, and though he has not advanced to the couch you feel the air in here is too close. No question, he wants to bed you, and tonight would be fine with him. But there is more, you must prompt him.

"And in what way can I aid the shifting of a crown?"

"With your name," he answers promptly, "all know that you see the future, Heaven's Eye of Argens. If he has favored you with the name of our next Mark…" he pauses in case you want to enlighten him. You consider telling him about the fire, the vision of flame, death and joy you've seen for a decade, since before the loss of the former Mark Kreel. Your personal prophecy, your hopes of a crown.

Not now, draw him in. Tempt him.

So instead of speaking, you sit, tucking the dress beneath you and crossing your legs so that the topmost thigh is aiming directly at him. Covered tight by the bright purple fabric or exposed by the slit, makes no difference. A man must look—and he does, dropping his gaze deliberately for a long moment.

"Keep your counsel, then. But let it be known that you are with me, and my choice will seem foreordained! If I could have the privilege to escort you, for example, at the theater, in the arena—should they ever allow the games again—and on parade place our litters beside each other. Then let Z'kammet Hammer rail in opposition, as we watch his support bleed away. But I need a place to begin; there are many among the lesser crafts and minor Colors who would send their leaders to me, if I could assure them of your backing."

This is the chance, it cannot go unseized. "Those you court will not come over to you?"

"They will not even meet with me!" Mias shouts in his excitement and frustration. "The only alternative is Hammer and the Blue, Gaspar Heugen, most likely," his voice dripping with distaste of the Fire Grip, leader of the Blue House. "But they shy away, each not wishing to commit first. Cowards, every one of them."

"Then meet here." Your voice stays calm even as you set the hook in the water. Carnad Mias chokes in surprise, his eyes come to you with a shiny alloy of joy and desire, and your heart almost flips.

"Here? Yes," he hisses at the unexpected gift, "I can see ten or even twelve here with comfort, and you—why, you won't even have to say a word, clever woman." He laughs out all his breath in admiration. "It will work, and Hammer can stamp and growl all he wants, but I'll wager none likes his hospitality so well. What think you madam? The smell of half-burnt halls and weak Hopeforger vintage—no wait, if Heugen's among them, probably only tea! Or the boudoir of the

Lavender Lady, and her intoxicating presence, which any man with salt in his blood would murder a brother to attend. Hah! Z'kammet Hammer never expected to be bested by any enemy, much less his most beautiful."

"And then too," he muses more calmly, "Our efforts will not go unrewarded." His gaze comes back to you, and it is clear the Red Cup has many ideas about what constitutes a reward.

"You flatter, Carnad Mias," as the goblets evidently refill themselves, "to think that the Hopeforger Patriarch would class me a foe." You sit and cock the head with interest, knuckles under chin so that one arm emphasizes your cleavage. Again, as a man he has no choice but to look, though he chuckles deeply at your artistry.

He shifts and brings his eyes back to yours, but slowly flexes one hand and lets the muscle-groups show all the way up his arm. Now you have to glance. Feeling his phantom-grip tingle on your leg, you nearly miss what he says as he leans forward and speaks low.

"Unhappy any man, dear woman, who found himself your enemy."

Now the chance presents itself, to let him take you. Would it entice trust, draw more information near the bed-pillows? Would committing your body serve Argens? Seldom an answer when you need one. You meet the stare of a noble elf, ageless like you, but older; versed in all the loving arts, who seeks influence beyond the musk of power already cascading from him. It's rare indeed, to meet a man who thinks himself worthy of the Lavender Lady. Carnad Mias believes he will bring ecstasy, not merely experience it. He might not be wrong.

But the rap on the door dissolves this potential future. Recognizing Kat's thin hand, you rise to open and cannot be sure whether the Red Cup behind you has clucked in distemper. Trying to frame how best to manage her worry, you gasp instead at the face of outright panic she has never worn before.

"My dear, you must not concern—"

"A man to see you," she manages, looking fearfully over your shoulder to where Carnad Mias has come to stand. This is unlike her, Kat manages your schedule to the last minim of the mundane. She must be hovering, fearing for your virtue with the Red House.

You smile and start again, "Well, my dear, he must—"

But she interrupts you again, like a human.

"A man with a silversteel token."

For a long moment, the only sound is that of three persons breathing in.

"That's, that is not possible," you say, and there is a band around your heart, not letting it beat hard enough to sustain you.

"I saw it with my own eyes. He won't let it go, just stands there in the chapel and says he will go with it as far as he is allowed."

"But there are only three in existence, and the church has hold of them all."

"It must be your rival Tanar'h then," Mias exclaims, and you sense his bitterness, thrilling as it is threatening.

You shake your head and turn to have them both in view. "Tanar'h contests with me, yes but, not a token."

"He wishes you for himself," Mias says accusingly; your shrug is meant to be modest, and brings a bitter laugh from the Red Cup. "Good taste! But you say only three—I thought there was one token in silversteel for each of the four elements."

"Ah yes," Kat nods, the teacher despite her worries, "but the Fire token has not been seen in over a century. Surely destroyed, we believed, melted down for its magic, or stolen away to other lands by someone ignorant of its, ahm, its true virtues."

"Virtues indeed!" Mias cries, his smile wide and crooked with emotion. "Any pass-key that reaches to the tower of the Lavender Lady is priceless. But I know who—it is Gaspar Heugen. My sources tell me the token of Fire was in the possession of the Mark, who held it for future favors. Heugen still occupies the palace, supposedly keeping to the Fire Grip's chambers. Bah! Surely he has rummaged it up and spends it now for your support." His face speaks volumes.

You turn to Kat before she can respond. "It matters not, I will see him whoever it is. Kat, bid him to wait five minutes and then bring him by the inner hall."

"Not to the outer door? Should I tell Chaktha he is here?"

You shake your head with a slight tilt towards the guest. "Let no one see the visitor. It is his privilege."

She nods, bows and hurries down the stairs as you close the door behind her. Before you can turn, Carnad Mias snakes one arm about your waist, lightly pressing you against his middle. He barely flexes, makes no show of force. But his hard, almost muscular midriff presses on the small of your back. Either you must step away, and lose face, or bend forward to accommodate him. There is a position for joy—you sense he knows it too—in which his girth can increase the sensation of joining.

"This bears further... examination," his voice buzzes in your ear.

You have him, but must let him go. With a breath and an effort, you turn smoothly in his light grip, so that now your breasts present a choice through his carnadine tunic. You place your hands against his shoulders without pressure, to frame attention already yours.

"I shall honor the silversteel token, milord," keeping your voice low and a smile off your face for once. This is Argens' will, however the token came to light.

You can see him struggle, but Carnad Mias knows the value of waiting for an investment to mature. He looks on you, lets you know his desire, then kisses you once, smoothly and without hurry, before stepping back.

"I bid you a good evening, milady. I feel certain it will be interesting."

"Spread word among those you wish to recruit. Bring them here tomorrow, after services and we shall entertain until late."

"And after they have been entertained?"

You swallow while pretending to consider. "Bring whatever you wish, and stay as long as you like."

Carnad Mias smiles then, and why not. His dreams both personal and political are being made. Bowing low again, he strides out and down.

Several deep breaths do not seem to help. The wine cup stays where it is; you need your wits. This man, you realize, could be pawn or puppeteer; there was no time to ask Kat in front of Mias, but by her face she did not recognize him. A stranger then, and if he wishes it, you will give him your body, for the silversteel token is sacred. Someone, somewhere divulged it for reasons only Argens knows. But the future is his province, and this night it returns, in the shadow of civil war when men and women everywhere may be asked to pay a price. Your life, you know, could be required of you at any hour. The Moment comes to all soon or late.

You glance in the mirror and see what everyone else sees, the most beautiful woman in the North Mark. Perhaps it will be a halfway-handsome stripling, or an Elf not unversed in lovemaking. But a voice whispers within your bosom, perhaps it is he, the love of your life, the man from the vision who will destroy or defend your home. You look to the window, and although the night is still, you feel watched. Argens, of course, sees you; let him be proud, whatever is required.

The wait only seems endless, as long as it is quiet. When the sound of boots ascends the treads below, time is suddenly too short. Measured, even paces, solid enough and strong. Another endless pause before the door—he hesitates? A sudden knock, enough to make you jump.

Only then, as you throw back the portal, does Argens spring the cruel joke.

He stands at attention, helm under arm, eyes ahead; it's a wonder he doesn't salute, you think he'd rather. In one outstretched arm he holds forth your destiny, a silversteel coin the size of a bottle-bottom, marked with the sign of fire. It is the captain from the arena, the Emperor's envoy the halfling told you would serve as a stalking horse for the real plan. The one sent to strut and insist and be a fool, while you scrambled to save the rest of these angry men from themselves.

And Argens has destined *him* to be your lover tonight.

You reach to take the token back for the church, its weight like a millstone on your future. Still he stands there, and you gesture him within or he'd have stayed at the door all evening. At least he hasn't spoken—a boaster, or nervous wreck rambling endlessly about himself, on top of all, would form a defensible case for suicide.

"Welcome Captain Thyme. Will you drink?"

When he does not answer at once you look up; he stands with his back to you before the statue of Argens, making a reverence. Indeed—a devout man, or at least one who wishes to appear so. He turns, and despite his proud veneer you can see he is nearly cracked with—fear? He glances at the goblet in your hands as if it contained poison, yet possibly worth drinking.

"I confess, mistress," he blurts out, immediately flinching at the double-meaning, "I am but a soldier, and completely unsure how to act. You must school me."

The honesty in this thrust evades every expectation, and you laugh in surprise, so hard he is forced to take the wine before you drop it. His fingers brush yours, your eyes meet, and the echo of his voice comes around to match what you heard in visions. The helmed warrior on the stairs; by the Flame, he is the one. Not a lover for one night, but all nights that remain to you.

He puts the goblet down, muttering "I think I shall need my wits tonight." You laugh again, your very thoughts. Now he regards you a second time, with suspicion and growing confusion.

"Well then, miss—Preacher Altieri. Will you favor me, with any knowledge of how to proceed? What do I, that is, what generally happens now that—when, that is, in such situations." He stands so straight, tries so hard to be proud and annoying. But the part does not fit him somehow, this brave, helpless fellow.

You can suppress your emotions enough to merely giggle. "While it may sound mysterious, Captain Justin, this visit can comprise anything you wish. I take it, no offence, you have not visited the Stargazers before?"

He shakes his head once sharply, declaring "I follow the Hopeforger" as if willing to suffer the consequences.

"A soldier's path, and thus a fine one. I invite you to attend our services tomorrow evening, which I think you'll find instructive." You move to take the couch out from between you. Should you approach him now, flatter, touch, caress? It is ordained, why wait? Not fear, or even as much distaste for this popinjay as you expected. He seems put upon somehow—strange, a pity.

"For tonight, however, we may sit and refresh ourselves, speak of life and Hope, seek enlightenment and your soul's best path in whatever—"

"Will you tell me who was to have been Overlord today?" He is so direct, and too honest by half. How could this be the fool you were assured was coming?

He throws his nose up a bit and tightens his jaw with conscious effort. "I presume at least that you had a unanimous vote in mind."

Better, that was more grating. But he is acting a part, and your stomach trembles to suspect hidden depths. He thinks you an enemy, of course; and so long as you move to seduce him he will only suspect you more. Try the truth.

"Well Captain, I rather believe, had you not arrived in such dramatic fashion, the vote would have gone to Et'run."

His face shows no comprehension.

"The Cliff Grip, or rather son of the former Cliff Grip slain in the war. The young red knight who challenged you earlier today."

The light of comprehension snaps into place, and he nods, adding a name to an enemy's face. "And now?" he asks bluntly, expecting an answer.

"Dear sir! Who can say, the process is—"

"I understand you can see the future." He interrupts like a human, sign of his excitement. But now his words spark your anger.

You step closer as the righteous fire builds beneath your folded arms. "Argens has gifted me with visions, aye Captain. Shall we snap our fingers now, and perhaps wave our hands like the wizards do? Would you have me summon him for you?"

You realize your breathing is heavy and fast, there is sweat on your brow. "The token, however you came by it, entitles you to much, Captain. My answers, my time, my body if you wish it. Until the dawn, I am yours."

The captain does not retreat from your anger, from the realization of his blasphemy. Another step toward him, close enough to see that he, too, is sweating.

"But my faith is mine, sir. At your behest, at the Overlord's, for the Emperor himself. I do not call for Argens Stargazer, Captain—he has called me."

Panting with you now, he does not speak for several long moments. You look up and see the pain in his eyes, leaking past his resolve.

"I am sorry, priestess," he sounds the honest man for an instant, but yields to the noble fop with effort, "That is, I trust you will forgive me, my ignorance of your customs prevents a proper response. Perhaps you will be so kind as to help remedy that."

Whatever insult you took from his words is redoubled now by this horrible job of acting. The Emperor's army has no chance with such half-hearted idiots at the tip of the spear. The sooner this night is over, the better. Part of you votes to bed him at once; Argens might be satisfied, and with luck his chosen would sleep through. But you decide to play out the farce awhile longer, though determined he shall not enjoy it.

"Well, let us see if we can read your future then, sir. Come and sit." The invitation, which should have been wrapped in love and desire, snaps from your mouth like a verdict; the Captain for his part strides stiffly to the couch and manages to take his seat as if still at attention.

"First, a short prayer for inspiration." With a deep breath you compose yourself and slightly lid your eyes, falling at once toward that familiar state of grace where Argens lives and watches over you. "Stargazer, hear us and show us your will for the days to come. Let the Hope you guide us toward shine on us from the heavens, and mark our course through the future."

You open one eye to glance at the Captain, signaling that he too should pray. He is uncomfortable with praying aloud—good, let him squirm. Deciding, he rises to face the statue and kneels—proper Hopeforger—clasping gauntleted hands and looking on Argens in stone with both eyes open.

"Argens, what must be done to save this Mark from war and ruin."

The chill runs through you as he sits again. No personal desire, no request to know what will become of him. In ten words he has shamed your example. This man, supposedly so stiff-necked and judgmental, wants to save a kingdom and does not haggle about the price. He asks of Argens … the same as you have. Indeed, who is this noble elf?

With another breath, you reach out and say "Now, we will attempt it."

As he moves to take your hands, you draw them back slightly, indicating his gauntlets. With a start he takes your meaning and hastily doffs them, stuffing the pair in his belt.

In the last instant, as he reaches again to take your hands in his, too late to draw back, you see on his smallest finger: a plain iron ring, set with the Emperor's ax-symbol. The sign of your secret contact! Did one murder the other, or—

32

But now his strong callused hands encompass your own, and the rush of Argens' answer nearly throws you from the couch.

⊕ ⊕ ⊕

A hot swirling wind blows over Cryssigens by night, driven by a dragon's breath fanning flames and pushing the glow of reflected Red down every street, into many houses. The scaly beast clutches a treasure-hoard to its chest and settles atop it like a lover, heedless of the chaos its flame has caused. In the stars above, The Arbalest loads a deadly bolt into his crossbow and fires at once. From the whirlwind many-legged creatures begin to drop down.

By the azure sea, shaded by the sounds of fighting, a raccoon carefully washes something in the surf. It looks up at you in the sky, and holds out a silversteel token.

The sounds of combat at your door; in the vision you see it swing open as the fighting blazes within. Sounds assail you, you nearly flee. The statue of Argens looks approvingly down on the warring forces, spiders versus fire ants. You hear your lover's voice, the Captain calling out commands, but still cannot tell which side he is on.

From the arena a gryphon screams in anger and blood rains over the walls like a shower of rose petals. A great black horse carries a burning salamander through the wrack to safety. You and Chaktha, an allegory of your past. Or will history repeat itself?

A small brown turtle calmly piles a few pebbles atop each other in the shade of a stone oak tree, whose leaves turn color. The fires of the city are visible, but turtle and tree are close to the sea, and safe for the moment.

Now the images come too quickly to make sense. A bright clever ferret snatches a silver-gold insect shape from the neck of a sleeping Arbalest, as it lies next to the Serpent. There are dark tunnels beneath the burning city, where the ferret flees from rats without number. Spiders clamber up the walls of a temple tower as fire ants defend it. The ferret changes shape, the serpent also alters its were-form to something verminous. Nothing is what it seems.

Then the crown- the Brow of the Ecclesiast, you are certain, its seven jewels burning brightly as it floats on waves of flame somewhere deep underground. You are there, you feel the thick, dragon-heated air hard to breathe. Then the enormous shadow of a giant fly appears, caught in amber behind a thick glass wall. The barrier cracks and shatters in a burst of brilliant, multi-colored light; splinters of something clearer, sharper, heavier than glass spin through you, shredding your

33

flesh. The Brow rises above your head and you feel the flames licking higher; the fly is thickening and hunching, its six legs combining into three.

Back above ground, blue sea and red fire are everywhere at war, racked or raised by the howling wind.

⊕ ⊕ ⊕

You come back to yourself, gasping and pummeled by tensed muscles around your stomach and heart. There is a sudden chill, the heat of the vision-flames left its mark in the fabric of your gown, but now perspiration clings like ice. The Captain, holding out one strong arm to contain you, looks battered by clubs-- his eyes also have seen everything.

Into the silence Argens' words echo at the end of the vision, as you have heard them before. You were just past twenty, and sought to know your future against the advice of all the preachers. Wait, they counseled, grow into your destiny. But you knew that decades were not left before your Moment. So you heard them, six years ago. You hear them again now, and through your flesh on his, the Captain also hears Argens' doom.

As the rule of men fails
A woman's spirit rises to lead them
Argens' Fire will not sear this soul
Nor wound and ruin impede her path

"How can you interpret such a vision?" the Captain whispers. He regards you now with awe, and a sense of your worth stripped of the body's beauty. It is a sight he never thought to see; one you never thought anyone else would see through.

Sitting close by, you also sense more than you imagined in him. This face is weathered, marked with several small scars; what a contrast with Tanar'h's glistening, unused smoothness. Hair tousled but thick and strong, whereas your rival is either bald or shaves meticulously. He still wears his chain armor, the sword in scabbard, perhaps he sleeps with them. Yet he has found time, today, to bathe. These muscles have borne mortal combat; his arm was cut recently and only hastily bound.

Unsuspected, a desire for him takes root—that arm to clasp you, his fierce loyalty conscripted to win your passion. The noble

34

fop was truly a mask; this man you could indeed love, for he too lives close to death.

And your heart takes a stab, as suddenly you are not eager for him to die in flame and wrack.

"The signs in the vision," you start slowly, "must be taken in turn, and then in sequence and finally in combination. Some are heavenly, we see them in the stars, showing most clearly the will of Argens."

"Like the Arbalest," he replies at once, "does that mean war from a distant enemy?"

"It could, or as he is often a hired man—what is the word?"

"Mercenary."

"Yes, then it could mean outsiders, or a conflict for greed. And the time is short."

The Captain's brow wrinkles, then smoothes in a flash. "Two months! The Arbalest is highest in the month of the Dragon, coming next after Hawk."

Good, you think while nodding, he is far from an idiot. "And more," you continue, "this is the year of the Arbalest as well. So his sign's power is redoubled in the fourth month, and he may strike all the sooner."

The soldier takes that in a moment. "This is the voice of Argens?"

"His warning, I would say rather. But we also see certain other signs of the zodiac: the Ferret, Serpent, Gryphon, Dragon, Raccoon, Turtle—were there any others?"

"Spiders, a fly and fire ants, briefly," he says. "Those last are a constellation and a zodiac sign. But what was the flaming thing on horseback?"

"A Salamander, one more-- the very avatar of flame, in a vision filled with fire. Eight signs, by the First!"

"Do each of these creatures mean someone or other here in the city?" the Captain asks.

"It is possible, but—well, so many heavenly constellations would tend to indicate large movements among the earthly populations. Or if individuals, then those charged with the power to alter life for the many."

You are both quiet for a time digesting this. He shakes his head, but you can tell it is dismay, not disbelief.

"You would have to guess all of those, I know none here."

You glance at the ring on his finger. If he is the Emperor's secret man, it is high time he learned some names. And if not, if he is merely the show-knight sent to bear the flag, then still no harm, or nearly. You rise to get paper and sit near him to make notes.

At the page-top, an empty box for the Overlord, then lines down to delineate his immediate vassals. Just beneath is another empty box, for the Master of Horse, then one for the Fire Grip, which you mark "GH". Three boxes on the next level down to denote the baronies, and one more to the side for the Highforge. You stop before going further down—enough for one night.

"The Overlord of the North Mark is served by several major officers, who naturally have sway over his successor in times when, as now, he has no heirs."

The Captain nods, saying "His son Kreelon was also killed in the rebellion. No other family, then?"

"Only his widow, who still lives in the palace as no one dares to eject her. The Master of Horse was slain in the Battle of Tor Perite, and his office—not hereditary—rests in the Overlord's keeping. You see? Thus, those three full votes lie dormant."

You glance up to see his eyes intently on yours. He doesn't ask how many votes there are in total—Praise Argens! You cannot be sure anyone knows. You tap the next box with your quill and he looks down to drink in whatever else you tell him. Truly, his focus is intense, rather thrilling.

"The Fire Grip has been Gaspar Heugen since the early days of Kreel's reign. He is a tightly-made man, I can tell you, formal and observant. A devout Hopeforger and one of the leading lights of the Blue House. His three votes would carry many others among the guilds and in the largest temple of the city. If, that is, he chose to divulge it."

"Could he be the Gryphon, from the arena?" Again, the Captain's thought is so direct, you have to smile. He wants things to make sense.

"I hardly believe! Heugen does not partake in any public entertainment I know of. He is indeed a solitary man, but I think the Gryphon much too fierce and intemperate for his character. The Fire Grip is a more deliberate spirit. Let us not guess too quickly.

There is also the office of High Forge, claimed at this moment by Z'kammet Hammer of the Hopeforger temple."

He glances up from the paper and still you have his full attention. "Three more votes with that office?" he asks, and as soon as you nod he continues. "You said claimed."

The tingle in your core is stronger than the first impact of rum. Yes, nothing wrong with this one's brain—he seems to sense the combat in everything. How much to tell him, though; and how to ask about the ring without revealing too much?

"Indeed, by virtue of the number of his followers, Hammer claims the title. But by right—that is, in times past, the title is held only by the curate who can wear the artifact of the office. A wondrous crown, called the Brow of the Ecclesiast."

"Surely, then he will wear it on the next voting day?"

"Why, then, did he not wear it today, my good Captain? He was the thin, aged gentleman whose prayer you interrupted by your rather dramatic arrival."

He nods, grins, flushes. "I was in a hurry. Still, interesting; why did he not wear it?"

You smile, still considering how much to say. "Suffice for the moment to note that he did not. His vote as head of a temple was only one. But the preacher that wears the Brow can cast three votes."

"And you plan to be that preacher." He looks you in the eye, not suspecting the danger in his words, but let that be. If you perish from donning the artifact, the plan is ruined. If you do not gain the Brow to even make the attempt, the plan is ruined anyway. For that, you need the Stealthic. But the Captain need not know of him.

"Well, good luck to you, I'm certain mistress," he says with a touch of the actor's sneer. "What of these others?" he gestures again at the chart and you return to filling in names in the bottom row.

"The barons have two votes apiece. Here is Pa'u Breret'n lord of Cesmir, who rants on about more ships for his fleet, and here the Baron of Gaden, Soln Ge'para, who only wants to hear about soldiers to defend the desert front. Cesmir is a solid Red House man, Gaden most likely a Blue."

"Wait. Hold a moment. I thought these Colors were guild representatives. What do you mean barons Red and Blue?"

You sigh in resignation. Tutoring this soldier in the niceties of Cryssigensian politics is no one's idea of how to spend a Stargazer token. While you think your hand unconsciously pats his and you feel again that spark as you did during the vision. He feels it too, the muscles of his arm bunch, and his star-clear gaze snaps up to yours. Perhaps if you finish quickly, there will be time for different diversions—you begin to like the idea now, and after all Argens chose him.

"It is indeed complicated, Captain. In this kingdom, the influence of our guilds far surpasses that in the other Marks of the Empire. The head of each major guild, it is true, only wields a half-vote apiece, sometimes less. But the wealth they bring the Mark supports all the feudal lords, and the barons know this."

"Because of the House Colors," The Captain asserts bluntly: your heart leaps again, your faith in Argens restored with every word. He is perceptive, he sees beyond the surface.

"Correct. Each Color has established itself in the various sectors of industry and manufacture. So in addition to producing items bearing the full Color that only they can provide—"

"Each house holds influence over the guilds associated with that trade, wielding power over the supply of their most valued products."

"You see the situation well, Captain. Thus each Color bears no vote directly in choosing the Overlord, but their guilds have many half-votes apiece, and together they could perhaps outvote the city officers and barons."

"Have they always been able to do so?"

"No, in the past there were fewer Colors, and fewer recognized guilds. Buying the right of recognition is quite expensive."

He barks a laugh. "Certainly. And as the years passed, I can imagine every time the Overlord needed funds he created another guild! Only he never counted on so many Colors—what are there, six—and the trunk leads the elephant by now. One Color or another, I wager, decides it needs more power and informs the Overlord that a new guild should be licensed, while making the appropriate donation of course. Your winner in two months may have to create more, to curry votes. So today even the barons kowtow, and the temples too."

This cuts too close. "The secrets of the Colors have brought tremendous prosperity to this Mark," you retort with heat. "You walked the streets today, Captain. How many beggars did you see? Starving children, none? By the docks, under the pilings if you seek hard, there are perhaps three score determined folks, half-insane, who refuse to take shelter in our schools and wards. Did the bounteous generosity of your Emperor provide this?"

Your hand is long since withdrawn from his, but the couch keeps you both quite close. He takes you in for a moment, admiring your fire without regret or fear, seeing again a potential enemy perhaps easier for him to confront than a beautiful woman.

"Are you a leader of the Purple, as well as the Stargazers?"

Will he never once remark with subtlety? Though you try to remain angry, you must smile at his impossible directness. "I am influential among my Color as I aspire to be in my temple, Captain. Am I suspect, then, in the conspiracy you spoke of today? Arrest me if you wish. Until the dawn you may even bind me."

Ah—that, at least got his attention, and you can tell whatever his proud noble act, whichever role he was sent here to play, he wants you.

"But not every pawn on this board, sir, moves so straightly as you might wish. My Color is not ruled by one person, and the Stargazer temple abhors compulsion."

"So their votes are perhaps still in play. One for your temple, I'll bet you obtain it; how many for your color?"

Maddening man. "Two full votes, with some surety, perhaps three."

He nods again. "But if you gain your prize, that Brow you spoke of, then just like a pawn reaching deepest into enemy territory you become a queen. Six votes, on your own."

You tilt your head in acknowledgement, and sigh. "Not enough. Carnad Mias, the Red Cup, has a dozen guilds under his thumb without question, and the Baron of Cesmir." You stop before voicing your deepest fears, still afraid this is the wrong contact.

"Carnad Mias," he says, "the fat man."

Your laughter is unforced and musical- only Kat ever made you so jolly before. Just a half-hour ago, you were trying to explain away his midriff. In the presence of this soldier, you could forget the Red Cup with ease.

"Yes Captain, compared to you many men are wide in the belly. And narrow in the shoulder, I might add."

"Could he be the Salamander, riding the black horse?"

"I must doubt it. The Red House could well be represented in fire, but in that case perhaps a Fire Ant, a leader of many. Truly, Captain Justin, I have never had such a puzzle to untangle before—like those chess games where every piece is still on the table."

Rising, you top off the goblets though neither of you is drinking. There are ways to move, bend, and pour that work wonders. Sitting now just a smidgeon closer, you reach to touch his hand again; while looking in his eye, you let your finger playfully trace the outside of his small ring.

"The Emperor's man also has a vote, if he attends the meeting."

The Captain's eyes flare as his hand stiffens; his nod is sharp, not a promise. He says only "How many other temples?"

No answers yet. You think about it. "The Demonbenders of course have been outlawed, so there's another vacant box. But there is the new cult, to the healer Telhol, he merits a full vote. And the Devout, that monk from Sinter—I must say I do not know if he can claim one."

"He was the tall one in brown, cloth over his face. Let us assume yes. So, the largest questions are—who does the Red favor? Where is the Fire Grip leaning? And what is the last baron's vote?"

"Tralmachia? Another empty seat, I'm afraid. The North Mark hears very little from its northern barony. Tralmachia exports wood and wool but imports hardly anything. And no one I know has ever met the baron T'yr or one of his many sons."

The Captain thinks on that a while, staring at nothing and absently turning that ring on his finger. When he looks at you, it is clear he has decided.

"I don't trust this Red House: a kingdom should be run by a noble strong enough to resist the pull of the marketplace."

Captain Justin rises to pace and continues. "I must speak with Gaspar Heugen. If you are correct about his character, then he may be patient enough not to risk war with the Empire for pride's sake, or money." He looks you directly in the eye. "Can you live with the Blue?"

Such an enormous question, yet he intends it personally. "My Color, Captain, stands between the Red and Blue in this city."

He searches your gaze, and you realize he is testing you for truth. A good thing, then, you had not tried to lie! He nods.

"Aye, like the sea and the flame in the vision." You had not thought of that.

"I will see the Fire Grip as soon as I can. Perhaps you could visit the leader of the Telholian temple, sound him out as a fellow preacher."

You realize with a thrill that he is committing your causes together. "Are we on the same side, then Captain?"

He gestures to the paper on the low table. "Count the votes. Either the rest band together, or Carnad Mias rules Cryssigens. And with all you've said about division, and those absent … we need more votes."

The thump on the door is soft but deep, from a large hand. There looms Chaktha, looking down on you like a giant, as he always has. His shield would cover your body by itself. He points to the Captain, then to his own chest describing an emblem-circle on his skin.

"Men, painted like him, in the arena."

"My company! The First's blessings on M'nesa Zetee, he's beat the schedule by half a day."

"Thank you, Chaktha," with a smile you close the door, noting your guard's face with an echo of Kat's worry on it.

"I will try to get you a message about my meeting with Heugen, before I go."

"Go?" You stand in shock as he retrieves his helm. "Go where?"

He stops and stares, truly biting his lip. "I have not … executed my orders yet, mistress."

Another moment, one glance at the statue of Argens, then he makes a decision. You can see it in every inch of him, he chooses a path and then no looking back, determined as—as a Fire Ant, you realize.

"There is someone here in the city, with whom I must make contact, before I leave. I do not know her name, but she will carry word back to Argens, of my progress. In any event there is not an hour to be lost. No sleep tonight."

Now you see Argens' cruelty, so different from the childish prank you thought me guilty of. Handsome, brave, loyal, and an elf who forgoes sleep as you do! And he is leaving? Before you tell him, you must know.

"Perhaps I can help you locate this person. But why can you not deliver the message yourself?"

"Because I am for the north and Tralmachia."

"You cannot!" You stand before him but do not remember moving. Your heart beats too slowly and too hard. "No one visits Tralmachia in force, only a few native merchants come out, once a season to sell their wares. Listen to me, my—Captain, the dangers and rumors of that barony are vast."

He only arches an eyebrow in response.

"Believe me! The Baron, Voev T'yr, has been alive, no one knows, but certainly for hundreds of years. Long enough to bear a dozen strong sons from many wives. They say he … I cannot bear to tell aloud what they whisper. But the hills of Tralmachia are infested with rustic tribesmen, never conquered even by Argens. And foul beasts of every kind haunt the tangled forests. Even the Overlord's army never reduced his central fortress, in elder days when rebellion was more common. Tralmachia has had no voice with Cryssigens since before the first Viridians, and we are better off for that."

You place one hand on his chest and his skin flinches like a startled horse. He presses his hand over yours and holds your gaze, still searching you for the truth. He wants to trust you.

But he says only, "There are two votes there and I will return with them if I can. If Carnad Mias elects the Overlord, this Mark will be drowned in war."

"You will die there!"

"My life," he says with conviction, "is the least thing I would lose for the prize I seek."

Your heart is hurling itself against your ribs in a desperate effort to escape. It doesn't matter if he is the fop of the flag—his decisive nature has kindled on your own flame now. You love him, and Argens is sending him to his death. This is a sacrifice you can understand.

"Wait here. I will bring you what you need."

Back into your bedroom—will he ever see it? You open the casket again, and slip the iron ax-ring on your finger. The way back to him is forced, you must tell each leg to move as you march in to send him to doom. Is there even a chance that he could live? Is there any hope for you?

You show him the ring and his jaw drops. He realizes, the need for pretense is gone; in you he has found the agent his masters ordained. Before you can think he has seized you in his arms, brought his mouth within an inch of yours; you note every spoke of his grey-green eyes and the depths of his hopeless desire for you.

"Someone set bandits against the flag of mission" he breathes into you. "Captain Valin T'lenthor, my riv—my fellow officer was slain. Bear this message back to Argens, and tell them of our plans."

"And is there then, no message for me?" you gasp, barely audible.

His entire frame quakes, towering over you as you hang in his embrace. Every important part of you touches him, holding the lightning bolt between your bodies. Certain death in a foreign hell-pit, he can face with calm. But this advance, this last inch to your lips, he does not dare. Resolutely he sets you back fully on the floor, smoothes the arms of the dress, gently takes and kisses your hand. The gesture of the rural knights, of centuries ago; your heart melts in charm, and drowns in separation.

"To the north then," you manage in a shaky tone, "and the power you can bring back from there."

"To the north, milady," he responds quietly, releasing your hand. He turns heel to toe, and the hammer-tap of his boots still echoes in your mind after he is gone from view.

⊕ ⊕ ⊕

You are alone, no idea where you could be until your hand puts the ax-ring back in the jewel-box. Standing by your bedside in the deep carpeted silence, you feel mourning flow into that cavity left in your ribs. Ever since Elle's father died, you had Argens' word, the life-love would come. You lived on that, until this soldier brought the token, and you suspected a joke. The strutting poser; you thought Argens had destined a vain fool for your body. But then you saw his soul, and he yours, in a vision of the future you both will strive to prevent. A noble elf, Captain of the realm, a mate worthy of your love and life.

And now he's gone. Less than an hour, one touch of his hands, that iron grip still marking your arms; but death will part you now. *To the north, milady*: there lies certain doom at the hands of the undying baron whose name is used to frighten unruly children across the city.

43

Why not weep, a part of you suggests, you have an Elf's lifetime separated from his courage and sacrifice. Argens' cruel joke continues to unfold. To think, you believed lying with a man you despised was the distasteful service required of you. So little faith, to suppose Argens would bring a lover you could not yearn after. Now you would pay all you own to have him here on your plush bed, for just one night. Instead, only the token of Fire remains from his departure. With a shock, it comes to you that he may not die in the haunted hills. He will return to your tower, you have seen it, to wage a desperate fight against unknown foes. But you will be elsewhere, unable to save his life.

Too late, you realize you are not, in fact, alone.

Spinning from the table, you discern across the brazier-lit bedroom a masked man-shaped shadow fixed atop the dresser above you. The Stealthic, Feldspar, come in answer to your commission. Now? Already, you must move on, speak, exhort this living legend to your bidding. No time for tears?

He sits, unmoving but projecting agility and speed from his high perch. You ask for his proofs, and he drops the matching gem into your hand, the same number etched on its back as the one the bard brought to Kat. No words from him—is he shy, perhaps mute? You prattle on, words to cover your uncertainty, and he listens well, still and silent.

To business, then. "What do you know, Feldspar, of the Brow of the Ecclesiast?"

He gestures that you should continue, and your mouth is happy to supply a bell-tongue melody to the heart's percussive dirge. You sail on about the sacred Brow, its unrivaled power to persuade, its mortal perils to the unworthy wearer. Until today, it was the key to all your schemes, the very stars and swaths of heaven took the form of its gems and twining metals. Wear it and survive, to save and perhaps to rule this city. But now—alone, without the Captain, you won't mind if indeed it does burn you to ash as the legends warn.

You move to the window, still speaking to the shadowed legend at your back while you look wistfully out, seeking any trace of your heart there on the glittering grounds below. Focus—the commission, before you start to weep. You turn to face him again across the quiet room.

44

"And before today, I will be honest with you, master Stealthic, I hoped to hire you to steal me this crown. With it, I could move the great stubborn stone that blocks our country's path to peace. I could—well. I believe I am worthy to wear the Brow, what of that? And the legends tell of horrible punishments for the one who dons it without merit. I am content to face that risk."

Indeed, almost eager now. Try as you might, your thoughts stay fixed on the sundered Captain, the raider who made off clutching your heart in his gauntleted fist.

With an effort, you shake your reverie and gaily ask Feldspar if he heard the arena news.

He produces a fluttering thing made of reeds and it circles down to land on the bed. Oh joy! He was there.

"Bravo! Yes, a remarkable interruption was it not? A day of surprises—" Such a marvelous gesture, you could hug him except he is so clearly uninterested in you, crouched high and unmoving. You carry him through your theory, that Z'kammet Hammer the Hopeforger patriarch does not have the Brow in his possession.

The black mask gives silent agreement, and you celebrate placing your warmed hands against the cool stone behind you, striking a seductive pose by long habit, without intending to. The fabric frames your body tightly; this posture exists to reward a man such as Carnad Mias. How you long to stand before your Captain in just this way. But the Stealthic—he looks aside, of course, his mind fixed on the risk, so you propose his commission even as your heart races. For if he refuses, all is lost with the Brow.

"I offer you five thousand pieces of silver, Feldspar, not for the return of the Brow, but merely for the knowledge of where it lies." You have him, you can sense it from across the room. Twenty thousand more, if it should require retrieval, but for now the promise is merely a Greatknight's ransom, to locate it. There may be other ways to get what you seek.

Feldspar will succeed—without benefit of vision, you were certain he could discover this hidden treasure of past greatness. Even as you exhort him to the imitation of his hero, your own path of danger aligns before your eyes. The room fades, and you see again *the swirl of fire, the rain of many-limbed creatures at war, constellations in their animal guises*

45

descending upon the city to touch lives and streets, leaving them bathed in water, light or fire. Through it all a galloping horse bears you closer to a matchless crown set with seven gems. A distant voice that sounds like yours is speaking to Feldspar, but before you is only the Brow. *Your Captain shouts to his men from the next room; they must bar the door to the stairs and hold out a few moments longer. Someone is battering the portal—*

The rapping hand on the outer door has Kat's weight but none of her usual delicacy. You feel dropped from the ceiling, breath rushes out and Argens' vision clears to reveal the bedroom. The Stealthic still sits atop your dresser and now the knock becomes insistent. You turn to the outer room leaving a sigh of resignation behind with your guest. All the city may troop through here before dawn.

Kat is bouncing, truly bouncing! She squeals like one of her own pupils; in her hands you see a lovely woven knot of vines and blossoms set with a red-white lotus at the center. You feel the strangeness of a jaw hanging slack; when was the last time you were truly surprised?

"Oh Kat, a love token! I am so pleased for you, come in and tell me everything."

You sweep to the couches, your dear teacher looking almost ridiculous with a love-struck face and such silver hair. So excited, she even eats.

"Left on the schoolhouse door, no one saw anything, I don't know *what* to believe."

"Who could it be my dear?"

"I swear to you 'Star I have no *idea*. It's probably nothing, I suppose- but oh, *look* at the workmanship!"

You giggle and admire the weave with her. "Yes, a message straight from the heart. One of your students I'm sure!"

"Oh, nonsense!" the teacher is properly horrified, which makes you laugh all the more.

"But Kat, no one else teaches such old-fashioned skills."

"I haven't shown the love-knot in *years*," she breathes, "not since your days in school." The mind moves rather slowly when one is in love.

"Yes, dear," you patiently lead her, "so it must have been a former student." Now that her brain is cornered into reluctant agreement, she begins to wonder with an almost painful expression, and your heart goes out to her. To know you are loved, and not to know who …

like your Captain, most likely. What token did you give him, except an ax-ring's permission to go and seek his own death?

"Perhaps Tanar'h," you suggest to forestall the welling tears.

Kat covers her ears in horror, dropping the woven flowers to the table. "The High Heart of the church! 'Star, such scandal! He wants you, everyone knows."

You laugh again, only a little forced. "Tanar'h wants several things, my dear. A fourth wife—or a fifth! Leadership of the church, probably the power to fly for all I know."

"Don't be silly. It's surely nothing—but oh, *look* at this marvelous weave!"

You have to smile, and together you admire the craft as she natters on about the symbolism. One corner of your mind just begins to wonder who, after all, might have done this splendid, thoughtful thing. Who has the time?

But before you dare ask Argens such a silly question, the Ferret enters the room. Your vision's echo, there are no loose animals in Cryssigens: beside you Kat still speaks, sees nothing. Snaking through the stairwell door, the Ferret's sinuous body hugs the wall as he makes his way over near the statue. He climbs it and looks about while perched on Argens' shoulder, then suddenly leaps down to the floor and scurries into your bedroom. Rising, you ignore Kat's bewildered questions and trail him as he climbs the sill and disappears outside. Your bedroom is empty, the feldspar gems taken, commission accepted. So—the Ferret's place in the vision, at least, is clear. But Feldspar will retrieve a necklace of some kind, not a crown? From the Arbalest?

Your steps have drifted back into the outer room and Kat's kind, worried face swims into view.

"What is it, 'Star? Did you have another vision? Did you see who my—" she trails off, her gaze falling on the silversteel token there on the table next to her wreath. Kat stifles her own scream with one hand, and looks desperately about. "What happened?" she hisses. "Is he still here?"

You hold out your arms to your friend and teacher. "Congratulate me, my dear. I too am in love."

She hops and screams again, her embrace surprisingly strong for someone so slender. You keep her hands on parting and make her sit with you. She has become tentative again, unsure and afraid.

"Is it, do you mean, Carnad Mias?" Her face twists in anxiety. Unhappy at the thought of you with the Red Cup, still she cannot contemplate the knight in mail.

"Later for that, my dear. I have had a vision, indeed, and I need your help to untangle it."

You tell it all and she does not interrupt once, though she stops smiling or eating. As you finish with your personal prophecy, her brow is already knit, the teacher working on a new problem with fervid energy.

"The bolt of the Arbalest will fall upon us hard and soon, I think."

"A foreign enemy?"

"Surely the Emperor's men," she concludes to your dismay. How could the Captain be author of this riot?

"What about the spiders and ants?" you ask suppressing an instinctive shiver.

"And that awful, molting fly," she avers, but shakes her head. "Argens protect us from all such mindless horrors. Again, enemy armies, perhaps more than one, come to fight in our city. And dear me! Right in this tower? Did you know this?"

"I thought it might be years away, dear heart, not part of our present tale."

She rises and strides a bit while thinking. "The Raccoon, Turtle, Horse are friendly signs I would say, offering some kind of help or shelter. Water and earth … the Dragon and Gryphon seem more ominous and threatening. Here are air and fire."

"But the Salamander?"

She regards you with arched brow and a hint of a smile. "I believe you have already volunteered for that role."

"And may do more harm than good! My thanks for your comfort. So I should avoid or flee the Gryphon, who is…"

Kat shrugs. "Why not the one we've already seen?"

Because, you practically shout, he is my lover's mount!

Kat continues before you speak aloud. "But the next images, these I think are important and the best sign of what you must do. If, that is, the Heaven's Eye of Argens will hear my interpretation." From the couch you play-kick her backside and she smiles before going on. "Whatever threat the arena portends, avoid it and seek some shelter or wisdom from the Turtle. The theft of the Ferret—seemingly also your friend—will bring him aid, which in turn may lead to the Brow."

Kat knows of your plan to risk the test, and her face creases now with dread. The end of the message, your prophecy, stands so clear that you have no trouble with it, but Kat only reluctantly admits the truth. "If you decide to wear the Brow of the Ecclesiast, you will survive. May Argens protect you."

"Yet why did so many alter their form? Who is truly our foe, that enemy who threatens to ruin the Mark? Is it the fly with the changing legs? That is no zodiac sign."

Kat is thoughtful. "No, the fly is from an old animal tale, one of the only stories we know from—from the children of Despair."

"The Spider and the Fly! Of course. But what an awful story, and what does he do in it, nothing but complain."

Kat looks on you with a face suddenly turned ashen. "He does nothing, because he is stuck."

You think about an evil thing held prisoner in this city, and a chill runs completely through you bringing a gasp. Not six legs, but three; the Shard Demon.

Kat continues, "I think both Spiders and Fly are the enemy here, as in that tale. Whereas the Fire Ant," she considers another moment, "also from the animal tales, is diligent and honest, a fierce warrior but loyal when enlisted. One of them, at least, could be your ally. It would appear the Ferret, reckless and intelligent, will take risks on your behalf."

You both know, at least, who that is.

"The Fire Ant, you make him sound rather attractive." You muse, whether to tell her everything. "Do you suppose, this Captain…"

She shakes her head at once. "Don't make everything so complicated, 'Star. He brought you the token, hence the Raccoon." She is the teacher, but something inside you rings dull at her words. The Raccoon is not a decisive, brave creature. On the other hand, insects have always made you shiver- and when you remember his iron grip, how close his mouth came to yours, you shiver again.

"It requires much further study," Kat says rising. "Let me go and write it down before I forget the details."

"Oh my dear, but here I have ruined your joy with work. You were so happy."

Kat's smile returns, small but strong just like her, and she picks up the love-knot. "It means nothing," she murmurs again, as if arguing with herself. "Just a kindly gesture, I'm sure."

Your eyes meet, and you prompt her. "But, look at the workmanship."

Her smile springs up into a grin, and she bounces and squeals once more. Snow-white hair and a spare frame, bobbing in childlike joy. You hug and laugh as she talks on of this unknown him.

"So *gratifying* to see a lesson well learned. That is all, I'm sure. Oh, it is *so* lovely." Your friend and mentor is positively beaming; she couldn't be younger.

Together to the stairwell: she will descend and return to her dormer over the schoolhouse. The bell across the grounds softly rings out the mid-eve hour. Your friend will diligently take notes on this vision, of course, and study them awhile. But then she will sleep, like all the others, dear thing. Only a bit past mid-eve. What it must be like, to lose hours at a time, doing nothing!

She turns back on the steps with a gasp. "But my dear! You have said nothing of *your* lover!" She seems eager and frightened, and it pains you to further the deception.

"I am quite content, dear teacher. Argens has spoken." Just a hint of your true disappointment allows her to believe you are following duty. And indeed nothing could be more true. She nods, hugs you again, and needlessly wishes good sleep upon you. After her steps fade, you can hear Chaktha below putting up his weapons and preparing to sleep on the bare floor of the antechamber. His slumber, you know, is that of the hunted wolf; he is only human, after all. Passing your door, you continue up the winding stairs, to the battlements.

The trembling in your thighs is not from exhaustion- when have you ever felt that? But a holy exaltation rather, from speaking with the sky where your hero lives and looks down. You did not sleep that first night either, after the preachers left you with tower and title—

you tiptoed past the guards and ascended to speak again with the Stargazer, to thank him for his vision and to ask, so many questions.

And tonight, the same. You spread your hands to the stars while intoning thanks; their argent light gathers in your eyes, a sting that pleases and grows beyond mortal sense. There is no past, no time beyond now, as all the sleepers below you believe. Between the scatter of gems above and the diadem of city-lamps below, you breathe in the coolest air of the predawn, tinted with an echo of jasmine.

The Arbalest, rising steadily from the southeast, bears his crossbow in full view now. By mid-Hawk he will stand clear upon the horizon. Ten weeks to find cover before his bolt takes flight aimed at the heart of your city. And the Shard Demon, the fly in a prison far below the palace that so few know to reach, may be breaking free. Can spiders ever help a fly?

Stepped out of your sandals, the stone pressing up into your feet lends a sense you might launch into heaven any moment. You drink the radiance of the zodiac, grateful for two more hours to soak in understanding, to seek the clearest path forward. Which of these constellations around you means well, or worse? Dimly, your heart pounds again to think of your honest, noble Captain and you sink now toward earth. He rides to question the Fire Grip, and soon thereafter leaves to court death in the north. No sleep for either of you—how could you fail to love him, though he might never know.

The Dragon sits atop that northern sky, the ally of flame and ruin, perhaps the captor of the Brow. Carnad Mias? Wealth and the greed for power he has, but what magic lore could he wield? Why try to kill you one night, seduce you the next? With luck, a few dissolute parties in your chambers will reveal the truth of his intentions. And if he demands your body—well, there are drugs to set on a man's mind and take off his loins, bringing sleep and forgetfulness. Argens would forgive such an impudence, now that your heart is taken.

Argens is indeed here, you can touch his presence while the stars draw close to your ever-wider eyes. Your feet feel nothing, your arms wide with a breath of jasmine breeze stirring the fabric. There is no tower, no city, no past or breath or need for rest. Stars, everywhere light and knowledge and tomorrow. He shows you once again the

Brow, and behind it a corona of fire, floating in air to your vision-hands. You reach for it without trembling and the oracle nears its peak.

The hero whose stars you gaze upon is making you worthy, because without your lover death holds no fear.

Indeed for that dawning courage, I shall always cherish you.

⊕ ⊕ ⊕

The accumulated light of the stars long ago merged into your eyes, a blinding wall of white intuition. You feel the usual regret as it dims and shrinks, warms and rises, leaving you in the relative dimness of another dawn.

Without a sound, Chaktha is there behind you atop the tower.

"Morning so soon?" you manage with a blink and a smile.

"Priestess," he answers, your private ritual, "the sun rises."

"Well, that seems to be all that's required," and you laugh but he does not. He smiles only once a day. "You know, Chaktha, you are free, no longer a slave."

Now it comes, wide and strong and powerful, as if he flexes his arms to do it. "As I was yesterday, priestess."

You place one hand on his chest, at the level of your own eyes, and smile up at him. "As long as that is settled," you breeze down the stairs with your bodyguard in train.

The ground floor room is set for breakfast—those ruby-fleshed tree melons that burst to life in the throat, warmed milk with chocolate, a sweet roll. Morning is the only time you ever feel truly hungry, low on vision fuel and eager to begin again. The melon fruit's cold juice thrusts down your throat as if shot from a bow, spreading a tingle of sweet and joy—a climax in reverse from top to bottom. Perhaps a second roll …

Through the inner door comes Tanar'h, a strange stare in his eyes making him oblivious to your shock at this intrusion. He wears his usual vestments, crossed leather straps the only covering above the waist, slit silken pantaloons in white, and today a plain golden torc around his neck. He crosses the room as if he might make a breakfast of you: such hunger, you've known it of him but he has lapsed to show it openly.

"High Heart, how dare you, we are not in some corner tavern and I have not—"

"Your sermon tonight," he cuts across your outrage, "what will you preach on?"

"My sermon!" you are honestly surprised. Tanar'h controls the slate of homilies, but never expressed any interest in your theme before. To suggest you would make one up is nearly blasphemous. "Never come here again unannounced!"

But his hand grips your arm, his eyes boring a hole toward the answer he seeks. Tanar'h has never lost control like this. You take a breath, and another, but no words come.

"Will you preach on the new Overlord? Will you tell us who he is to be?"

"Will I—? " You scan his face, seeking out the reason for this violation. His demand is an unspeakable insult, you always thought he knew this much about you. With icy melon in your throat you growl, "I shall speak as Argens instructs, preacher. As I *ever* have."

"Who shall you name!" he thunders, immune to your anger and rattling you like a scarecrow. Not unmoved—he is shaken by something else. The handsome face, smooth dome, the naked arms and the torso hardly concealed by the leather straps—but Tanar'h is practically quaking with desire or fear. You knew he believed in your power, doesn't doubt your prophecy. But Tanar'h was always a bit jealous, unwilling to openly acknowledge the frequency and accuracy of your visions. It gave your rivalry life. It made you want him, a little—to win his respect. But you thought he realized, even he, that visions are not pumped from Argens like water from a cistern.

Now you look on Tanar'h with new eyes. He is all glistening smooth muscles, but you desire stubbled cheeks, unkempt long hair, scars and dirt and honest manhood. Before today, you would not have chosen to break his arm-grip, not sure you could. Now you pull back so quickly his fingers snap together.

"You will leave now, ere I summon Chaktha. Shall the entire temple witness your shame?"

He looks to the door with a start, as if only now remembering. Again, his reaction is—all wrong. Tanar'h despises and fears your Nubian; but now he pulls a rueful face and smothers a curse, as if it would ruin his plans to kill the guard. He has no such power against Chaktha—does he?

Again he stares unblinking; this is some tragic play where everyone has forgotten their lines, you feel lost in this horrid present hour. With a final glare at you, devoid of his old desire, Tanar'h retreats to the inner door and slams it behind him. You rush after, throw the bolt and break into tears without knowing why.

The outer door opens; Chaktha effortlessly blocks the portal from a bustle of men in livery behind him. "Priestess," he intones, "the petitioners, if you are ready."

You nod, already sapped of the dawn's exhilaration. Tea, perhaps, nice and strong; you pour a cup as the men—all men!—file in. At their head, three proud bearers of the Red House, one holding a small darkwood box. A trio of crimson palean-bird plumes bow in unison, three red-gloved hands extend low with one holding the cask.

"A gift, Heaven's Eye of Argens Stargazer, from our master Carnad Mias. He instructs us to say that your beauty can admit no improvement, but must be honored nonetheless. You would fulfill his wildest dreams to use it."

Bemused, you flip open the golden catch and behold within a paste, for use no doubt on the skin. A scent of jasmine, tinted with something else, something wondrous, tickles you and restores your spirits. The cream is slightly red, of course, but as you rub some on your shoulders and neck, it disappears at once. Wonderful! Except for Kat's occasional prodding, you never use such ointments, but this feels as if your morning's energy now flows back in, on a tide of … yes, a smell something like the sea, mingled with your favorite flower. The gesture is well-timed, and using it thus publicly makes the point clear to the other suppliants.

"Please convey my thanks to your master, and remind him that I expect him at service, and afterwards here, this evening." You take one moment to consider, and add with a small smile, "We may discuss the extent of wild dreams at that time."

They are well-mannered men, but at this each shivers beneath wide eyes, before covering with another unison bow. Behind them, Welles the jeweler looks at you with a worried face; you cannot imagine why he is here, but with other clients in attendance it isn't safe. A small gesture, to reassure him that you will speak in private:

he hesitates briefly, but bows and withdraws without further word as the mason's representative shoulders his way forward.

"Priestess, if I may". Your dread rises expecting a carefully-worded political request, salted with vaporous promises of support. When Chaktha opens the door you turn to his interruption with relief. For a moment.

"Fighting at the arena, priestess," he says "the newcomers."

The Captain under attack? You see the arena in your prophecy, *the scream of a Gryphon* drowns out whatever the clients are saying, *the lick of flames* warms your forehead. This is the vision-grip, and even as you move to the door you feel as if you have done this before. Past the black Stallion who shoulders his shield and spear to follow, you make your way toward the scene of dripping blood and the ruin of men, a scene you well recall from childhood as well as last night.

Dimly, you hear people in the crowded streets as you pass—calling to you, offering aid, asking questions, stepping back at the Stallion's command. The Heaven's Eye of Argens Stargazer, traversing the city in broad daylight, with only one attendant, is too strange for any citizen to ignore. Behind you swells a buzzing tide of human confusion as you tread the main avenue leading to the coliseum; a louder wave ahead, spiced with the sharp ring of steel and sudden shouts of the wounded.

Feuds are the meat and drink of the city—Colors wrestle for control of key guilds, the Grips contest for higher ranks, even temple guards will bleed to preserve their imagined place. Now the men of the Emperor are here, no doubt a magnet of common hatred for an hour, to bring some mob against them, offending with their presence. The Captain, you believe, would have prevented fighting if he were with them; but unwise to this danger, he is probably still at the palace. A stab to your heart just to think it—if his men are to be saved, you must do it for him.

You think of the day your family died in that arena, and your eye drifts to two boys, the age you were then and starting a scrap as only young boys can, over close to nothing. One has a Yellow bandana, the other a Green belt, probably pinched from their father's rooms. No doubt they saw the bands of men entering the coliseum and think to do their sires proud. Why so easy, for men seeking reasons to fight to the death?

The ritual insults of the pair die out as they notice you looking upon them. The lad in Green, you have seen him before—a regular at services without his parents, and his eyes filled with love though only eleven. You resolve to save the son outside the arena walls as well as the father within. This city creates too many orphans—and you do not wish to lose this boy to the Hopeforgers, who take in all the city's wards.

Beckoning him with a finger is as effective as a hook in his mouth. "I remember you from church. Can I trust you with a message, young sir?" He gapes and bows still gaping, missing your quiet giggle. "I left my quarters in haste and need to send a message to my—to the schoolteacher Ekaterinye. Can you deliver it for me, please?"

They both drag off their head-coverings and murmur assurances—an alliance begun, even for the wrong reason, still ends the fight. "Please tell the teacher that the Salamander and Horse approach the Gryphon now, and will return from the arena before noon. As Argens has foreseen." They nod, stare another moment at you, leaning slightly down toward them, like camels at the fountain-pool. Then they are off, shots from twin bows, careening without collision around cursing adults, lamp-posts, rolling carts and other things that have no chance to hit them without their will. A good message—not that Kat needs to know, but the words "As Argens has foreseen" will do wonders when they spread.

Chaktha moves ahead now as you enter the gates, emerging from beneath the interior arch to view the red-spackled sands of the show floor.

Lightly-armored men lie dead in the House colors of their sponsors, and a crowd of thousands gasps in horror at the raging monster roaming free, reaping bloody rows of guards and forging toward the stands. Just behind the Overlord's dais, among the noble families sits a small girl, already quite beautiful in a light purple gown. Heedless of the nagging present hour, you stand enthralled by the waking nightmare, seeing the child from below, as if she were someone else. *The monster running amok plows into the stands—the Gryphon? No, a young dragon some genius thought he could control long enough to profit by, which he had assured the crowds could not yet breathe*

56

flame. The guest's seat of honor probably seemed less desirable to the man, as the maturing wurm's first fire-roar incinerated him in his chair. And your parents, without weapons but standing together between her and the horror—Chaktha snatching the girl up like a tea-tray and bearing her off; all you saw then had been his back. But from here, you see—what foot-long claws and teeth can do to the flesh of the Altieris …

Chaktha says "Priestess," noting your gaze. Suddenly the honor-dais in the stands is empty; you plunge once again into the current day. Shaking your head to get present-bearings—*your mother, she stood right next to her husband, her body helped gain another moment for you to live.* Today, the sand is not bloody, not yet; these are rose petals, or most of them, the council table is still there. A beast screams, but this is the Captain's gryphon, now chained. Men are skirmishing in a ragged double-oval, Imperial sun-blazons in the center, Colors to all sides around them. Several men are wounded and hanging back; the emperor's company has repelled assaults so far and now the men of the city lob missiles and insults into their shields.

No one has died yet, as far as you can see. None should die again, not here, not if you can stop it. *You hear your mother's high-edged scream.*

You slip past Chaktha and run for the council table, just within the circle of Emperor's men. The sand pulls at your stride and you slow, because dignity is more important than speed for the miracle you want to invoke. Besides, many already notice your entrance—irrelevantly, you wished you had brushed out your hair a bit more. Cheers and calls, as those from the Red, Blue and Green assume you are there to support them. But the hails turn to warnings, and finally to gasps of astonishment as you move on to the deadly space between the two forces. For a few moments all eyes are back on you, where they belong. Now you can save them, from themselves.

The heat of the sand is quite noticeable, lending haste to your stride again. The fighting has turned desultory, one last group rushing the imperial line, rattling metal against wood for a few moments and then falling back. A shoving contest, more than anything; but a few men hold an arm or side, weapons ready and panting for payback. Scanning the emperor's company as you approach, the Captain is not here. But you never doubt your safe-passage: why that should be, you do not even question. Argens guides you now.

You stop at the shield wall in Chaktha's shade. Within the ring, a slim elven dekentar comes up behind the row of bowmen standing atop the raised dais. "May I, help you, priestess?" he asks with deference but not looking directly upon you. A cool one, and mannerly; without him you feel sure things would have been worse.

"I am here, rather to help you. Please let me pass, officer—you are on city ground and I am its representative at this time."

"You parley for these, these citizens?"

"I will undertake to prevent bloodshed, which I presume would accord with your Captain's wishes."

Looming up next to the elf, a muscled mortal has only two bars on his shoulder to distinguish him from a thug. "Nothing wrong with a little bloodshed," he rasps gleefully, and this Man has no difficulty looking at you steadily. "So," he muses aloud, "that's what a silversteel token can get you."

At a word from the slim elven dekentar, the line breaks to admit you to the raised dais. Chaktha waits on the sand just beyond the shield wall, with ill grace. In three moments, you try to take it all in.

The men of Cryssigens range about in clots and bunches of the brightest Color livery, swords with a few shields and some order to their ranks. Blue, mostly, with just one squad of Red on the side furthest from where you stand. Perhaps one in every five Color-guards is female. Green is also there, half as numerous as the Blue and looking a good deal more aggressive—your instinct for fighting is poor, but you would bet that they started the quarrel whatever it is. And thinking of that, you note several crossbows among their ranks—the Arbalest is already here.

Scattered between the Color squads are "undressed" citizens—those unable to afford a suit of Color—in number nearly equal to both sides of fighters, yet poorly armed with whatever they could seize on the run to wherever something interesting was happening. Few stay close enough to the Emperor's men to bear much danger—most might prefer to sit on the benches and watch.

The Imperial soldiers surrounding you stand in a neat ring, uniformly armed with large shield and spear in the front rank, bow-bearing men behind. Several officers range in the hollow circle at their backs, dressing lines and pointing out the troublemakers. There is a hardened look to all the company; even without orders there is no stray step or feint. In Cryssigens, dueling and brawling are pastimes; but this troop has seen war, and won. They don't even look back, now that you stand in their midst. Just beyond the ring, with no one close by, the gryphon hunches alert between two neck-chains driven into the hard-pack beneath the arena sands. Near the entrance, several small wagons smell of fresh-butchered meat. The creature looks as if it could consume the load, wood and all.

High time to begin the miracle, if Argens wills it.

Spreading arms wide and pitching your voice to carry as in church, you call "Citizens!" Just three syllables, backed with authority and invitation—this is key to the miracle of Engagement. The energy rushes out and in at once, lifting you on toe like a dancer. Echoes of that word carry over the patter of weapons and muttered curses; as you turn in a full circle you can see they all look up at you now. Even most of the emperor's men turn their heads, excepting that slim dekentar—clever boy, he fears an enchantment to twist his will. The Hopeforgers, now, with their ritual of Awe, that would do nicely—Z'kammet Hammer might be able to give marching orders standing where you are now. But the Stargazers believe in persuasion and consensus. The miracle quiets the fighting and settles the air a moment, leaving you to talk.

"This fracas does not become us," you are speaking over the emperor's men to your fellow Cryssigensians on all sides, hoping to mask the fact that the words protect your lover's band from harm. "Our future must be decided through the cast of ballots, not the spill of blood. These warriors are guests here, and must be accorded decent treatment. Do not welcome them, if you prefer—but leave our honor unstained with these base feuds and pointless hatred."

This is more difficult than in church—the miracle requires eye contact and the direct path of the speaker's voice, but the fighters are ranged in a circle. You turn slowly as you speak—best of all to face away from the monster, for only a few of the imperial cadre guard that side, yet you cannot quite give your back to the beast.

"They started it, priestess!" someone calls over by the Blue; interruptions are bad, you must find the speaker at once and maintain the Engagement, or you'll just be a woman standing amidst the battle.

One of the females catches your eye, tall and tough, she gives you a nod filled with admiration and peril, as if to say 'I'll attack you last of all'. But behind her, with the townsfolk, a larger working man has a sash-belt of cobalt Blue, and is gesturing like one who has spoken. A leader? It doesn't seem—

"What, by being here!" the burly human dekentar roars back. "We follow orders, damn your tinted clothes."

"Citizens, this boots nothing" you begin, loud and with arms spread, turning to try and include them all. But now that blasted monster screams again—everyone flinches and you feel the miracle shredding about its edges. Too many distractions, so much happening at once, as it did on that day …

Chaktha holds you as gently as when he lifted you into the trees on your parents' manor, but he is forging back through the panicking crowd. With your face against his back you can hear the butt-end of his spear smacking a way through the press, catch a glimpse of bodies beneath his sandaled feet, hurt but alive at least, unlike your mother and father a few feet on. It's a bumpy ride, your forehead sometimes bangs on his muscled shoulder-blade, and once your skull raps against the shaft of his spear so hard you see stars. Even then, the points of light had meaning.

Men are shouting everywhere, and Chaktha yells "Priestess!" which is strange because you were only a girl then. The pain in the back of your head is resounding and sharp; one of the stars you see is bright green, like a Color in the night-sky which is strange because it was not night then. A voice of command quietly says the same words your father did to Chaktha before he died. "Take her". His face, so kindly and noble, but not looking directly at you because the peril is nearby, and he fears what he might lose if he looks on you now. And this too is strange because he is not your father—

It is the slim dekentar, and the fighting has broken out again. In the table near you a poniard quivers, its pommel set with bright emerald and the hilt wrappings unmistakably Green. Your head-someone threw at you when your back was turned, only the random spin of the blade caused it to strike hilt-first and rebound. You feel dizzy and sick, slumping near to falling.

Your miracle broken, now the Color-feuds and other jealousies within the city are drowned like sandbars beneath a tide of ancient hatred from Cryssigens for Argens, the North Mark versus the Empire.

This is the price your people will pay, for a civil war you did not avert. The city, your new family, torn to bits by a monstrous threat while you hug your skull achieving nothing.

Men throw themselves against the shield wall, yet the dekentars call out "Hold!" and the bows remain taut, unfired. Imperial spears reach well beyond the edges and blunts wielded by the City; men are bleeding in numbers now. The view is suddenly cut off by Chaktha's shield. He has muscled inside the circle and covers you against the renewed fighting. Your protest is cut off by a sharp *thunk*, as two inches of a quarrel appear in the wood not half a foot from the bridge of your nose.

"Like for like, Zetee," the brawny human calls, and the slim elven officer nods once.

"Loose!" now the bowstrings thrum, and with five fallen bodies the matter is instantly decided. Colors and cityfolk rout in all directions; Chaktha herds you along towards the nearest of the exits. The emperor's men are up and moving now, away from the raised center dais toward their camp area, still holding as a group. Suddenly the men in Green are on one side, the crossbows that started it hanging slack from their belts. They notice you, look to each other, and spread in a semi-circle arresting your progress. Chaktha presents shield and spear while backing you up, onto the dais again, by the council table to limit their field for attack.

"No truce with Purple," one of them says leeringly, "nor with the 'Gazers.'" One of their number puts his hands up and backs off, saying "Not me; my father's a vineguilder." Seven left, five with crossbows, smiling like jackals at the chance you've given them. Eliminate a rival, claim accident—one of them already tried. You step back again, and the table bumps your thighs. The Green men reach for their windlasses, but stop as Chaktha hefts his spear overhand.

The Nubian never wastes words. "Who dies first? Crank your bow and show me."

They freeze, buying precious seconds. Chaktha stands ready to hurl the fencepost-spear like a dart, training it smoothly back and forth across their ranks. You need to do something, but the smell of blood and sound of wrack have sent your dizzy mind elsewhen. Facing the stands beyond the Green line of death you *see the dragon mauling your parents in an instant, ruining their flesh and creating an orphan of the small girl over a Nubian's back, just beyond its reach; she flees, always fleeing danger. Not a mark on her, beautiful child-*

"Idiots," one of them snarls, "he can only throw once. Use your blades. Take her." People die on those words.

They draw short swords and start crab-stepping towards Chaktha. It would never surprise you if he killed three, but they are seven. Reaching behind, perhaps to ascend the table and try another miracle, you cry out as your hand scrapes something sharp. The dagger slices your hand but you grip and draw it forth anyway. Instead of wielding the blade, you hold it out toward them emerald pommel-first, like a talisman; were you thinking to offer it back, and did you believe that would buy your life? Or is Argens truly guiding you, despite the appearance of a useless coincidence?

The Green men are close to grips now. Chaktha, with no good options, prepares to sell his life dearly. All is shattered by the sound-force of the gryphon's scream, tinged with the snap of chains. With one leap it is there on the dais, fierce and free and colossal. Faster than thought, it turns its head toward you, a beak the size of your waist reeking of slaughter; its eyes focus for a split-second on your outstretched hand; then it turns to make a shambles of men dressed in Green. Blood patters like rain at last.

And now again, *again,* Chaktha has hoisted you and is running; will he never stop saving your life. Your screams and kicks are not much more effective than they were at age eleven; but you have learned saltier curses and somehow you manage to make Chaktha put you back down for just a moment. The gryphon has savaged the men of Green, two of them reeling back alive with just three arms between them.

"Weapons *down!*" The familiar voice you never heard in such anger before rings out now from the horse-entrance. Gaspar Heugen, the Fire Grip and virtual regent of Cryssigens checks his brown stallion at the head of an enormous troop of City guardsmen rushing in to surround all and sundry. The undressed empty their hands at once, either fleeing or groveling. The other Color-guards lower their points and stand sullenly, hopelessly outnumbered. The Blue, by contrast, grin and make to join with the City militia—you note many sapphire and cobalt accents marring the uniform effect of the latter's garb and something in you deeply misgives.

Heugen gestures someone forward, and your Captain canters to his men on a dappled mare, dismounting while the horse still moves, hearing reports before his second foot has touched the sand.

He has been up all night, but you see no sign of fatigue as he sets the camp in order. The company is clearly preparing for a march; not knowing their destination the men snap to it. You hear the ribaldry in their feigned complaints, though the tasks would do credit to the real thing. One squad regains control of the gryphon, Justin standing fearlessly near the head to calm it. With quick looks and salutes, the men convey a respect bordering on awe. They love him too.

The two leaders met predawn and conferred; then heard news of this melee and came from the palace to investigate. The three of you form a triangle two hundred paces on a side now, no way to read faces from here. That they met, at least, is a good sign; but has the Captain made a mistake by committing to the Blue? One of their men broke the miracle that would have averted bloodshed. And Heugen seems to hover near attempts on your life—arriving so soon after this brush with death, the last to leave the Hopeforger temple before the previous one.

With an effort you tear your gaze away from Justin's back; the priestess of Argens Stargazer has no business with a lackey of the Southern Emperor, her charge is a report to the Fire Grip. One sleeve ripped from your gown makes a stylish bandage for your palm; the seeping blood shows purple through the gauzy fabric. You hand the dagger to Chaktha; his pace parallels your own until the last step before Heugen's horse. The Fire Grip oversees the detainment from horseback and you await his pleasure. Even mounted he looks as if there is a board stuck up his back.

The City guards control the arena; several captured men groan with their injuries, as the fighting slaves used to do here. From the entrance a brace of courtiers and attendants swarm up, who must have lagged the Fire Grip on foot. They look askance at you, but press closer with official papers, a wax seal, murmured imprecations. Even as Heugen continues to direct his officers regarding internment and hearings, he removes a gauntlet to seize proffered quills and sign upheld documents. You note his remarkably clean nails as you wait, thinking he has perhaps forgotten you. But no male can conceal the effort not to look, and he is making one now. The last attendant insistently holds up a tray with food, and when the Fire Grip shakes his head, the servant points to the washing-bowl on one side. Defeated, Heugen removes his other glove and cleanses his hands before taking up one roll, then gestures to you over the tray.

"Priestess Altieri, some refreshment."

"I have broken fast, Fire Grip, my thanks."

He consults a report handed to him by an officer. "The Green House will be brought to task for this assault," he remarks neutrally. He holds your gaze a moment, and you know there are webs thick underfoot here.

"There was much confusion, milord, the beast broke free and all was chaos." You are reversing events somewhat, but a rift with the Green is too high a price to pay for your dignity. With more confidence than you feel, you say "We cannot assume the Color was behind this, this regrettable pass."

He raises an eyebrow—approval? "Merely the axe for your attackers then."

You see a rain of blood, hear the creature behind you still chewing. "The men—those who survived—have suffered enough. Let there be no charges brought, I pray you."

Heugen's face goes still, long enough to imagine you have pushed too far toward lenience for his taste. Or maybe he wants you to think this favor is hard to grant, maneuvering for the vote ahead. Worth it, in either case; you smile winningly up at him and curtsy as if he has already agreed.

"Well, praise The First you are safe, priestess." Before you can frame your thanks, he undercuts any noble sentiment, adding "This will be difficult enough without losing someone to keep that stallion Tanar'h in hand." With a shock you realize Gaspar Heugen, the noble whose influence you were hoping to gain just three nights ago, plans to use you in turn. But again, to what end?

"The last of the Altieris is quite pleased, I assure you, still to serve the Stargazers," you insert a gentle reminder of your influence.

The Fire Grip looks down on you again. "I remember well your parents," he replies, a rather direct assertion of the difference in your age. "They were square in dealing, honest at least, in their opposition to my counsel to Overlord Kreel." His gaze comes again to your eyes. "I opposed the introduction of a dragon here, on the day your parents died. Wasteful, needless risk." Such raw candor in referring to their loss—you can scarcely breathe. He speaks with no gentleness, though he means it kindly. "I think, perhaps they sensed their Moment had arrived. They were resolved at the end, that their purpose would live on in you—you bear their meaning now. Those were different days, priestess, though not so long ago."

He says more, and the Grip's words are always important, but you live again in the day they were taken away. The Gryphon of your vision screams and only you can hear its prophecy. With a fierce anger at confinement it promises that any who try to harness its power will meet with trials, and loss. Your parents, the men in Green—everyone has a family they plan to see again, in the moments before a monster rends them to shanks. That boy from outside—despite your efforts or perhaps because of them, he is likely an orphan now. This is the meaning of monstrous; that which cares not about hopes, joy or family. The Gryphon warns of the price you all will pay, if the Arbalest and the Spiders and the Dragon succeed.

A small man in brown robes edges through the cloud of Heugen's courtiers, his face crossed with concern for those behind you in the arena center. It is the healer, the preacher to Telhol; the death screams of years past, and the vision-sounds of combat to come, both yield to the cries of today's wounded. Heugen's men have all the Color guards detained, and bar the way to the wounded among them. The preacher turns back to face Heugen up on his horse.

"Fire Grip, let me pass, I must practice my faith."

"Those men are bound for trial, Telholian," Heugen says, in the tone of an immortal nobleman explaining matters to a human émigré. "By custom, if they survive till their case is heard, they prove worthy to bear the consequence of their misdeed. Of which you know nothing."

65

The little man will have none of that; without rancor he responds at once. "You intend to apply the law of the arena, to free citizens of the Empire?"

Heugen almost smiles. "That law applies to the location, sir, and takes no notice of rank." He is fencing semantics on tip-toe, perhaps to annoy the newcomer.

But the preacher seems unruffled. "You gave me license to build and practice devotion in this city, milord. Without regard to location: this is my practice, deprived of which your license means nothing."

"Let him pass, milord," you say on impulse, to remind Heugen of his promise. "I beg you, as a favor." No harm in cultivating this newcomer with a vote, as the Captain has asked.

Heugen shrugs and the spears draw back, letting the Telholian through to the dais where the wounded lie on the council table. For a moment, the gryphon rouses and pulls against the chains as Imperial soldiers strain to hang on. It is several lengths from the dais, but some of the wounded scramble up to try and escape. The preacher looks across the space at the monster, eye to eye—to your astonishment he does not flinch though unarmed and barely taller than you. His face shows concern but no fear, he only waits to see if he must do something. And could. For one instant the gryphon looks on the preacher; it settles back, still angry but willing to let the soldiers make it sit again. The Telholian turns to the wounded, calling out healing incantations as he helps with bandages.

You turn to thank the Fire Grip, hoping for further conversation, but with a start you see the Captain has ridden up close, just on the other side of Heugen's stallion. For a moment it is not possible to speak; barely able to breathe you wait for some sign from Justin. But he too is making an effort, not as well as his elder.

"My thanks, milord, your arrival here has saved my men the trouble of dispensing a lesson." He is playing the role of the fop again, though he dissembles no better than he did last night. You must help him.

"My old teacher would say, captain, that it is usually the tutor who learns the most."

"Indeed?" he sneers barely polite. "I would say my men and I have learned the extent of Cryssigensian hospitality."

"Well, sir, you hardly took advantage of your opportunity," you purr, suppressing a tremble, and the point scores. The Captain shifts in his saddle as if the horse had started, instead of himself. Now his eye drifts to your torn sleeve, the makeshift bandage, and his eyes flare with a moment of fury.

Without moving his head, Heugen glances at both of you and the vision slams down again –*the meticulous nocturnal scavenger holding out a token of treasure.* The Fire Grip knows, and he sees that you know him now. With clean hands, the Raccoon sent you a treasure in the night, for reasons unknown.

A commotion in the center draws everyone's glance. Part of the arena floor heaves and bulges like lava; suddenly a large trap door flips open shedding a wave of sand. A team of Justin's men emerge from the ramp beneath pushing a large wheeled cage with thick bars. The brawny human officer rides atop it and laughs gustily, spreading his arms to the cheers of the troop. "What did I tell you?" he shouts, slapping the back of his hand. "Like *this* I know the place!" They begin to herd the gryphon carefully, and it rages again, well aware of their intent.

With alarm, you see now that the imperial company is ready to march. "So soon?" you exclaim, looking dazed and silly before these military men.

"I shall send messages as I find the opportunity," Justin says to Heugen, but his glance flickers to include you.

"More than a week, to reach the seat of Tyr," Heugen remarks. "On foot, that is. Two months may seem longer now than once you arrive. The vote will not wait for anyone, Captain."

"The ides of the Dragon," Justin nods, "I will not fail."

Heugen's eyebrows reflect his judgment on that—he manages to convey doubt of success and indifference in the same gesture. Wheeling his mount, the Fire Grip calls out orders, directing his men to take the prisoners in tow back out the main entrance toward the Dock Quarter and the gaol. You see that among those arrested, several wounded men are now walking, only the one worst hurt being carried on a shield but quite alive. The small robed preacher leans alone against the council table with both hands, head hung low and clearly exhausted.

Before you can go to him the sounds of Justin's company swing you around, the sight making you dizzier than the turn. They march out the grand exit opposite, closer to the city's east-facing gate, and the road north to Tralmachia. Such a tiny company, not even five-score men. The Baron of Blood will drink them in. You cannot run after him, cannot stop his march to death with your tears or some girlish plea. You can even credit, though grudgingly, that he must take this risk, so that your city might survive. But still you wish his men would turn back, or his horse at least stumble, anything to slow the loss of your heart.

Then he checks his horse, turns abruptly as if to oversee the team pulling the gryphon-cage in the rear. You see his face again—his effort not to look back dissolves, the eyes returning your gaze. He tries so hard to appear an indifferent enemy of the city's fate, and you just another beautiful woman who means him harm. You wave with a mocking laugh, and the laughter comes easily because he is so brave, and alone, and because the hysteria of your separation breathes close upon you.

But when he waits until the last hoof and boot has turned the corner, and still looks upon you without witnesses—then you can stop. The arena is a vast empty space, like the world outside it; there is only him, for you, and he is far and will most likely never return. He stares back as if he can hoard the view of you, and ration it out over long leagues and weeks ahead. Such an expert horseman, he seems to use only his mind to turn the dappled mare. He is gone and your world is empty indeed.

The sun near midday beats on the sand like metal, and part of what blurs your vision may be heat-vapor. Only a madwoman would hug herself and shiver with a chill. Suddenly exhausted, you turn once more to the dais—but the Telholian too has left, removing your chance to speak to him. Praise the First for a small favor.

"Back to the temple, Chaktha. And let us discuss, along the way, how to break you of this bad habit you have, of saving my life."

⊕ ⊕ ⊕

Afternoon light already shades the contemplation garden behind the temple. The low surrounding wall, many fulsome trees, valley landscaping and more cast the aura of privacy even in places where the benches have a view. Though it lacks an hour of sunset yet, some of the night-blooming jasmine has already begun to open in the relative darkness. This is where Kat or any other Stargazer curate would seek you, with your tower unguarded. Chaktha stands beyond the garden's arch, some say because he would be embarrassed to come upon a love-pair within; you and he both know, it is because he mortifies them. Besides, you are safe here. The garden is wrapped thick with enchantment, layered on by preachers of the ancient day, promoting the contemplation and intimacy that brings enlightenment. Violence of any kind is prohibited here, by more than a temple rule—preachers find it difficult even to argue a point of law or of sport within the walls.

In the summer mornings the strolling devotee can pluck fruit from the trees, and flowers of every variety enhance the senses, promoting thoughts of higher things, the future, and the heart's desire in growing warmth. Even now, with the relative cool of winter, the emphasis merely shifts to the evergreen ground-cover, the small blue and white flowers that dot the hillsides; their scent is more austere, but cleaner, enhancing the coolness of that time when the heat of the day begins to turn. Thoughts of closure, discernment of meaning and new resolves take root. In any season, it is not unusual for your friends or clients to find you in some corner, staring at nothing and needing to be aroused as if from sleep. The hours dissolve here, and the future beckons.

But today you have no recourse to timeless ignorant bliss; the garden is delightfully cool and understanding of your vision deepens, but you cannot forget where you are for one step. Your love is no longer a dream, a helmed voice in combat; his face now defined, his honor rings in thought and his fate marches north into peril on the edge of a razor. The Fire Ant, no more doubt, a Captain among his soldiers but obeying orders without hesitation or regard for his own life. In Tralmachia, he will burrow at the roots of the Stone Oak until they crush him, so that his successors might triumph. You will surely never see him again this side of death. But then, how can he return to defend your tower? And why would he need to?

A woman's gasp ahead sounds close to ecstasy, so you turn aside. But the next sound is clearly a sob—the two so close, betokening their opposites—and you sense she is alone. The young priestess on the bench is one of the novitiates, graduated from Kat's classroom but not yet fully under vows to the temple. It is love that breaks her heart, you can tell.

"Dear one, what troubles you so?" The girl turns with a gasp, but before she can launch into some ridiculous apology involving your rank, you gather her up in a warm embrace that asks no questions. She sobs full on for a time—Talishaya, you recall her now, such a lovely girl when not crying. When she can stand on her own, you hold her shoulders in appraisal. So tall and willowy, she must already be making an impression on the congregation; but too soon, by a year yet.

"Now then."

"Heaven's Eye, I am sorry to have disturbed your reflections."

"Nonsense, I am bored with thrones and struggles, truth to tell. It is high time I did some real good today. What troubles you, Talishaya- not a lover, I hope?"

Her eyes go wide and she curtsies, clearly flattered that you remember her. Your mind for people was always a good one. "You are from a crafting family, in the Red house I believe, down by the docks?" She nods and you both sit on the bench.

"It is my sister, priestess."

"Is she in love then? But I thought her younger than you—"

The girl cries out, almost a laugh but too hard-edged. "Certainly not! Keilee is just a child- missing, priestess, and I cannot find her."

"Missing? How long?"

"More than a day, since before the arena gathering where—when the vote was not taken. We returned and she did not—that's hardly unusual, but overnight, and by the time I came here for service, still nothing."

You knit a brow, already deciding to ask Argens for his help in navigating to the girl, for your acolyte's sake. You need to know more about her. "She should be in school. Is she not fit for study?"

Now her laughter is unforced. "Is the swallow suited to dig a tunnel? With ropes you could not tie Keilee to a school desk, priestess. She is always out and about—why just last week she scampered on the river-pilings, almost across to Old Cryss! But a kindly gentleman, our neighbor, managed to retrieve her—poor soul, he nearly drowned."

Focusing in your spirit, you draw on these words to seek for the girl. The miracle of Sending works best with those well known to you, but perhaps a glimpse of the future, if you clear your mind of the vision and other thoughts about yourself.

"The kind neighbor, has he seen her, then?"

"He is missing as well! Or at least, we have not seen him. He sells stone or some such, and we sent Keilee to work for him as a penance."

Well then, you think, it may be nothing.

"It may be nothing, priestess, but I cannot help worrying. She is a terror, and will be the death of my mother."

"Let us see what may be done."

She shakes her head, eyes wide again. "Oh no, Myster, this is not a matter for the church."

"And whom, then, should it concern, young priestess? The Stargazers are specially charged with the care of the lost and the safeguard of family. The miracles Argens sends to us are not some hoarded gemstore, but grain to be sown forth and returned to us a thousandfold." You hesitate as hope springs up before you. "It may be that my talents are insufficient to locate her. But the sincere attempt never goes awry. Let us pray, and try it."

Talishaya swallows, nods, and closes her eyes with whispering lips to ask The First for news of her sister. You smile on her, and reach for her hand as you extend your spirit in quest of a little girl you have never seen. Contact with the querent brings only a chance of success. And you must cleanse your mind, of course, of all lordly claptrap about crowns and successions.

"Argens, lord of navigation," you begin, "send my spirit in voyage for some word of the young Keilee, keep her in your—"

The rush of vision is nearly as strong as when you were with the Captain. Instead of clearing from your thoughts, animal-forms and zodiac signs crowd in once again, as if Argens is not listening to you. *A jeweled crown lies at the Ferret's feet, in an enormous sacred space defiled by a throng of rats. A brave urchin prisoner stands and shouts defiance at the king of the vermin, hurling a piece of stone just missing his head and bouncing gently off the Ferret's heart. Insects the size of pillars loom behind her, as the rat-king laughs. The Ferret places the stone in a large balance-scale; the crown on the other side is outweighed. The girl is doused in perils yet you know the Ferret will keep her safe from them somehow.*

Your vision pulls back, beyond the cracked walls of the colossal temple into the darkest night. Strange statues here, and horrible rows of stone markers behind a fence; cold, and buildings made for a race of unsleeping giants. In the sprawling courtyard, the Dragon searches everywhere for that crown—The Brow! He comes ever closer, and behind him a hot wind destroys the chill of this haunted place, presaging a storm of fire, and legions of spiders. You must warn the Ferret, and the Fire-Ant Captain, but you cannot speak. Your mouth opens but only water flows forth, you are not allowed …

"Star! Are you hearing me, he's done it!" You swim toward Kat's voice, she stands in a garden with Talishaya near a drooling idiot in a purple gown.

"Heaven's Eye?"

"Star! Listen to me, and close your mouth."

You clap your jaw shut on the edge of your tongue, and the sharp pain brings you fully back to the present. Breathless, you wipe your chin and try to redress yourself. "What—how long have I—"

Kat holds your elbow sharply in her concern: she sees you return from the vision-grip but still hesitates before deciding to simply say, rather than try to explain.

"Tanar'h has replaced you in the order. You may not speak. He preaches tonight, not you."

"He replaced me?" The blow would hurt more if you could believe your ears. Tanar'h indeed controls the slate of preaching as High Heart—did he mention something to you last night, before this morning's outrageous intrusion—but now, to simply change the names, no consultation or vote. In your adult years, it has never happened once.

A new resolve takes root in you. Today, you and Tanar'h will settle something. Your feet are moving toward the postern-door before you remember the need. You turn back to Kat still standing with Talishaya before the bench.

"Tell Chaktha I will be in the temple, await me there as usual."

This violation cannot be borne. You weren't planning to contest with Tanar'h for the leadership so long before the vote, but he has forced your hand. Tonight's service—Carnad Mias will be there, with many clients and aspiring allies. You imagine the scene, Tanar'h grinding on about the manly virtues from the pulpit while you sit with folded hands to one side and watch their faces drop into boredom. No, not if Argens forbade you—well, for The First of course, but not for any mere man.

With dismay, you realize you have said no word of comfort yet to Talishaya and turn again, now many steps away, to see her standing alone and staring. How much of the symbolism to relay?

"Your sister—she is brave as a lion. Nothing affrights her, and she will be well. Under Argens' protection; I believe you will find her soon. Be of good heart—" No, this won't do. You run back to hug your acolyte, whispering, "and tell me when she is found." She giggles with relief, and promises though you doubt her courage—still so awe struck by the higher ranks, such a dear.

And now, at last, you can run to the postern. These are directions you learned as a child, a lucky discovery only two years into your newfound position.

From the rear garden exit, you trot back up the winding path until it nears the north side of the temple proper. The directions are in your body's memory: duck beneath the magnolia and wend through a hedge that shows no break until up close. The wall here is smooth, and from the bottom of the light-slits to either side you can spy the hallway within, empty as usual. Pressing here and here, you engage the pivot and soundlessly slip through unseen from either side. Furious as you are, yet the giggle overtakes you a moment— there was no reason not to stomp around to the front and enter the chapel with Chaktha by your side. But temple intrigue, usually the province of your mainly-male elders, demands some tribute. You found this passage quite by accident, and no doubt there are others known only to Tanar'h and the rest. Let them wonder, a bit, how you came by this route from the gardens to the preachers' entrance of the sacred space.

You start toward the chapel, away from your tower—you think with a thrill that this is the passage Tanar'h used this morning, and the anger returns. He is trying to subdue you through his control of the schedule, playing on your desire to speak before the congregation to win your influence, perhaps your vote, or even—no, surely even

Tanar'h would never stoop to this blasphemy in order to win your hand? Still, the man of this morning, a total stranger to your rival, the man who stared, and seized you, and insisted. Tanar'h is overconfident, and prides himself on his virility; but he is a Stargazer. You shake your head even as your stride lengthens near a run. He is in the grip of something, perhaps fear over the new Overlord. You must correct him, if only you can master your anger enough to argue rationally.

You glide into the main cathedral space, one glance acquainting you with the present moment. Your entrance is level with the altar. Worship-benches fill the enormous space to your left split by a wide carpeted aisle leading out the main entrance. Just two or three solitary worshippers sit scattered around the back, enough to pay witness to any unseemly argument. Tanar'h kneels at the statue's foot, praying as is his habit before service. The lamps are not yet brightened, and in the ceiling, thick circular windowpanes show more of the stars than would appear outside in dusk's aura; the air holds enough secrecy to speak in quiet tones, but loud words will carry.

There are eighty full paces between the altar and the main entrance arch, but all is so still within the cathedral that you dimly hear the temple guards remarking in surprise at the Nubian's arrival.

"Where is the Heaven's Eye then, Chaktha?"

"Within."

"It cannot be! We have stood here since mid-afternoon, and she is in the garden."

Tanar'h stirs from his devotions, roused by the warning at those words. Looking up from his knees, he starts with recognition and surprise, but none of the guilt you expected.

"W'starrah! You are, I suppose, that is, you—" he deserves to be interrupted as the humans do.

"Favor me, Tanar'h. Am I punished for failure to fulfill a sacred temple procedure? Or is this simply chastisement for refusing your suit?"

Still on his knees, he boils but retains his poise and outward calm. You put just enough emphasis behind the word "punished" that it echoed among the benches. But he too, is master of this space and knows its acoustics intimately.

"You speak of two separate causes, *love*."

74

You involuntarily glance out to see a half-dozen early arrivals now, all looking over at that word.

"The first matter is trivia, we agree I need not rise to defend my actions. As to the second—" he pauses, and looks up at you with a familiar, once welcome intensity, "I should again stay as I am, on my knees, to beg before Argens and the world, for such a priceless object as your hand."

He reaches up to take it, inches away from another proposal, and this time in public. With a shock, you resist the urge to back away and instead put the intended hand on his shoulder. Now the pose is more collegial than you wished, but you can lean in a bit to whisper.

"You think of yourself too often, trying to steal my moment Tanar'h!"

"And you of yourself too much, W'starrah," he snaps back, the hiss-edges making his emotion clear. "This is a scheduling matter; why should you care when you are allowed to preach? Argens will gift you on any night, I have faith."

And in this, you sense Tanar'h speaks his honest mind. "But why tonight?" you counter. "Are the farm-guilders among your Yellow house allies so urgently in need of inspiration?"

He tries to chuckle, getting a dry cough instead. "Hah—no doubt, they must return to sow the winter wheat." He pauses, and you sense your usual familiarity with him ebbing away. He looks uncomfortable, not simply because you have the right of the matter. "But you, W'starrah," he counters finally, "even you are not above the protocols. I warned you yesterday, we must discuss the schedule, yet you were too busy nearly getting killed in a street brawl to attend to it. Heed your priorities, then, and I will mind the church without you."

"The church? Or your growing *harum*?"

"Will you learn humility!" Tanar'h stings from your banter, which you regret the moment the words escaped you. "Not every matter of the Stargazer temple has the same person standing at the center of it, Myster Altieri. The favored of Argens is not his only concern." Though still on his knees, the High Heart projects more and more confidence as yours begins to fade. "I do as I must for the good of my clerical brethren, who are my true family. And should be yours."

You straighten with a gasp at the insult. Tanar'h keeps his voice low and bores on.

"I preach tonight for—yes, for certain elements among our population, certain guests, that must hear the words of the Stargazer. This city needs leadership, and our congregants, our family, are my first concern. The marriage, my proposal, that is another matter, though it should march alongside the first."

He looks up, with a need so sincere it makes your heart ache. "I have already bespoken Eline, Bereshutha and May'stra about you, and they made clear to me they would welcome you as a sister among them. I have told you that I love you, W'starrah, but not yet that I loved you that first day, the evening you came to us."

In an instant, though he is on his knees before you, *Tanar'h looms, on this very spot, over a little girl brought in breathless and weeping. As Chaktha sets you down among the other elders, men and women stand around you at the interrupted service, and you see also the smiling countenance of Argens in marble looking over their shoulders right in your eyes. Ekaterinye, brown hair and only a few wrinkles, bends down speaking kind words, trying to distract from the dour mutterings on all sides. Only one preacher- handsome, nearly-naked, muscular- shakes his head and argues for some other course.*

"You came to us an orphan, W'starrah, on the death of your parents in that horrid arena. And by rights the Hopeforgers should have had you. But I alone called for you to stay; I said that the Stargazer himself welcomed you, and that this was your family. The spirit of The First moved me to speak those words. I am not ashamed to say, I was struck to the heart by your beauty even then. And I waited ten years before I spoke one word to you."

He urges his suit, finally rising to face you before the statue, with more than a dozen persons in view. High time for tonight's preacher to take position outside the main door, and begin greeting the congregation.

"Put aside your pride, W'starrah. You remain Heaven's Eye among us, and may visit your tower whenever your heart draws you from the chambers I shall set aside. The Stargazers cannot exist alone. Your previous lover, that sailor—and your daughter Ellesmera; these are casualties to your delay. Join the family and take your proper place with us."

You tremble despite yourself, but you can no more speak the lie here, where Argens first saved you, than you could knock his statue to the ground. Tanar'h is sincere, he is handsome, and he is wooing you in a public place, before The First and anyone else who comes. But the love of your life, the Captain brave enough to fly upon a heaven-wrought symbol of fierce destruction and purpose, would never dream of making a "no" so difficult to say. Which thought makes it easier for you to voice.

"How I attend to the Stargazer, High Heart, is a matter between The First and myself. On the other hand," you say "I believe this is yours," drawing forth the token of Fire and handing it back to its warden. His jaw drops and he stares at the silversteel disk, unable to wrap his mind around all the consequence of this find. "I think always of my family here, this I swear. And that remembrance shall not lapse tonight."

"The token of Fire!" Tanar'h draws a shaky breath, passing his hand over the marvel before stowing it at his belt. "This—this, changes nothing, W'starrah," he says with quiet urgency, struggling to keep his jealousy in check. "I know you courted the influence of Carnad Mias last night—his wealth is greater than I imagined—but these intrigues have no place here. And the speaking order remains unchanged."

So, his best thrust misses the mark completely. "Never fear, Tanar'h. I would not stand between you and your saffron-support. Go back to them, and wear again the golden bauble at your neck they gave you." You see puzzlement cross his face, and your anger bests you a little. "But never seek to enter my tower again to lay unbidden hands on me."

Now he is absolutely stunned, and despite your warning he reaches to take your arm again. "W'starrah, what? You must—the order—"

"Never fear, High Heart," you cut in, pulling your arm smoothly away and turning down the aisle off the altar. You drop a word behind your shoulder in audible tones. "The order remains unchanged. Live in Hope, Tanar'h."

He stands there uncertain, and quietly adds, "And light of the stars to you, Heaven's Eye." Never before has the traditional word sounded so much like farewell.

But his confusion and sorrow give you the time to defy him. Before he realizes your treachery, you are at the entrance nave and through the arch, to stand at the open doors. Chaktha is there on the portico, near two temple guardsmen in Tanar'h's favor that start with surprise and bow so quickly their spears knock, catching as they straighten. You smile past them to the arriving worshippers, as if nothing is wrong. The Stallion takes up his usual position behind you, as if nothing ever was.

"Myster! Revered Heaven's Eye, we did not, that is, we were told to expect—"

"—perhaps not told, but that is—"

"My thanks, Jal'i and Tamess, as I have already conveyed my appreciation to the High Heart. No doubt he anticipated I would be late returning from the garden today. I'm all a fluster, so much has happened!" You pat Jal'i's shoulder and straighten the lovely decorative braid admiringly—sunrise Yellow, of course. "But I am here now at last, so kind of you both to greet the early arrivals."

Of course, neither did any such thing, but an exit is easy to take when you are confused, so the pair turn and enter the temple. They stand looking to the altar a moment; you can see from your eye-corner Tanar'h stock-still and fuming, deciding what to do. He sharply waves them away, then sits in the preacher's seat defiantly. So the battle is not yet over.

There is pain from the stabs he took at you in there. The Stargazers embrace the image of Argens as father, lover, husband, and Tanar'h has thrown your alone-ness in your face. No surviving family after that horrible day in the arena; a brief, illicit love producing a daughter always estranged and now absent. The great Myster, Heaven's Eye of the city, lives alone in her tower. Men desire her body, everyone comes to hear her speak of the future. But she remains apart, no arms enfold her to assuage a moment of loneliness, no child brightens her days.

Ellesmera—you promised not to contact her with a Sending anymore, but she has been so often troubled. A preacher's oath means nothing to a mother. You agree with yourself not to speak to her, only observe. Even as one or two scattered arrivals nod to you on the stairs, you smile back and send your spirit in quest of your only child.

With such a familiar face the contact is instantaneous and strong, bereft of Argens' playful imagery. Your daughter sits in plain robes on a bench in a stone cell silently discussing something with two others you have seen before. There is no outward distress, no suffering or wound. If she is jailed, it is at least not the same prison in Wanlock, when you went out by gate last fall to post her bond, and she fled before you could find her. With a sigh you close the contact and return to this place, heavy with loss and empty of inspiration. Even if you defy Tanar'h, how can you deliver a sermon worthy of The First?

You turn to greet the growing stream of worshippers, seeing many faces you recognize. Not only staff from the temple, approaching along the portico to either side, but folk of the city down the main avenue from the precinct gate. More of them since you began preaching here (you flatter yourself with a broadening smile); but also it must be admitted, many of the fashionable and wealthy have recently turned to the Stargazers since the banishment of the Demonbender sect. Even a few nobles- there is the cousin of the Cliff Grip, proudly wearing Green and no doubt preferring death to attendance with the Hopeforgers. He passes with only a nod, and you can see on his face the firm intention to nap. But the crafters and common folk, they greet you warmly, generously, some even with hugs of relief. At first it is hard to make sense of their effusive compliments and outspoken thanks for your safety.

Their story comes to you slowly, in pieces. The arena! That fight happened just earlier today. The cut on your palm is nearly invisible now, you must probe it to feel any pain. The rash choice to follow your vision has grown to an heroic exploit of ridiculous proportions: facing down the savage gryphon with only a dagger, waving one arm to make soldiers put down their weapons. Even the Emperor's men—the villains, of course—could not keep you a prisoner in their ranks, and now they flee to parts unknown, good riddance. Such hyperbole grants you ample leeway to deprecate without lying, and the air fills with light jokes and even cheering.

The crowd thickens, too many to greet individually—there is Welles, bowing and still looking serious—a carnival atmosphere as the time before a worship service should be. The elation that your devotion to Argens brings is starting to work within you again; your feet feel light and if you don't dance or preach soon you may fly away.

Here is Kat, up the side path and hugging you hard. You bubble with public greetings for a time that all can hear. Then she leans in to whisper, "I am *so* glad, you managed to convince Tanar'h to relent."

"Well my dear, we shall see," you murmur coolly, with a point of your head within.

She squints in the fading dusk, and squeaks to see him seated in the preaching chair with his arms crossed. "'Star! What can this mean? What are you *doing* here?"

"What, my dear teacher, is he doing there?" You give Kat a long glance that she may see your determination. She shrinks, bites her lip; but before she can speak again you hear the excited cry of a young boy.

The lad with the Green belt waves with one arm while dragging his reluctant father with the other. It is a Color guard, the one who refused to attack you; his wife and another, elder man, possibly his vine-guilder father are behind them.

"There she is! See, Preacher, I have brought my father to service!"

The man looks as if he wished the gryphon had gotten him instead, but faces up bravely to his fate. He bows low on the step beneath yours, and takes your hem to his lips, the homage paid to lords, and to owners before the slaves were freed. "I owe you my life, Lavender Lady."

"Your life? Credit instead your own common sense, sir, knowing when to step away from a monster. But we are delighted to have you here. This bright young lad, Ekaterinye, bore my message I trust."

"Yes," Kat says gaily, "he came to me tumbling over his friend and between punches in each other's ribs they told me your story in turns." She regards the boy with a serious face and a twinkling eye, "I thank you, young man for your service to the church." He beams and stands tall.

"He should be in school with you, wouldn't you say teacher?" And now it is the youth's turn to look condemned. But his mother laughs and agrees. You shake hands with the grandfather, who sports a thin bright violet sash. "Your son chose to honor your Color, sir, above his own, and for that I praise him."

"I had no orders to kill a preacher," the Green guard answers, and his father nods along.

"I am glad of any happy chance that keeps my family and loyalty intact, priestess." He leans in to whisper to you, and his hair is neat, his cologne in good taste. "I believe I may have advanced our Color in a way that would please you. Perhaps tomorrow or the next day, at audience?"

"I look forward to it, sir, you intrigue me. Welcome, all of you, go within. Ekaterinye, take your latest student and his family along, and acquaint the youth with his new schedule."

More laughter then, at least from the adults. Kat peers again at the altar, then kisses you quickly and hurries within, where the other curates sit to one side. A seat there in the front rank is yours, on nights you do not preach. As you shake more hands and greet all who hail you, a rare feeling steals over your heart. The tingle spreads and you almost forget where you are, until the meaning comes clear.

Will you preach tonight, or will Tanar'h? For a wonder, you do not actually know what will happen. Is this the incredible anticipation that faces other folk? Is that what attracts them to you, to hear you speak of the future, because they themselves do not often glimpse it? What a miracle, to be alive and so uncertain: no wonder you love them so.

From the side-path again strides the tall thin ascetic, with a pair of attendants in turbans and robes like the Bedou-uu of the Mindsea. Teretheny nods curtly and stops to stare, only his eyes showing above the face-cloth, so like a desert-dweller himself.

"I trust we shall hear a meaningful message this evening, Myster Altieri" he comments, eyes flicking within before coming back to you. Of course—this guest, likely Tanar'h's real target and the one he hoped to influence.

"I guarantee it personally, Devout," you lilt back, taking in his guards with your smile. They are indeed sunburned and mortal Men, Bedou-uu among the settled folk. One tall, the other short, one mustache and one beard, they are a pair suited to the variety of a rich child's toys. Only the shorter one wears jewelry, a plain dark torc around his left arm. He seems slightly dazed, unusual in a bodyguard, and his taller fellow looks on him with some concern.

"Come," Teretheny snaps and they bow to you before following the monk to a front row seat. Hundreds are in place, whispering with more animation than usual. Some story is making the rounds, and you think you know which one. See if Tanar'h can deny you now.

A crowd has gathered on the path but comes no closer, a riot of Color from two dozen guilders and lesser nobles chatting quietly among themselves and forcing the common folk to squeeze past on either side. At last like a bolt of ruby cloth the Cup of Red arrives with guards in train; the clot of hangers-on parts to let him through and reforms in his wake. Fire through a sea of people.

Carnad Mias takes your outstretched hands and kisses them. "I look forward to this ceremony, preacher," he says in a public voice, gesturing to his entourage. "See where all of Cryssigens has come to learn from your foresight."

It is indeed a glittering array- potters, porters, the Captain of the South Gate, one of the shipguilders, the wives of two noblemen who attend the Cryssian temple. Some are in Mias' camp already, but most wear other Colors and you know them to be undecided. Here is the bounty of unharvested votes, and you must risk letting him gain their influence if you are to get closer to the conspiracy your lover seeks to unmask.

"All of Cryssigens, honored Cup?" you laugh, "Our cathedral is not nearly large enough. But all are welcome, most welcome, both here and after service as you shall deem fit to invite." The very words he needed; the guilders look to him like dogs after a tidbit now, realizing that his favor is needed to gain yours. Carnad Mias for his part grins with undisguised delight at this gift, then settles into a smile much more intent and personal. His evening is starting well, and you must not let it go awry. The Cup of Red longs to fill you, to entrust you with his intent among more carnal transfers; his energy ironically helps inspire you, lifts your view and bolsters the devotion you need to speak. Whatever it takes—a public fight before the statue, their horror, your reputation's ruin—Tanar'h must not preach this evening. And if the Devout Teretheny fails to gain his way, perhaps all the better.

They have begun to sing now, greeting the evening heavens and calling for the Stargazer's blessing as is tradition. Squaring your shoulders, you move down the main aisle and whisper to The First as you take every eye onto yourself.

"Let your will find honor in my actions; to speak with foresight, or to serve with humility. But oh, let me speak, Star-finder! Let me speak with your tongue and win new souls to your devotion."

As the altar steps seem to propel you into the air, you approach the statue with Tanar'h in the preaching seat to the right. In those first years you used to steal here in the wee hours, kick off your sandals and hug the savior's marble knees for an hour at a time. His saving grace has always been with you, and letting him speak through your mouth seems a small repayment for his vocation of purpose. But you are grown now, and everyone is watching, so you merely bow with respect. You turn upon Tanar'h with your best, most friendly smile, saying to the world that all is well, and he is close to your heart. His return look is stern but steady, as if to say he will hurt you if he must. You take your seat with the other curates as the hymn closes, and a few murmurs slither around the enormous space, questions and answers that go well with shrugs. No one knows, not even the Heaven's Eye, what will happen next.

Tanar'h rises and gives the ceremonial greeting, hears the ritual response as if nothing were amiss. He leads the assemblage in prayer.

"Stargazer, remake us now to be fit instruments for such unique and challenging times ahead. Change our hearts, turn us to your will and show us your way, that we may show the city, the kingdom, and the world the one true way."

Your next breath is hard to draw—you stare at Tanar'h as he returns to his seat, and must remind your jaw to stay shut, your eyes calm. In a single breath, to speak of remaking and turning—so like forging and bending—is a unitarian stroke combining tenets of all the major sects. You glance out to see the Green-garbed noble, still quite awake, and the multi-hued clot sitting so near Carnad Mias you could segment them from the others with a velvet rope. He rests his gaze on you more often than anywhere else, smug and unaware anything is wrong.

You have underestimated Tanar'h; instead of his usual fare—bluntly encouraging all present to be manly and confident in love like himself—he is making a play to gather in converts here, a real theology if one that flirts with heresy. There hasn't been serious talk of unity among the heroes since—certainly before your lifetime, or his—since the days of Old Cryss and the holocaust.

Despite yourself, you want to hear him preach tonight. It occurs to you only now that perhaps The First has Tanar'h in mind.

As you wrestle with your pride, the people stand whenever they are moved to give thanks. The first to speak, as usual, are of noble rank and their gratitude concerns large matters; the recent security of their house, continued prosperity in their dealings. For most, simply a question of hearing one's echo in a holy place, but little harm in that.

Carnad Mias rises slowly, so that anyone behind him has a moment to reseat themselves with grace. "For another day, for any day, that the life and safety of our magnificent Heaven's Eye is preserved for us." This triggers a squall of follow-on claims, from those who seek either your favor or his.

"Aye, for the safety of the Lavender Lady, thanks great Stargazer!"

"Praise you for saving her from death today."

Now there is cheering and applause, not unheard of in a Stargazer ceremony but not usually so soon. You and Tanar'h exchange a glance; you can see he is pricked sore by his dilemma. Who else to preach, with what you've done and what has happened to you this day? Smiling, you gesture for quiet to still the wave of repeated thanks.

"Faithful, I am quite certain the Stargazer hears you." Laughter and seats retaken. "I am grateful to you all, but this will not suffice to make him save me again!" More laughter, while you sit back, little dreaming how rightly you have prophesized of me.

The poorer folk begin to stand then and thank Argens for decidedly lesser, more earthly things: that a day's work went well, a child no longer sick, a husband on a ship come safely home. Occasionally a curate of the faith will add a word; Kat rises to softly thank the Stargazer "for a lesson well remembered" and you reach to grasp her arm as she sits again. You have more to be thankful for than most. But you will not speak again, you decide, until Argens calls you to preach. And if not—when you try to think on that, nothing comes to your mind but a great white wall.

The time until the presentation only seems interminable; here comes the chosen family with a basket of winter crops, and small handiwork from the craft guilds, each representing much larger donations in kind. The preacher who rises to accept this basket is invariably the one to give the sermon. Your eyes lock with Tanar'h's as the murmurs grow. His pupils of the deepest blue come off as black from this distance, yet you can see the furious dance of anger, fear and anguish. The offering basket comes ever closer, one of the family puts a foot on the lowest step—and still you defer, in strength not to move first.

Tanar'h rises, steps down to meet the offering family, and takes the basket reverently in both hands. The colors of the food and crafted items reflect their various materials, yet each container, ribbon, tie-cord and the basket itself are all the most brilliant Red. Today, the wrappings are worth a hundred times the gifts themselves: the congregation gasps as the crimson hues reflect under the central lamps near the altar.

Tanar'h turns deliberately and smoothly to bring the offering to the foot of the statue, where he sets it down from one knee. Surely, he can move well, like a dancer without a shred of nerves. The High Heart turns back to face the assemblage, takes three steps down to center, stops.

And extends one hand to you.

The utter silence of night floods the chamber; no one is breathing. You stand, and move to take his hand with a broad smile, and he gives you a look filled with meaning as he gestures to the podiate with the other. He returns to sit, while the people begin to cheer and shout congratulations to you both.

Your mind is working slowly—to share the preaching duties is unprecedented, but what can they mean by this praise? You hear a random word— "proposal", and in a flash the puzzle resolves. You spoke to him before the altar, he on his knees; and then you gave him a sacred token!

You catch Tanar'h's eye, filled now with bitter amusement as he also apprehends what you have done, and you cannot forbear to laugh at yourself. You are caught eight ways to Argens' Day; the High Heart and Heaven's Eye will marry. Everyone knows this marvelous farce to be the truth, and no amount of reasonable explanation will ever erase the fairy tale you have written with your actions today.

Never mind. Let Argens speak now.

You lid your eyes and let the state of grace overtake you, the boundless energy you felt on that first day as a child, speaking his word because without a torrent of speech to hold you on earth, your feet would leave the ground.

"We face the fire." The susurration of agreement is barely audible. "And so often, we misjudge fire by its distance. A few embers spill from the hearth near our feet and we leap up for water. But in the sky the Arbalest rises, with a threat to us all and we take no notice. Ember and star, about the same size, to our eyes?"

"We misjudge by heat. Qellen—" you gesture to the armorsmith, faithful churchgoer and solid Purple man who rises, "tell me what hue is your forge when the shield and plate must be of the highest quality."

"Nearly white within, priestess; even the walls of it become a bit red before I'm through. And it must last at that level, six hours or more, with only the purest coals."

"White heat. Useful to you then. Like those stars." You give them a moment to take it in; Argens' message presses against your chest, unknown until spoken but heavy with importance and joyous expecting release. "Yet what say you, May," gesturing to the back row of the clergy in attendance where May'stra, Tanar'h's third wife, is shocked to be called upon. Her husband never asks anyone else's opinion when he preaches. "When you baked those magnificent rolls this morning—" how long ago that seems! "—what fuel and what heat did you seek?"

She looks to her husband as if for permission, but stands and answers with a shy smile. "I—I'm glad you liked them, W'starrah. My oven is only clay; a quarter-hour over a birchwood flame is usually enough, but you must watch closely."

"Just so—we gain profit from the flames Argens sends through calculation and reason. A mistake, should we try to exchange them: ten years in May's oven would not be enough for Qellen's plate, and ten seconds too long for the reverse!" The laughter is easy, and you note the Green noble is yet awake, perhaps to his surprise he is interested in spite of himself. "And we cannot choose only one fire to use, my friends. Unless you would willingly go to war armored in pastry, or settle back at table to eat a shield!" They roar and guffaw and you smile down to them; their approval sustains you, or else with so much of The First's message to relay you would faint.

"Just one more twist to our tragic tale, if I may." You pause, and the murmurs of encouragement rise readily; they are listening, they are yours. "We also misjudge the fire, at times, through the matching not of distance, nor heat, nor size, but in our persons. The flame itself is suited to different tasks, and so are we." You look kindly on the pair of them before continuing, that all may know you mean no insult. "Unless you would prefer to eat cakes prepared by Qellen, or wear the armor—" and the rest is lost in a tide of amused comprehension. The smith and his wife must lean on each other for support, they are laughing so heartily. And one of the clerics next to May holds up her arm mocking her muscle, until she pulls it down though giggling. The laughter and comments swirl into applause, which lasts some time; a few are standing as they clap, to honor your words. But you know it is The First speaking, as ever. And the rest of his message is becoming clear, a path through the coming days.

"We face the fire!" The squall of laughter calms and they hang on your voice. "We have all come to know flame, in our way. But will we stand where and when we are called? Make no mistake, the heat will be forge-hot, and its flames will leap perhaps higher than the walls of our city." This extinguishes the laughter completely but leaves them open to encouragement. Not yet: you must tell them more, that they are not caught unawares.

"The signs of the stars seem small and distant, but they are clear. I see them. The Dragon comes against us", a sigh of dismay, "and the Arbalest, as we feared, but with his bolt come legions of Spiders", a few shrieks of denial, some cursing, the Elves despise insects of all kinds, "and even the crown which brings our salvation is wreathed in flame!" They think you mean the circlet the new Overlord will wear, but you see only the Brow of your vision. It stands there now, between you and the people, and you describe it to them. "For these glittering golden bands dazzle the eye, their gems tempt the heart, and we become focused on gaining them, until it is too late, and the fire has done its dread work unattended."

"We must *face* the fire, my friends. You know your work, head down over a wheel or kiln; but if those scattered embers smolder unwatched, what next? Your neighbor's house is aflame. A cinder, think on it, needs only our ignorance or cowardice to grow until it burns a home, a shop—"

"Or a temple!" yells a lusty voice from the back, and the laughter returns. He means the Hopeforger cathedral of course. But this bit of smug rivalry is not to the purpose.

"Or a temple, aye—and all those within." They gasp in recognition at that. You drive each word with emphasis. "Or a city. And all those within." The poor fellow in the back practically falls onto his seat again. You exchange a glance with Carnad Mias—he was there, when Z'kammet Hammer's church was set aflame by unknown enemies. No one slain, except that pair of assassins. And Gaspar Heugen had only just left.

"Fire destroys the bonds between citizens as surely as it incinerates a city's walls. Burning of all kinds awaits us, friends; fire is the test Argens gives to those who follow him."

You turn your head to take them all in, like Kat when she has asked the class a question and is determined to await an answer.

"We need the Overlord!" one voice, joined by a chorus of others.

Without looking, you can feel twin points of pressure from a front row seat. Why is it so hard, to treat the Devout as one of you? Why must he know the answer to this question? You breathe deep and take refuge again where you belong, in the will of The First. He will say what he desires. Perhaps he will have you utter your own name? But neither is this to the purpose.

"And how will we know the Overlord, friends, when Argens reveals him to us? By what sign shall we recognize her?" Both man and woman? The First never mis-speaks. "The ruler of our city, leader of the North Mark, will be the one who does not mistake a far off white hot star as harmless, nor scoff at a tiny glowing ember and wait."

There are familiar gasps and exclamations among the faithful. The aura of sanctity around your person becomes visible—they see some echo of the marvelous energy pulsing through you this past hour. Tanar'h signals; Jal'i and Tamess are lowering the lamps, to highlight the miracle. There in the center of the benches is the Blue color-guard from the arena, she nods to you now with respect. Your mortal frame can no longer contain the full essence of Argens' inspiration, an ecstasy cleansed of doubt, or sweat or exhaustion. You cannot be sure if your toes still touch the marble step.

From your eye-corners you catch sight of separate men. Carnad Mias, formerly bemused as at the theater, wears a face stamped with shock. He apprehends now, your devotion is not some mundane thing to be bought or bartered. He is thinking, for perhaps the first time in years, of the world beyond this life, and about consequences that will not yield to a tally-sheet, however large the sums inscribed upon it.

Opposite him, the Devout Teretheny can barely hold his seat, driven throughout his frame by an emotion very much like rage. You refuse—no, Argens only—to give him the name he so desperately wants to hear.

"To raise the alarm, yes, to put our resources in order that we may fight it. To put body and life, if needed, before the danger, an example to us all. These will be the signs whereby we recognize the one worthy to lead us."

"But this fire, the next test, will not await the new Overlord, my people. Once beyond control, a flame does not tame itself. The star-fire will not hold its course an extra day to serve our convenience, the dragon's breath will not distinguish your rival from your firstborn. It consumes all before it, destroys any semblance of order and love and life. Either this, or…"

You hold until the last echo dies. Without breathing, you ask The First to bear you up just a moment longer, to complete his message before you swoon.

"Or—we face the fire, ourselves. We know what to do! Which of us has not run to fight a flame, from the next street, or in another precinct? The call goes out and for our Color, for our temple, we take our places to help a stranger. No! Not for an alien. We declare, with our sweat and toil and risk of life that there are no strangers among us! As you have done, as our forefathers taught us to do, we stand before the flame for each other. As I would gladly stand for all of you—"

"No priestess! I for you!" one anonymous shout grows into a chorus. "For you, preacher!" "Argens pick me—for this city I stand!" "I face the fire!" Everyone is on their feet, defying peril and ardently declaring their willingness. The curates join hands in prayer, and the energy of their mutual Blessing washes over the ecstatic multitude. Tanar'h is smiling honestly as he gestures for the final hymn to begin. He shakes his head slightly in admiration, and perhaps a bit of jealousy, that he cannot stand in the favor of The First so closely—but you both know he made the right decision.

Through the orison-ceiling windows you can see to one side the head of the Arbalest, inching higher in the sky and seeming to look down on you. You throw wide both arms, daring him to shoot now. Let the bolt fall on you, rather than any of these you love so dearly. The jeweler, the boy, Kat, greedy conniving Carnad, Tanar'h's guards—all of them you would gladly give your life to save, though you doubt that will be price enough. Yet worth it, to fulfill your destiny, to repay The First for his gifts. And worth it, too, a small voice reminds you, to spend no nights grieving over a life-love lost. Yes, if Argens wills it, let it come now.

Through another ceiling-pane you spot the northern constellation of Sword in Crown, perfectly centered to view. As the song begins, you think on its message—rulership, change to a new order, and ascendance. A crown of star-fire beckons to one already cut by a blade. Let the consequences be what they may: Argens has chosen.

The roar of the congregation blends into song, the final hymn. Hands support your back, as you finally let slip your conscious mind, you can hear voices new and familiar.

Mark me, Eternal Flame! The Moment could be soon,
Let legend bear like yours my name, bright as unending noon.
Come now the test to bear, I burn to glory see
And find my soul not break nor tear, through all eternity

Tanar'h has such a fine tenor—normally he sings quietly, ashamed not to bandy a bass range, but tonight he is inspired. Kat's soprano so airy and joyous; Carnad Mias, it must be he so close by, the voice of a man better spent in counting coins but sincere for the moment. Towards the back you dimly see someone hands a song-sheet to the Green noble, and he nods along dutifully. They all sing, or try to, your real family. Tanar'h was not right enough; for this orphan only the entire city will do.

he city is aflame and from atop your tower you can see spiders in all the streets. The Dragon's breath lights the sky momentarily, all the way to the old abandoned city. You see as if with the eyes of a hawk. There an enormous alabaster insect crawls across a statue of Argens, blindly seeking something stolen.

You awaken out of breath and soaked with sweat. The dream seemed so real it exhausted you. How you came to be here, what happened the night before, everything that followed your sermon is a blank in your mind.

But none of that is what has you shaking with cold sweat. The awakening did that by itself.

You have not slept in almost ten years.

You lie facing the window and wonder—as a bright sun peeks outside your sill and a heavy heart thuds inside your chest—whether behind you on the mattress lies Carnad Mias. The only cloth touching your body is the bright purple coverlet, soft and thick and entirely unsuitable for use as a dress. It takes an age to muster the courage, but you finally roll back a half-turn, to glance at the rest of the wide bed.

Empty, praise The First.

But the coverlet there is matted and mussed, as with a large body. Or two.

Think, get up and put this together, for the sake of the city if not your own. Morning chill on your naked skin brings some wakefulness along with the goose-bumps and nippling. You check your jewel-box-foolish to believe you would be robbed, but the iron ring is there and unmoved. You put it on now, turning the ax-face down in case you continue to forget yourself.

There, on the opposite bed-stand, a second goblet sits like a small life-raft in your ocean of turmoil. You almost don't dare approach, but it is the next thing you must do. Drained, and the smell of the passionsleep posset you mixed still clings. Praise the First; you sink to your knees by the bedside and fight back welling tears, pushing down your selfish relief to give gratitude to Argens, that he vouchsafed you this respite. Mias was here, drank with you, probably petted, and then fell unconscious to awaken later and tiptoe off. With fortune, he remembers either bedding you or that he was too drunk to perform. You have a chance to perpetuate the masquerade, the next time you speak: be kind, engaging, discreet, let him fill the blanks. And perhaps by then, you will remember on your own. You hold your head and stroll back into the meeting chamber, straining to recall and gasping with more than the dawn-cold, to suffer such a void in your memory.

The statue in the outer chamber has two heads, the second one white and eyeless. Extra arms grip the sides of Argens-- vision, dream, real? No matter, it is a Bug, and it seems to hear you now. The scream is quite involuntary.

Bounding steps down the roof stairs; the massive teakwood door bursts half-off its hinges as Chaktha breaks in by foot, spear and shield ready. He looks about and then only to you—the statue is no longer encumbered by nightmare. You are still naked.

"I thank you, Chaktha. A bad dream."

"Priestess." He turns to face the shattered portal, intending to stand guard. This is full faith, you reflect as you run back to dress; if your guard feels any dismay at this broken habit, he shows no sign.

But you missed the dawn! Belatedly, you hold your arms out to the rising disk beyond your window, but feel no echo of the elation, the energy that the fading stars always left with you. Instead you slept, and are exhausted. As you throw on your gown and adjust the slits and décolletage to best advantage, your eye falls on the small red box. The ointment within is nearly gone- did you use it last night? Twice or three times perhaps! But behind it, now another; Mias is thoughtful if calculating. As you slather some on, your eye comes to the small statue of Argens by your bedside bringing a flash of memory with the sight.

"You're sure it is safe to speak, Red Cup?"

"Gentlemen, please, I urge you to consider everyone here our friend and ally. The Lavender Lady will do as she pleases, no doubt."

"Or so you hope, Carnad Mias!" *A general cackle of ill-smothered laughter.* Standing with your hand on the proxy, you can practically hear his grin. This is the previous night, the party in your room, with a dozen conspirators perhaps ignorant of their treason.

"The vote is within our reach, gentlemen. The Cryss temple is already flailing about looking for the best deal in return for their support, and guilds bleed away from Z'kammet Hammer by the day. If it is made of wood or weave, it is ours already—" grunts of agreement *"of course, Cesmir's vote will be in accord with our own, I assure you."*

"And what of the new preacher? Is he sound?"

"The pacifist? What harm could he do?"

"Nay, Red Cup, the Devout, the monk who is guest to the High Heart of this very temple."

"Ah, the anchorite," you recall the slight hesitation in Mias' voice. *"Never fear, gentlemen, the Heaven's Eye has him well in hand."*

The memory fades, but certain fragments of the evening slip in. They all came, the clot of guilders and crafters hanging on Mias' hem after the service. You were here—recovered from your swoon, you played the gracious hostess. Of course there was the endless dance of compliments and innuendo, from men and women angling for tokens. Did you promise any? And Mias—he kept the same seat all evening, you remember that with clarity, the couch where you interviewed him previously, his back to the statue and his head swiveling to follow you everywhere you moved. It was easy to excuse yourself, more than once, to your inner room. You used the proxy to listen to them make their filthy suggestions and drop a few hints.

Still you only pull in the emotion of the party, not enough specifics of what was said. They are tempted, but still cautious—it will require more such gatherings, and the ruin of whatever reputation you may still have with the respectable elites like Gaspar Heugen. You drift down the stair behind Chaktha to the reception room, ignoring the breakfast setting while you try so hard to recall.

Should you contact the Emperor's Hand, give him the Captain's message? Too soon: Morinack's instructions were that the ax-ring could only be used three times. Perhaps a visit to the Telholian should be next—but the back of your head is buzzing with that unpleasant, yet familiar sensation—so much forgotten, things out of order.

The knock and Chaktha's question echo only dimly—as if you still dream, men enter the chamber and arrange themselves to petition for the day. But just as the door nearly closes, you hear an elderly tone of command calling "Hold!" The portal widens to admit the tall frame of Z'hammet Hammer, Patriarch of Argens Hopeforger. Suddenly you feel wide awake.

"Patriarch, we are honored," you say trying to sound as if his visit was expected. The snow-haired elder looks down on all of you as he does most fellow elves, standing more than six feet tall and as thin and hard as a mannikin built of iron rods. His glare sweeps the silent room; though crowded with more than a dozen supplicants you hear nothing, until one by one they rise to bow to you, mutter an excuse, and leave. Hammer empties the room with his eyes, but the fury in him only seems to stoke with more air to feed it, until you are left alone with a living forge, heat already past red and close to melting ingots. One false word, or light joke, and he will explode.

But you can't change your habit with ease. "Well," you chuckle, "that lightens my calendar considerably, thanks."

You turn to serve yourself at the table—suddenly you are famished, nearly light-headed. When he says nothing, you turn back to offer tea. You should have been prepared, but the sight of his red, furious face is so abrupt you drop the cup and step back.

"You dare," he advances slowly, his words rasping in counterpoint to the ground glass beneath his sandals. "With the fate of the entire Mark resting on a razor, you throw it in the dung heap and for what! A night of pleasure with that brazen mountebank, a childish dream of power! Your orgy last night is the talk of the city!"

Think fast—Mias would claim the same no matter the truth of it; you knew this was where your deception led. "I never thought him such an early riser," you jibe, "though I must object, Patriarch, it was hardly an orgy. My guests enjoyed fruitful conversations, no tokens were distributed." Or so you believe.

He is too incensed to care about the details; something deeper has Hammer not just angry but unnerved. "Bed him! Let him boast of you everywhere, you think I care a fig for the reputation of the Stargazers. Marry the polygamist Tanar'h, or live in chaste seclusion out at Sinter with the Devout—each one better than the last, yet it means nothing to me, girl. But your guests. Have you any notion what damage you did to the fragile tapestry of peace that your betters are trying to weave?"

Physically, your Hopeforger rival has become a trial. Standing so close, he does not threaten with his clenching hands but has backed you into the table-corner now, looming above you as his robes nearly smoke with the cloying tinct of incense drenching every fiber. You cannot move further away from him without loss of honor, and you dare not breathe deeply or else lapse into a fit of coughing.

But emotionally—there, you have him nearly in hand. Z'kammet Hammer has hardly stopped shouting since his arrival, moving too fast and nearly spitting in his fury. One or two more calm ripostes and he might suffer a seizure of the heart.

"Please, reverend Myster, tell me more of this wondrous tapestry. Shot throughout with Blue, no doubt? Highlighted at all corners by the Flame Eternal of the Hopeforgers, and showing an admirable man as Mark of the North in its center? Gaspar Heugen, no doubt."

He flinches at this—could his opinion of your political acumen really be so low? Now you begin to feel some fury, while he steps back, still angry himself but beginning to calculate.

"No doubt," he counters, "the tapestry would look better to your eye with that fool E'trun holding the rod of office. And Carnad Mias, or even you, standing behind him?"

You laugh uncommonly loud, and say "Behind him?" in an attempt to shock, which scores. Hammer's white eyebrows ascend beneath his hair as his jaw drops open. In the space he created, you step to the table again—not tea, your hands might shake—but some grapes to quench hunger and thirst, and perhaps cool your center. This meeting is important; Hammer's support is probably out of question but his regard still matters. You or he will back a winner—there are uncounted years to live once the Mark has been crowned.

"You, you would dare to reach so far beyond yourself?"

The grapes aren't countering the heat. "Indeed, Patriarch? Tell me, is it my sex, my marital status, or just that I dare follow Argens along a different path than you? Are there any other critiques you would offer while here as my guest, sir? My outfit: I know the color is all wrong, but by all means advise me what else I should wear to please the highest ranking preacher in the city."

"What matters it," Hammer spits back, "you evidently believe the less clothing, the more votes you'll get. And you might be right," he says with bitterness, "just parade naked down Altair Way with a cheering mob behind you, so long as it ends at the palace with a crown on your head."

Part of you says not to, but he has gone too far now, and deserves it.

"Speaking of crowns," you say in a low tone, "where is yours, Patriarch?"

He steps back again, and you can see the rivets on the forge starting to come loose under pressure. But your control is also fraying so you step towards him and keep stoking the flame.

"You came here today, no doubt to dissuade me from my course. Why not use the artifact of the Highforge? After all, I'm only a loose woman, not a respected fellow preacher with a full vote at council. Why not sway me, revered Hopeforger?"

Even as furious as he is, the devotion of Z'kammet Hammer makes certain actions habitual, faster than you had guessed of him. He raises one hand in finger-spread invocation, and says "I call upon Argens to detect the truth".

Stunned, you stop and feel the power of his miracle wash over you, into you. Whatever Z'kammet Hammer asks you next, you cannot lie. The shock knocks you clean out of countenance; prisoners before the docket get better treatment than this.

Before commencing interrogation, Hammer compounds his insult with another miracle. Raising both arms he cries out "*A'mirar!*" in the Ancient Tongue, invoking the Hopeforger ritual of Awe. Now he has done more than expose the lie, and is attempting to command that you speak only the truth. "Did you hire the Stealthic Feldspar to steal the Brow of the Ecclesiast?" he thunders.

You had recovered your wits in time to resist his second miracle—or you believe so, at any rate—but now you can literally laugh in Hammer's face, while praising your own cleverness. "I specifically and clearly did *not* ask him to do any such thing." Your aura shows bright blue, and you gaze at your hand admiring how it sets off the purple of your amethyst bracelet.

Hammer is unhappy but unmoved, reaching into his belt and throwing down a kerchief made of the brightest, most brilliant Purple lace you have ever seen. "How then? It matters not which stooge you hired, but where is it? Return it at once!"

He is truly beside himself now, to give away so much information. The artifact is indeed missing—and more, someone has taken care to implicate the Lavender Lady in the crime. You pick it up and compare it to your sleeve, a match; as you catch the subtle scent of jasmine on the cloth, it feels colder now in your hand. Someone has taken great care.

"Reverend elder, in all sincerity, I do not have it. Whether I aspire to find or wear the Brow, that is my business. You are not welcome here, whatever your merit, to lash a Stargazer Myster with questions like some felon under irons."

"If you believe that you can foil the will of The First by seizing either crown, you deserve no better than gaol, intemperate temptress! Do not confuse the attraction of weak-willed men for power—there are those who care nothing for a pretty face or lilting voice, but think only of how you may be used to further their own ends. Those who will shred your pretty flesh like so much parchment to get what they want."

"Patriarch, why fret you so? What weak man or foolish whore could possibly frustrate Argens' design?" You have him now, arguing predestination like a schoolchild where no answers will be to his purpose.

He stomps his foot in fury. "Wretch! Have you the temerity—do you realize, the presence of Farnh'y and Trothfer…"

"Ah yes, two of my guests last night—so the Glassblowers will move to the Red side," you toss back casually, "what of it, Myster Hammer? The support of that business is fragile, and how not—it's based on hot air! Argens will see us through, as any good Child of Hope knows."

"Us! Your parents would have been ashamed." His spare, intelligent face is twisted with the need to win this argument. As you regard him you know the face he sees is calm, perhaps smug. Z'kammet Hammer was by no means your friend. Head of a rival temple, pious to the point of intolerance, unyielding in any trivial matter touching on the importance of his sect or position. And he reeks of incense. But you always regarded him as one of the family, the city you love. Now as he storms toward the outer door, you must let him go, and he must leave angry. But a twinge inside, a sudden recall, moves you before you can think.

"Patriarch," as he pauses by the door, "please, no matter our differences, whatever you think of me, my sincere regards to your lovely wife." She had always been friendly.

He snaps a nod. Again he turns to leave and again you arrest him with words.

"Let her know, if she needs anything—she has not called on me for certain supplies in some time."

"I have forbidden it," Hammer spits, and the portal slams to behind him. The depth of his enmity is now revealed. Elves of more than a century's age at times need herbal remedies, to provide the spark of love. But the husband has cut off even his occasional marital devotion, in service to his politics.

You could eat or drink in comfort now, but pace the circular chamber instead. You don't recall when the tears began. Everywhere, it seems, stand men trying to confine you: Tanar'h to a bridal suite, Mias to a bed, and Hammer to some imagined position of prim subservience. They crawl across your tower like insects. And if you flee this sanctuary, to the world beyond, there is Gaspar Heugen, doing his best to ignore you, and the Emperor's Hand, the halfling Morinack, demanding information. If any of these become too threatening, too monstrous, there is only Chaktha—another man—to save you.

Except your dear doomed Captain, you realize as a wind from the northern road seems to tickle across your arm. Nothing about soldiering is familiar to you; would he be still on the escarpment beyond the city? The second day, surely no; but not yet to Tralmachia. The lonely tween-lands of scattered hamlets and herds; still safe, you can hope. And he asked you to do something for him, gave you a role in his desperate scheme, will put his life, as yours, at risk to save the Mark. Only he, and Argens, want you to act. To the Telholian preacher, and it is also time to know more about the vision. Your clients conveniently gone for the day, the morning is free. You know Kat will be found with the students in the school.

⊕ ⊕ ⊕

The white wood dormer schoolhouse with the broad red door sits at the end of a gently winding path between two shallow ponds. The loose ring of surrounding trees blocks your view of the temple precinct walls. You could be out in the country, but for the distant sounds of the city and the even fainter thrum of the sea. The garden patches have coordinated blooms, the pattern of letters on the stones below, the glint of afternoon sun on the small bronze bell in the front-tower: this is by far the most inviting, welcoming place you've ever known, yet the closer to the door the slower you walk. You try to lie, that you're working to remember the meaning of the stones, or the flowers, taught to you so long ago. But the truth lies deep down: it's the woman within, the one who taught all those things and so many more that you also forgot. Seeing her again, remembering such deep love and devotion, this thought drags your pace to a crawl. For surely today, with this transgression, you will anger her beyond repair. The feel of the metal latch makes your hand jump as if grasping a snake. Get in quick, before you lose heart.

The single room within is well lit, crowded and still—the air is redolent with that sense, when many have just learned a thing. It's a portrait; Kat faces the room, the table before her piled with winter apples and plums, something of sums and proportions. And three dozen children of all ages, facing her from the benches and completely intent, completely in love. On every side, faces come alight by twos and threes. The teacher continues speaking, looking to those whose brows are still furrowed. She towers high over her little congregants, reaching out to call upon raised hands, spreading insight, converting them. Teaching.

"Yes, you see it well now, Pieri. As we add the same number to each side, the difference remains the same in number, but—"

"- shrinks in proportion!"

"But how is this important, teacher?"

"Right, teacher, the difference is six, and always six."

"Very true, but what if the task was not simply to count, but to achieve a balance, as with mixing ingredients for food, or—"

"Or for a majority in voting." You interrupt, because you were always mischievous. The heads all snap around, and the children gasp—no one is supposed to watch them while they learn, now they must act their parts. Some become even more dutiful, while several others—mainly the boys—slouch back a bit on their benches as if this lesson were less interesting than watching their own hair grow. Kat, bless her, absorbs this unwelcome interruption with grace and rallies.

"Why yes, voting is another case, though one that is rarely exercised by children. In the example on our table, the red apples are in the majority, but it is shrinking. Depending how many votes are left, purple may be catching up." She looks back to you with such a smile of prim innocence, you feel the hilarity bubble up as always. But you must not laugh, or hug her, in fact will likely outrage her immediately. This is hard, this particular lesson.

"Indeed?" You respond coolly, "from my perspective, it would seem the Red is in no danger."

Kat frowns, because you have deliberately made the Color reference explicit. Now the intelligence she has sown in her classroom will run loose, and for that she can blame no one else, nor would she want to.

"It's the election!" one yells, "Carnad Mias will win and E'trun will be Mark at last. Hurrah!"

Denials pour in from a dozen mouths; one girl runs to the table and puts down a lemon, another a melon and Kat cannot control them. The table is jostled, fruit rolls to the floor and jumbles together. At last the teacher resorts to her sternest measure, clapping her hands once and placing arms akimbo. Everyone shorter than she sits down as if death was the penalty for tardiness. You have to stifle the urge yourself. In a moment of wonder, you cannot recall anyone ever being punished for crossing this final line.

But your part must be played. You step forward and survey the citrine wrack on the floor, saying "Yes, this is about how the first ballot went." The children all laugh, as you reach down and snag an apple to bite into.

"There! The vote is a bit closer now." Pieri cries, to more giggles.

"Look," another boy crows, "Heaven's Eye is kissing the Red Cup!"

You see it then. Children gasp, and stop learning anything. Now their minds skirt around the edges of sex instead, and their innocence irretrievably slips. The younger ones whisper questions to the older, the boys recall how much they desire you, and Kat stares across the table with a face of true anger. That was the punishment, the line no one dared cross as a child. The thought that the teacher might love you less was unbearable to any student. Grown now and forced to pretend, still you are not sure you can pay this price.

Your voice is a little forced breaking the silence. "Is it story-time yet? I want to hear about the Spider and the Fly."

100

The smaller children are again asking questions. Only the older students have heard this tale, once told to the little ones of Despair. Kat's face is as hard as flint now, and she takes her seat with determination. You thought she would refuse, scold you, try to send you away; but to your surprise the teacher places her hands on her legs, takes a deep breath and begins.

"In a high rafter of one of the castles of Man, there lived a Widow Spider of great size and age..." You sit as well now, drawn to wedge a woman's curves into a student's seat by the power of her voice taking you to childhood again. The story itself is fierce and hopeless, yet the sound of the teacher's voice somehow makes it alright, though no less sad. Kat's high light tone, the notes that mean patience and interest and love, is like a calming hand through a nightmare. The spider's uneaten mate, weakened and dying, vies with a webbed-up fly, her forgotten victim, whining as to which of them suffers more. You relive the dismay, the sour humor, as if for the first time, until the end when one leaps to his doom and the other is devoured.

You realize with a shock that this is a different ending.

As you lift your eyes to meet Kat's steady gaze, the older children complain.

"Wait! Teacher, what of the bird?"

"Yes, the swallow that soars through the web, and frees the fly!"

Only when everyone looks do you recognize the echoes of your own voice.

"That is in the version of the tale that the Rom tell," Kat says with a small smile. "Not the original, which of course comes to us from the Children of Despair. Thus they taught that obedience to authority was the only virtue, that death comes to us all, and that our perceived slights and differences are truly minor things." There is a tear on her cheek now, and several on yours.

"And perhaps," you manage, "that those we take at first as enemies are indeed just victims of cruel fate."

A streak of puzzlement crosses the teacher's face, pushing her anger away to both sides.

"And perhaps also," she allows quietly, "are truly friends despite all seeming."

In the moment of silence following, you can feel again everyone around you learning. And you are with them, you are twelve years old again and there are no burning crowns or monstrous beasts before your path. Only love and the classroom and she who was a hero alongside The First himself, before she became your friend. The tears come steadily now and you wonder how to maintain this charade.

"But teacher," Pieri insists, "what if the Rom version is the true one?"

Kat faces the pupil, her face shining with pride. "How indeed?" She pauses and looks back to you while the pride steals away. Cocking her head the teacher makes a decision. "You should repair to the High Heart of the church and ask him."

"The High Heart!"

"Certainly," Kat replies with a twinkle in her eye. "It was the Rom who brought Myster Tanar'h to us, many years ago. He traveled with them from his family's home to the east, when they sent him to study. Yes, go and ask him now. Class is dismissed for the day."

The schoolhouse rings with the sudden cheers of a race freed from bondage, however light the burden had been. For the second time Kat's control is imperfect, as she shouts a last reminder to fleeing heels and backs.

"Tomorrow as usual. And take this fruit for your lunch, lest it spoil."

Quick as the lightning, some turn back and grab, one evidently intending to begin business as a grocer, and then they are all gone. This was the plan, to ruin her teaching with saucy insults and lascivious hints. The news of your impiety will spread faster through children's mouths than wind could drive the flames. And Kat needs to be in the dark, beyond that fire, to help your scheme and to protect her life. She stands now and busies herself with matters of straightening as if alone, back stiff and shoulders slightly shaking.

Just a few more words, delivered from your feet and with a dry-cheeked grin, will be enough. Ekaterinye will leave your service, the final proof of a conversion to Mias' seduction. No one will doubt you have taken up his cause, given him your body, joined his inner circle and can be trusted with his darkest secrets. Assassins will leave

Kat alone, no one will involve her good name in your ruin after this break. You need only stand and do it.

The desk wobbles ungraciously beneath you as you rise; you feel dizzy from the height of your own head. Papers rustle and it is like a hiss of disapproval. Worse, your eyes refuse to clear, there is a kind of film over them that makes Kat's back, the walls, the sunlit windows shimmer as if from heat. And in your mouth, where there should be words of innuendo and cruel wit, there is only an acrid taste, that of an old fruit eaten too late and filled with regret and pain in the stomach.

She turns, her face resolved to bear up under any new insult. She is slight and short and old. And before her pained face you crumble to your knees, weeping and grasping her hem to your forehead. Because you cannot pay this price.

"Oh teacher, do not leave me!"

Two hands raise you back up and you hug her fiercely for a time. The hiss and horrid taste in your mouth only grows worse, and now you feel something like panic. You must explain, that is it, and hurry.

"W'starrah, what has happened to you?"

"Kat, please, please don't leave me, I cannot pretend to you any longer."

"What do you mean," she coughs through her own tears, "are you, is this about the Red Cup?"

"Yes, I have been play-acting, to draw out his plan, but you—"

Kat cuts you off with a hug as strong as her tiny frame can make it.

"I should, oh I should *slap* you."

You feel a release inside, though the pain in your throat only grows.

"But Kat, you must pretend I have angered you, or else the danger—"

"The danger, don't be silly, I'm so *relieved*," and whatever else the teacher would say is drowned in coughing. Your eyes are dry now, but your vision still blurs. The hiss of papers ceased long ago, but you hear it clearly. Reeling apart from your teacher, you find you must yet lean on her to stand and look around.

There on the table, the bright yellow lemon is rocking slightly back and forth, surrounded by shimmers. You haul Kat with you towards the table, stumbling forward to grasp the fruit in one hand, trying to quell the flow of poison from inside it.

"The color!" Kat gasps on her knees next to you, and now the wealth behind this plot is made plain. A living thing, subjected to the mysteries of Color? Unheard of. But now the goal is to get out.

The door to the schoolhouse seems a thousand steps away. With Kat on your arm you don't make five.

*T*here is a hiss, like flames burning without fuel, and the clicking sound made by a giant insect which towers over your vision of the stars by day. You are on the wooden floor, and nearby Kat lies very still, her face covered by silver hair. There is something wooden and bright Yellow in your hand. You throw it away, and it bounces across the floor into the statue of Argens by the wall, where something the shape of a beetle and the size of a mastiff is advancing.

In the stars behind the enormous insect you can see the Arbalest, his crossbow loaded and aimed in your direction. He must not hit your friend, and you pray he means for you to die instead.

"W'starrah! W'starrah, Ekatarinye!" The voice is familiar and urgent but distant; the shimmering air muffles sound as it drowns the breath. Your throat hurts too much to answer. A sharp *bratch* and the gentle clatter of wooden splinters is somewhat closer. The beetle-thing stops, cocks its head, and scuttles back from Kat's body behind the statue again. Someone is coughing, but there's a thread of clear air to breathe. From the touch of smooth skin and hardened muscle you can tell it is Tanar'h, cradling you in a single arm while steadying Kat over the opposite shoulder. He carries you both with ease while coughing and cursing, kicking desks from his path and stumbling out through the shattered door into the light, and air, and life outside.

Soft grass, the cool winter sunshine and air sweeter than melons pulse over you.

"W'starrah! Are you alright, can you speak?" Tanar'h's face is filled with concern bordering on terror. Your first thought is of Yellow. But Tanar'h's neck is still bare, with no gold circlet. He has never been a good play-actor, the fear of death is stamped on his face. After rising slightly, your vision swims clear to reveal the door to the schoolhouse looking as thoroughly smashed as if hit by a catapult-stone. He couldn't have known.

You manage to ask, "Where is Kat?" before falling back into new coughs. Tanar'h starts, then turns away to check the teacher. You can hear the voices of children gathered nearby, Jal'i and Tamess admonishing them to stand clear. Kat is on her back, unconscious; it takes an eternity before you can see the slightest rise in her chest to indicate breath.

Tanar'h taps Kat's cheeks, puts one hand on her forehead. "I cannot awaken her," he says, "I have no healing." He looks back to share regret with you, who never learned to Draw Poison either. The heartbeat hammers up against your ribs as you lie there weak, and the chapel bell rings an alarm.

Folks run from everywhere down-vale to the schoolhouse; you feel a little stronger, from fresh air and the strength of their concern. Using Tanar'h's shoulder for a handhold, you sit up and look around to see everyone—including guards from the outer gate—rushing in to see what has happened. You have to smile at the lack of discipline; these charming folk do not think of monsters and bolts from heaven raining down death, they think someone they know may be in trouble and they wish to help, or watch.

The basso pound of sandals on the path precedes Chaktha scattering idlers on either side. He stops when he sees you, pain on his face and his hand tightly gripping the spear, in hopes he may bury his guilt by using it soon.

As he raises you in one hand you ask "Check the school," putting out one arm to stop Tanar'h. Moving aside with your bodyguard you say, "Look for any children" and whisper "giant bug". Eyes ablaze, Chaktha nods and charges in.

With one eye on the door you return to Tanar'h.

"W'starrah, what happened in there?"

"A poison in the air. How did you know to come?"

"I was, well, I was going to ask—" he looks down to Kat again and grimaces. "I was in conference, with our guest the Devout, when suddenly there were shouting children everywhere, buzzing about the Rom and asking if I was a Gypsy!"

You have to grin at this, the reliable way youngsters will exaggerate a tale.

"I was angry. Ekaterinye knows I have no way with children. But now—eyes of the First, W'starrah, why are you so constantly in danger?"

It is time to test your friend and rival.

"Why indeed, High Heart? The vessel of the poison was of the brightest Yellow."

Tanar'h flinches as if struck, but not surprised. He searches your eyes, swallows hard before responding.

"Do you have a dagger?"

"What? What do you—"

He draws a slim blade from the back of his belt and hands it to you. "Here. With these events you should always carry something." Stepping in, he reaches to your wrist and places the point on his own chest. "If I thought that I or any of my followers had intended harm to you, W'starrah Altieri, beloved of the Stargazer, Heaven's Eye and my love, then I would this moment help you press the blade home."

He is leaning into the point hard enough to draw blood, and the blade shakes in your hand, perhaps because you are still weak. Beneath your feet, you hear Kat cough and start to rouse. Both of you are on your knees at once, and her faint voice restores your spirit with every word.

"What happened?"

"Rest, teacher," Tanar'h says.

Chaktha returns, blocking the sun and shaking his head. "Nothing, priestess."

"Kat, the fruit, do you remember, which child had the lemon? On the table."

The teacher shakes her head, then begins to quake with some frenzy. She sits up and rolls to her knees.

"Fire of the First, no, please no Stargazer!"

"Kat, what is it?"

She crawls toward the nearer pond; you half-tackle her or she would be in the water.

"The child!" she cries, then whispers, "I never dismiss school early, except you had…" She chokes in horror, and you realize the

106

truth of her thought. "Everyone was intended to be there, by the stars. Someone—some parent gave their own child—"

Kat is overcome by a new fit of coughing, collapses to the grass and passes out again.

Tanar'h calls to his guards, "Carry the teacher inside the temple."

"No," you respond. "The healer. Tanar'h, send them to the Telholian and beg him to come at once." He nods and points to Jal'i and Tamess, who salute and flee up the hill toward the city.

Chaktha scoops up the teacher like a kitten in one arm and follows you back to the tower. Most of your thoughts are frantic with concern for her, but there is also the horrid idea she voiced by the water. And more; you have never visited the schoolhouse by day before. Has Kat been the target all along? Or does your mysterious enemy, like a monster, like a flame, not care where it wreaks destruction?

Kat lies on the divan in your room, not conscious but steadily murmuring of the Dragon and spiders, her children dying. You pray for her health, but all you can see in your mind's eye is a horrid pale insect crawling over the statue here. Did you only imagine it, at the schoolhouse? Was it real, here the previous night? You rise to look behind the stone in the alcove, but notice nothing.

"Priestess," Chaktha calls from below "the High Heart asks audience." Tanar'h hates being announced as a suppliant; Chaktha is aware of this and cares not. Kat is safe, so you descend.

Tanar'h looks drawn and worried, and you sense this is not on Kat's account. "Heaven's Eye," he begins formally, "will you walk with me?" As you consider, Chaktha moves to the stairs to guard her. You gesture and Tanar'h leads the way outside into the gardens.

For the first time, you notice some who see you coming and turn aside. The work you did hosting the Red Cup and interrupting the school day is having its effect. Perhaps they believe the High Heart is drawing you aside to lecture his intended. Perhaps he is.

Perhaps he should.

The trees are mainly bare of buds, but soon now; the worst of the mild Argensian winter is already over. Tanar'h is silent, staring down as he walks, gathering his thoughts. The alone-ness of life without Kat and the goodwill of your temple family presses down. You never cried when brought here as a child; you loved the preachers without restraint and they welcomed the beautiful girl who spoke the words of the Stargazer. But today, to look upon the paths and hedges you could navigate blindfolded is to feel homesick for a place while still here.

"It is clear that I should apologize." He stops and swallows, looking up as if in hope this will suffice. Unsure of his meaning, you take a guess.

"For what happened today? Some ally went beyond your intent?"

"What? No!" Tanar'h is shocked and stung, but something holds him back from his usual short temper. "I have already addressed that, Heaven's Eye; use that dagger if you don't believe me." His burnished chest bears the dribble of dried blood like a medal; he could not be guilty of this, at least.

"What then, Tanar'h, for trying to take my preaching away?"

"Hell of demons! I have much, it seems, to atone for. I refer, W'starrah, to that morning, in your tower, when I, for what I said to you then."

You recall, the fit of passion and fury that held him. Yet truly, this was the least of his affronts to your mind, and the furthest ago in time.

"Please believe me, I would never—that is, when those words … it was most unlike me, to do that to you, and it will never happen again."

"You are kind, High Heart, to make amends. Why now, may I know, do you feel the need?"

"I have only now learned, that is, upon reflection I realize my error. Remember what I told you, W'starrah, last service, at the altar, what I confessed to you. Ask me again, should you ever doubt, ask me when I first loved you. I shall gladly repeat it before the preachers or the city, whatever the shame; and thus will you know me."

Before you can unravel his meaning, Tanar'h stiffly bows and withdraws. What could he have meant by this bizarre admission, a half-apology? Does he think to cover his part in a plot? But even though he courts you with the subtlety of a stallion, a rival does little to advance his suit with such talk. Instead he seemed to think it proof of something, and part of you believes this secret worth discovering. Perhaps you are still too weak from the poison, the mind can make no progress.

A slight cough from behind reveals the elderly vine-guilder, who has been waiting to attend you. He bows at once and gestures to various bulky tubes and bulbs of glass at his waist-belt.

"Myster Altieri, if you are endowed with a moment's leisure, I hoped to demonstrate my art."

Here is one, at least, who has not embraced your scandal, or perhaps he runs in circles too dignified to have yet heard. At a gesture he proceeds, indicating a small jasmine shrub, one of the first to bloom here in the second month; he begins to lay out tools and other apparatus as he speaks.

"You have no doubt noticed, priestess, that the jasmine is not always white?"

"Certainly, it is my favorite flower, and sometimes the blooms can be yellow." That word puts a clenching hand around your heart, but the elderly gardener does not notice.

"Indeed, yellow is fairly common, and on rare occasions I have seen them with a reddish tint." He looks up to you a moment, with a slightly impish grin; so then, he is not completely ignorant this fellow. You chuckle with him.

"But I bethought me, what color could better improve the plant than ours—provided of course it caused no harm." His things are ready and he kneels back a moment with his hands on his thighs. You survey the equipment he has laid out and connected, but there is no pattern to it. None of it looks to be normal gardening tools. He is clearly proud of his effort here; never once has he alluded to how long this work has taken, and of course it would be rude to ask.

First he sets what appears to be a dry paste or putty around the base of the tree. A few thin rods of wood, set into that base, align with the stem of the shrub in the same way as a supporting trellis would. These are tied with cord around the top. Finally, using a needle-thin nail attached to a small pot by a hempen hose, he punctures the trunk near the ground and holds the pot overhead. Perhaps something liquid is running from there through the tube and into the trunk, but it is silent. Every item whether soft or hard is made of the purest, brightest Purple: your mind boggles at the expense.

The gentleman holds your gaze as he sits there, smiling gently. You smile back, then furrow the brows slightly to indicate puzzlement.

In response, he breaks into a grin well beneath his age, and indicates with his eyes that you should look up.

Every single blossom attached to this stem is changing before your eyes, from bright white to lavender, then fuchsia, deepberry and amethyst. You cry out in joy, clapping your hands and rushing up to take in the unchanged, glorious scent. To you, jasmine always smelled like Purple.

There are tears in your eyes as you raise up the vineguilder and hug him.

"I hope, priestess, that you are pleased then." His voice is also thick with emotion, for here is a dedicated son of your Cup seeing his life's work come to fruition.

"Dear sir, I have no words, this is a priceless gift."

"It is no temporary stain," he says, eager to assure you, "this plant will remain truly Purple all its life; through the trunk, within the cross section of every leaf." Indeed, even the stem is changing hue now.

"And the next generation, drawn from its seed?"

He sighs and looks down. "I have no such sway over nature, priestess. The children of this plant will return to white. I have tried, a dozen times—"

You cut off his confession with a kiss and another hug. "Never mind, sir, this is an inestimable stroke, a work of genius." He smiles and fidgets, having lost a third of his age under your praise. Then the thought strikes like a bolt, and you seize his hand.

"Good sir! Do you know of any other Color that has achieved this mastery, over a thing still living?"

He slowly shakes his head and raises a silvered brow.

"Will you consent to do me another favor? I have something to show you, it is in the schoolhouse."

He bows. "I am at your disposal Heaven's Eye." He stoops to retrieve his things and comes with you.

"It needs great discretion, but surely the First himself sent you to me."

He wraps the oblong fruit of bright sunlight in a cloth and carefully stows it in his pouch, nodding at your injunctions to be careful of the poison.

"I am delighted, priestess, to receive this mission and hope to prove worthy."

Such a graceful, poised elder, and of course he charms you to pieces with refined flattery. He kisses your extended hand—the old-fashioned habit, just as your Captain used—and strolls with you out of the schoolhouse.

There would have been more time for pleasant chat but a crimson-clad retainer, leader of the three who came from Carnad Mias, approaches and salutes you. The vineguilder bows and directs a somewhat frosty glance at the newcomer before taking his leave. The retainer smiles, bows and presents a folded, red parchment addressed to you and sealed in purple.

"My master the Red Cup invites you to tour the Crystal Street Festival as his guest."

"Is that today? Already?" With a heart-thud you realize these details are slipping from your grasp. The attack on Kat was a major distraction.

"The precinct by the southern gate has been preparing for two weeks, Myster Altieri. The Red Cup invites you to make full use of his carriage now at the temple gate, and to join him at your convenience in his box for the parade."

A perfect opportunity: everyone knows of Mias' suit for the glass guilds. He rented the perfect viewing-box for years now, at prices no one dare ask. The gate-path is smooth ahead.

Belatedly you think of Kat still helpless, and turn back. Yet the Red man anticipates your thought.

"That bodyguard, priestess, told me when I checked for you there, to say that the teacher—whomever that is—has recovered with the healer's help—a swoon, I suppose—and is now resting in her chambers." Clever, discreet fellow.

"My thanks, good sir, I shall inform the Red Cup of your assistance. Would you be so kind to return there and tell Chak'tha that I shall not require him this afternoon? Ask him to look after the teacher."

"The Nubian, mistress?" The retainer turns a bit pale, sketches a half-bow and bites his lip. "May I, that is, would it be too troubling to have a note from you to that effect? I doubt he will be pleased."

111

This brings unforced laughter and a few words quickly penned on the back of the invitation, followed with the mark used to signal Stargazer business. "You will need to read the message to him, but this sign will remove all impediments."

He retreats with a grin and you glide past the gate into the magnificent cherry-wood gold-posted chaise. The driver and footman resume their places and snap up the team of deep chestnut bays, hauling into an immediate turnabout, scattering peasant traffic to either side. Fitting, you think, to treat them now with the same disdain as Mias and his conspirators do at all times. A bit wistfully, you wonder if there will be any reputation left to salvage when the month's business is done.

This dour reflection is interrupted by the sight of the Devout Teretheny, walking ahead of the chaise and trailed by his two mismatched guards. An instinct prompts.

"Driver, please slow down. I wish to take in the sights."

He walks deliberately toward the southern gate district, no doubt to the same festival but likely with a different purpose. Where does he fit in this web of schemes? And what hold does he evidently have on Tanar'h, other than the proximity of his monastery to the High Heart's childhood home? For a man who talks so much about family, your rival has been at great pains only to show you the one he constructed for himself since arriving in Cryssigens. A family he invited you to join. Your heart is settled, but doomed, you cannot believe your Captain can survive his quest. Perhaps a decent widowhood with May'stra and the others …

The Devout turns down a side-alley and you only notice when he calls to his guards, who had trudged on straight. It will look suspicious if you stop the chaise here. But the Stargazer smiles; two guilder carts with last-moment supplies for the festival feast are arguing the right of way just ahead. Some sixty steps down the alley looms the tall figure of the Devout Teretheny, his earthen robes stretched nearly taut over too-long limbs, facing away and regarding a small wizened figure lurking and gesticulating before him. It is difficult to make out many details, but something about the stranger's pointed features and furtive movements speaks of power. There are two flames in the alley, both dangerous you sense.

Just as the held-up wagons decipher their order and move on, the little man hands a pouch or canteen of some kind to the Devout, who stores it in his robe. The other man's eyes are visible for just a moment, and you shiver from the sheen of their rabid vitality. Here is someone who you would never willingly approach. Even knowing that Teretheny clasped hands with him is a warning. But of what?

All at once, the chaise passes under a street-bridge and turns left onto Glitter Mall, and thoughts of anything other than beauty are banished. The cheers are deafening, largely for you, but they are nothing compared to the sights.

The Red carriage joins a line of wealthy coaches slowly circling clockwise on a broad divided street, surrounded by tall, close-set manses replete with balconies, viewing boxes, or connecting bridges thirty feet and more off the ground. The median between this elongated cobblestone oval is a grassy sward set with dozens of crystal statues; heroes on pedestals, figures in groups, beast-combats and famous miracles life-size and larger. The noonday sun of late winter flashes into the mall and reflects in so many directions that it hurts the eyes wherever you look. Even the mortar between the cobblestones is speckled with glints of finest glass and bright gems, so that it seems at times the sun is rising beneath the wheels.

The people cheer the informal parade of celebrities, calling out to leaders of their church, their guild or Color as well as to the nobles who partake in the procession. Returning their praise is easy and comes back to you redoubled; the citizens have always been eager to celebrate. Many wait until the chaise has passed to surreptitiously point, as if the presence of the Lavender Lady in the Red carriage needed explanation.

There, in the finest balcony above the center of the near side, the gorgeous box of the Red House, and Carnad Mias sits looking down with a face as pleased as a napping cat. He rises to bow to you as if your station were higher than his own, a great compliment; you blow him a kiss and he mimes that its force knocks him back to his seat, creating a wave of jubilation. Every man's rib is elbowed by a neighbor, with remarks about what the Red Cup may expect soon. You sit back and drink it in, your ruin means the advancement of your cause. How to avoid Mias' meaty grasp in the dead of night, you are not sure; but let it rest for now.

As the carriage turns through the narrow end and starts back on the far side of the Mall, the statues on the median naturally attract attention. Most of the carved groupings are quite old, several are huge and multi-figured; all are completely beyond mortal price. No single Guild, no Baron by himself, could have commissioned one of these monuments, requiring the highest skills in the Empire and decades of careful measurement, assessment and cutting. In a way, the guilds of glass united the city, by requiring such widespread efforts to engage their services.

One set shows the founder himself, Cryss Altair, raising the palace through magic. Another, depicting the famous Storm March of an early and failed rebellion against Argens, showers a set of head-bent knights with rain from an adjacent fountain. Clever lanterns set with lenses in all the Colors rotate at intervals tinting the entire set of statues and the constant rain to the continual delight of the eye. More, the patter of drops striking crystal helms and cloaks is musical, suggesting a melody that you cannot tarry to make out.

With a shock, you see again the Devout Teretheny ahead, standing with arms akimbo before a colossal glass diorama of Argens subduing the desert dwellers. Behind him his two guards wait uncomfortably, as boos rain down from the crowd. No one is supposed to walk on this median, but of course your visitor neither knows nor appears to care. What a chore Tanar'h has had with him, you suppose. But this reflects also on your church. Calling to the driver, you open the door as if welcoming a snake into your bedroom.

"Pious Devout, won't you join me up here, I assure you the view is unsurpassed."

He whirls around, face brimming with outrage and suspicion, but appears to calculate before signaling to his men and climbing up. Boarding the steps requires both hands briefly; the robe beneath his face-mask falls away, revealing again something on his neck golden and sparkling with gems, arching away from a center like multiple legs. He takes the opposite seat and the statues no longer seem to interest him. Between the wrapping around his forehead and mouth blazes a flame from his whirling pupils.

His guards trail along behind. The tall one need only walk to keep up with the slow pace of the horses, yet he constantly attends to his companion, tugging him by the sleeve lest he fall behind, or even down. You are in sight of thousands who still adore you despite your scandal, he would never dare any violence now. Still you fear this anchorite.

"The festival displeases you, holy sir?"

"The veneration of the heroes is an abomination."

"What!" Who could keep composure at such blasphemy? Anger like Z'kammet Hammer's rises inside, but must be throttled if you are to discover anything. Following with a silvery laugh you manage, "Too much time alone has dried out your heart, reverend Myster."

"So then, you admire the spectacle, conquest of a foreign people? Crushing war, with its loss of life and the confinement of the defeated to desert lands? This is heroic?"

"That is a Hopeforger statue," you respond carefully. "I think you are mistaking courage—"

"Bah," he plows on pointing to the passing displays, "or then here, Cryss Altair and the first of his many fruitless, pointless rebellions. Teaching the nobility to value independence over peace. There, Argens and his pleasure-drunken *harum*. That one, at least, you Stargazers would own?"

"Is it simply that so many examples of virtue confuse you, sir?" Little point pretending that this fanatic, at least, will ever be an ally. Mock him, draw him out.

His lips are covered by the wrapping, but his sneer shows through it. "Confusion, aye, sown by preachers to keep our people divided and weak. Heroes aplenty, but no true heroism."

"Our people, holy sir? Do you speak of all Cryssigens? Then why should we disagree?"

"The city! Hah—the nation, all nations together."

"The North Mark forever united with Argens?"

"Elf and Man, Bedou-uu and black, women equal to men in all things, no gulf between peasantry and nobility. This is how we should advance."

"All the same," you gasp, "like … mindless insects." Fire Ants, or Spiders.

115

"All together! Following one who can draw all ranks, all races, all colors to—" he checks his speech and settles back. Your mind is swimming, desperate for a handhold. This vision is a blasphemy beyond the old Unitarian chatter, and before which the election of a Mark would only be a stepping stone.

"This explains your toleration in selecting desert men as guards."

"They are useful to me," he replies shortly. "I found Sanhim and Elehar near the edge of the Shimmering Mindsea, men with no tribe, and took them in. We have an arrangement."

"It seems to me, holy sir, we are not so different. Argens Stargazer welcomes all, as I—"

"Argens Stargazer does not exist." At this affront, your mind reels back and into my arms. There was no way to brace you for this thrust, but at least now you recognize your enemy's shape, if not his aim.

"None of the heroes exist. There is only the hero, if you will. That was the true message of the service last evening, which you interrupted."

Teretheny is avid now, every word slicing sharp-edged at the heart of your faith. "You with your fantasies about seeing the future, while holding out hope of multiple marriages to give yourself an excuse for lechery. And the Hopeforgers who rail on about being first, as if their place mattered more than another's. Telhol, and Astor and all the reverence given to names of myth in the northern barbarian lands. All a distraction, and what should be a crime. Courage, honor, foresight, purity, these are all to be found in one spirit, and each must try to achieve that without distraction of statues, and song, incense, flashes of light and pretty dresses. Brother Tanar'h sees this, though his thoughts still drift." Your eyes flash together at this, and the disdain in his gaze is like a punch.

A deep breath before you reply, to gather your courage. "Fascinating sermon, holy sir. I had no idea the devotions at Sinter were this … original. It's clear you can have no use for an old-fashioned girl still clinging to her beliefs. You are always welcome at service, and who the High Heart chooses to host is of course his concern. Driver, my guest is finished."

The chaise slows and stops; Teretheny's guards lumber up to await him. As the monk rises to debark, you lean slightly forward and speak low while covering your bosom.

"I think it best, holy sir, that you not return to my tower. A mere courtesy, you understand. It could be that Argens will insist on taking insult, despite not being real. And he has been known to wield the fire of Solar on those who displease him."

Teretheny snorts, saying, "A storm is rising that will fan all flames to its will. Let any who resist its coming be swept along."

Without instructions, the driver stands until you hear the shouts of those behind who wish to continue the parade. Coming around again you see Mias at his balcony and signal the driver to pull aside to pay respects in person. Though the gathered crowd waits for you to step out, it needs several moments to calm the breathing, and be sure your legs will obey without quivering.

A quarter-hour later you are having nine-tenths of a splendid time. The ruby-silk cushioned chair feels as if it had been built for you (and perhaps it was); the view from the balcony can admit of no improvement; servants are attentive to your goblet and otherwise their crimson livery blends into the curtains of the alcove as if invisible. The weather is crisp and fine with the prospect of warming. Music from the passing parade cars is never discordant, the miniature plays shown at each stop—one directly before you—are meaningful and sincere.

Yet Carnad Mias rests one hand continually on your thigh, below sight of the crowd, with an occasional sensuous squeeze of familiar possession that makes you want to leap the rail and take your chances with the fall.

Aside from murmured praise for this or that bit of the pageant, there has been no conversation yet. With small glances you fence his gaze, trying to determine if he knows about the attack at the schoolhouse. Surely the Red Cup hears all, but he has not expressed regret, surprise, anger. So many questions. But let him feel the smart one.

"Augh," you exclaim as the Goblet Guild float rolls past, "too much gold for me at least. Perhaps I'm less partial to yellow after today."

Now his squeeze is strong and sustained, bringing your eyes around to meet his. "Yes, my dear, I heard. And I might say the news left a sour taste in my mouth as well."

The mutual chuckle dies when he adds. "I shall find those responsible, and the census will run short, I assure you."

You take in the metallic sincerity of his eyes, and the meaning is clear. A woman protected so masterfully, whose lover pulls men down and cuts their throats, will be grateful and enthused in public, later soft and yielding in private. He will earn you, like a month's wages drawn from a new and interesting employer.

Was it only two nights ago that you felt some thrill at his touch, thought him attractive in a way? But that was before Justin: the Red Cup has a seductive stalk as smooth as the Captain's skin is rough, his manner refined like thin-beaten gold compared to the Argensian's halting, comic candor. When tasked to protect your honor and life, the man before you now would raise a finger, whisper to a lackey, sign an order. The other, far from you and close to death, would reach for his own sword, putting his body between you and danger.

You smile cat-like and trace a finger on the back of his thigh-grasping paw, tempting it up off your leg to chase the bait of your hand. Light banter, pretended gratitude, wide-eyed innuendo, these roll from your tongue with ease as you think of your Captain. But before you let Carnad Mias take your body, the dagger Tanar'h gave you should find your own breast.

The passing parade wagons bear live actors and beasts, playing out featured moments in the history of the city; each rolling cart is adorned with a full-size glass figure at the front, figureheads for the fleet of civic pride sailing in stately circle before the cheering crowds. Attendants have rolled out thick carpets over all the cobbles, to lessen the lurching that could otherwise bring irreparable harm.

"How like our situation," you muse loud enough for Carnad to hear. "We glide along lightly now, as if nothing could threaten our fragile future." You look to him with as much sincerity and worry as you can muster, and when you think how the Red Cup might be involved, it is not hard to pretend.

"Cryssigens is a priceless jewel indeed," he answers, studying your face intently. "All who love her are working hard to keep her safe."

118

"But can Et'run lead us effectively? If he should bring war with Argens—"

Now Carnad Mias smiles: he thinks you have missed the mark, and there is something in that. "As for that, my dear, worry not. Our army is reduced it's true, but the lad has ... hidden resources I assure you. The knights of the Empire—"

"Are no longer its strongest weapon," you interrupt, and it discomfits him. "Have you seen the Imperial troops, their discipline?"

"Ah yes, that fracas in the Arena," he returns, "I'm glad you came off safely from the clutches of those invaders. And now their captain has scuttled away with them, I'm told, off doing the Firegrip's bidding Argens knows where. With fortune, that blasted gryphon will eat him soon."

You find in his face only scorn, no hint of jealousy. The Red Cup sees nothing but a rival's pawn in your lover's actions, and if he knew the certain death Justin marched to, it would concern him even less. Carnad's gaze softens now into a leer. "The soldiers of Argens, the Green and Yellow Houses, you must take care my dear, to make no further enemies."

You laugh and drink, taking his kiss on your cheek as is proper in public. "I suppose I have only four Colors left to annoy!"

"From the Red, dear one, you are safe as houses." Mias pauses to gaze blankly at the parade again; the final wagon is about to enter the plaza. "By the way, have you heard anything about a new Color?"

This is a shock, and you shake your head numbly. "What do you mean? The Brown, of course I had nearly forgotten—but they never enter politics. Has someone created White, or even Black then after all these years?"

Mias shakes his head, and shrugs with a smile. "Grey, milady. But I don't know if I can trust the reports."

"A new House, are you serious? Where is their chapter, what industry do they—"

"Nothing so substantial! Just a Man, I mean a mortal, spotted in the docks and poorer districts, dressed all in drab down to his hair, bearing strange weapons and an oddly-shaped talisman about his neck. Only rumors at this point, and I thought perhaps you had heard more." He shrugs again as if to be sure, and you grin with a hand on his shoulder.

"It is a thing you do not know for certain, great Cup of Red," you accuse playfully, "and this annoys you."

He turns to you and his face holds a reptile's grin, too tight against his skin to be sincere. "I like to be sure of things, that is true. In all my dealings."

The final float has moved into the parade now, to a rising tide of the crowd's awe that drowns out private speech. But you cannot look to this wonder, for Carnad Mias has risen from his chair and draws you to him. His eyes are cat-wide with desire, hands cupping your elbows; at the slightest exertion of his massive arms you rise from the ground toward him.

You knew it was coming, this poker game has an ante each round. Kiss him or be revealed. But you have a plan, and I am with you always.

You close your eyes, and at the first touch of his lips *you feel the grip of his hands more like talons. His tunic front is finest wool yet the brocade feels like melded coins against your silk shift. His tongue licks into you with an expert flicker, feeling forked. Every ounce of breath expels under his embrace,* and you must not writhe, nor scream nor call Justin's name to ask forgiveness. The Dragon of your vision, you cannot question the Red Cup's place in the city's future. Fire, and ruin, and one of those present when the demon breaks free.

Your plan aligns with reality; hanging there in Carnad Mias' crushing embrace you do not need to fake fainting. Blackness, and an airless vise around your soul. For the second time in as many days you are not awake; and in this handful of seconds there are no dreams but the vision is always there. You see *the Serpent, the storm of multi-legged doom from the whirlwind, and the star-formed Arbalest cranking his bolt into place.*

Someone has set you back in your chair, one talon still on your arm but with a more tender regard. A deep voice chuffs orders, an iced cloth chills your forehead. You open your eyes and see everything at once.

The main parade float does not hold just one statue at its prow, but is completely paved in glass. The city of Cryssigens itself is on deck, all the major buildings placed just where they should be and nearly

120

large enough for a child to crawl into. Figures everywhere, taller than your forearm and carved in matchless detail. Gaspar Heugen stands before the palace with a sash of brightest Blue. Carnad Mias in a ruby carriage by the arena, and atop your own tower of the Stargazer temple stands a small gorgeous replica of yourself in lavender-tinted crystal. The guilds and other sects are all represented, it is too much to take in and the sunlight makes it too hard for the eye to bear more than a blink at a time. But your vision-view is supernal, you see it all in an instant, and more. You see beyond.

On the plaza opposite your box, down on the street stands the cowled Serpent, tipping back and draining the last quaff from a canteen before speaking to his two guards. The taller one jogs his fellow, who rouses from a standing sleep and says something. The monk drops the canteen and spreads arms to the sides, eyes closed and breathing in deeply.

The windstorm emanates directly from his body, and of all the crowd around the square only Teretheny is unaffected. No one else sees whither the cyclone begins, as they scatter and fall and scream in shooting panic. The cone of the twister grows more visible and increases in size, steering a path in curves out into the square, engulfing the wagons. Wooden rails and wheels splinter and crack, but the glass figures vibrate, then explode. Crystal statues larger than life, the entire city of the main float, all detonate in turn and throw their armloads of gash and maiming into the storm. Scores are falling to the ground now, striped in red, missing limbs, impaled through the skull. It is a fire of wind and blood, and from its wrack drop shards of glass and flesh like a many-legged thing. You see a sun-yellow arm with a sharp severed elbow, sea-green hair in separate shattered strands, the pure quartz head of a lovely child; a rainbow of shards swirls, collides, shatters again and again until there is only one color, with all differences annihilated.

The shower of deathly rain reaches the box level and you feel its stinging patter in a dozen places at once. Carnad Mias reacts as quickly as a gladiator, throwing his thick woolen cloak between you and death, cursing loudly and hunching down to shelter your body even with his own. Safer, you wonder, with the Dragon than the Serpent? You hear the cries of agony and confusion coming in waves, between blows of the windstorm as it destroys every beautiful thing in the plaza, whether it struggles still to live or now slays in the deadly image of life.

⊕ ⊕ ⊕

Ｙou are certain of only a few things by the next day. What day exactly it is does not number among them.

You did not sleep again, though the dawn was thankless and empty. You stood there in the breeze the morning sun sometimes brings, feeling a sting beyond the chill, the smarting pain of a score of tiny wounds on your cheeks, arms, neck. And heavy, your soles flat on the stone and none of the elation that had felt so accustomed, an entitlement. For the first time, your morning prayer feels more like a duty, pulling time and strength at the very start of the day and giving back nothing but a dim echo of satisfaction, guilt averted, a chore tallied.

Chaktha is there behind you, as always and this time you hug him fiercely. Your arm span is far short of an embrace around his enormous muscular frame; it is like hugging a corner of the temple. But his flesh is solid and warm, years later the jungle heat still in it, and his heart beneath your ear beats enough to gently move your head.

"You should be free," you whisper to his chest with anger, "you should leave my service and go somewhere honest and honorable."

"I should stay more closely with the priestess," he rumbles back, a mild reproof. You nod, but you both know it is not a promise. Chaktha follows you back down the stairs, and you are relieved to see the door repaired, but slightly ajar.

Chaktha has already brought the workers up here, since he had battered his way within. He steps through first now, as alert for human foes as the monstrous Bug you keep imagining. But the suite is empty, and once the disappointment has crossed his face, at not being able to perhaps spear Carnard Mias as an intruder, your bodyguard leaves to once again stand at the lower entrance.

The Red Cup was here again last night, another thing of which you are certain. He escorted you away from the disaster in Glitter Mall, a cadre of blood-clad guards to all sides, your chaise an ambulance in what became another parade back to the temple. Of course, all the city would know that the Red House took W'starrah Altieri under its wing, its Cup her protector against any foes and naturally an ally in the coming political battle.

He barely feigned hesitation when you begged him to come to your chambers. Pretending to fuss about your comfort beneath the thick purple coverlet, he let his hands roam by accident to graze those parts of your body which they would have explored long ago with any other woman. Men like Mias need to know their manner is seductive, since they have no love in their hearts to draw them. But there was a shred of decency about the man, at least regarding sexual pleasure; you kissed him again as best you could, gasping without pretense from the painful cuts where his arms enfolded you, and he managed to stagger back and control himself for the moment. He lay beside you as if from gallantry, pretending he would just abide chastely and not arouse from sleep a few hours later, pulled by his midriff to take you at last. And you let him pretend, since he drank the posset seeming unawares, to your health no less! Truer words never spoken. After four hours staring wide-eyed at the ceiling and counting his snores, you stole away to greet the dawn. And now he is gone again, your chambers are your own until tomorrow night. Another party. Perhaps then, you'll hear what you need.

The bedroom is empty and you see in the mirror a woman with the pox. Ragged red dots speckle her flesh, the damage done before Mias covered you both with his cloak. He had several as well, and a gash on the back of his neck. But neither the Red Cup nor anyone else you heard shouting and wailing at yesterday's catastrophe could say from where it had come. Only you saw Brother Teretheny, the empty flask, the strange words with his bodyguards and the spread-armed invocation that brought down the destroying wind. You never liked him, and you admit there was a certain satisfaction in hearing his fanatical rant as he rode in your carriage, to know you would not need to make common cause. But this; you had never suspected the willingness to wantonly slaughter helpless citizens on such a scale. What enemy could be a greater threat to the city's safety? Who else indeed could be the enemy?

And does he know that you are aware of him?

Barely past dawn, and you feel the exhaustion that normally comes after an evening of preaching. The cuts never stop reporting pain, as

123

if the glass were still embedded there, or had been doused in vinegar. You are not sure you remember Kat, the night before, salving and cleaning each mark, wailing with worry as if your complexion were a greater matter than scores of the innocent dismembered. She left to attend to any wounded brought to the hospice here. Forgiving her, you do recall that; she was not there, and she loves you.

But who else would love this speckled visage you see in the glass? Without noticing, you have already fumbled among the small mountain of wooden boxes to find one with ointment, and are slathering it on. Maybe Carnad brought more with him last night? But who else could be using it, you wonder. Kat perhaps, she is always interested in such things, poor teacher. The crème disappears quickly and you feel a tingle something like the energy you once took for granted. Praise Astor, it is enough to continue, though you sense it won't last for long. Before you leave, on impulse you don the plain iron ring and turn the ax-face away from sight. With this, you sent Justin on his lethal mission to the north, and with it you can make a report to your mutual masters in Argens. Part of you wants to do so at once, but you need to know more. The Emperor's Halfling Morinack said it would work only three times.

The breakfast goes down without taste, as well made as ever but doing little to sustain your spirit, and nothing to dispel the memories of that bloody square wizening your stomach. Mias blocked much of the view while carrying you, but the wrack of flesh lay everywhere.

And your reputation, it seems, is also ruined. The audience room has but one occupant this morning: Welles, the Orange house jeweler.

"Myster Altieri, praise the stars you are safe."

"My dear Welles, are you quite alright, you look as if you haven't—"

He smiles at the slight nearly spoken.

"Slept, I know milady. I work hard and am not ashamed to admit that I take a few hours most nights, just as the mortals must. But I came to ask, rather, after your, em, your comfort since, that is, whether you have been, ahm, completely alright?" It's clear the crafter with no embarrassment for his own habits is too afraid to inquire about yours. He wishes to ask if you have slept well, assumes you do, but knows he mustn't say so to a noble. You think on this as you look

124

him steadily in the eyes, then pour him a cup of tea and hold on when he reaches for it, to draw his gaze in return.

"You have had bad dreams?"

He nods in misery, and more, in fear.

"And you wonder—dear sweet man, you wonder if I have had the same."

Another nod, and he whispers despite the empty room.

"I may confess to you freely, priestess. I searched everywhere for that stone, both of a size and quality that it might hold the spell you wished. I nearly despaired of the effort, but then it just ... fell across my view, as it were. It is curiously ... light for gemstone, priestess; I should have guessed when my source was so willing to sell. The perfect piece! I knew when I paid that I would need to make a few polishes, feared I might have to cut it. I set it on my lapidary bench and decided to, well, to sleep on it once before working."

"It is a splendid job, I assure you, and it works to perfection."

"Milady! I made no cut, barely a single buff to that gem. When I awoke, it was already in the exact form of my vision, with Argens as my witness." Welles is clearly much moved, his voice constantly rising as he tells his story. "I thought myself fortunate. Hah! And when my friend Oshuwen the mage came to cast the sorcery he too found hardly any work was needed."

"I can have no idea what you mean, sir."

"Oshuwen said," now Welles was back to a cutting whisper and his eyes whirled with agitation. "He said it was as if the stone *knew* the purpose we intended. He spent less than two days, rather than the fortnight he expected, to complete the job."

Welles stands back and shakes his head like a wet dog. "I shall never accept such a commission the rest of my days."

You sip your tea and regard him carefully. "What is the nature of these dreams?"

Welles flinches like a man stung, and mutters, "Bugs, milady." He looks to both sides in the empty room, and any relief you feel to think of your own visions erodes while he continues. "Seeking, probing, down unfamiliar streets in darkened ways. But I know, I can feel it, they are looking for it. For me."

You take a deep breath. "In your dream, you mean."

125

Welles looks back at you with a face full of misery, and now you are truly concerned for his welfare.

"You must rest, my dear Welles, you've become distraught. Tell me, have you redeemed the token I gave you?" His face lights up a touch on that, and he meekly shakes his head. "Use it tonight, if you will be counseled by me, relax and take comfort in the arms of the church. No need to say more! Only go in peace and may the stars watch over you."

He bows and leaves you to the unaccustomed silence of your audience chamber, the untouched board of morning foods, the distant chime of the early hour. It is comforting to know the truth now, that the gem you are using to spy on the Red Cup bears this odd curse of dreams. Since you do not sleep—or hardly—it assails you through your waking mind, in visions. Surely.

The Devout Teretheny is a threat to the city, perhaps the only one. Was that storm an attempt on your life? No, it is too horrible to contemplate that a man would willingly countenance the death of scores for such a clumsy assassination. And the previous attempts—at the Hopeforger temple where you were saved by Chaktha and that mysterious interloper, and yesterday in the schoolhouse—those show the mark of someone familiar with the ways of the city. Hiring assassins and commissioning that dreadful poisoned fruit should be far beyond the resources of a monk from the distant Sinter monastery. Does he have partners then? That thin man in the alley was no guild leader or nobleman, yet he seemed so confident when he gave the monk the flask. Who could—

With a chill, you recall that Kat was with you both times.

And the second attack, at least, was as indiscriminate as the storm in the plaza, which you saw Teretheny create. The knot won't unravel, but you feel certain that Tanar'h, at least, must not know any of your suspicions. He has probably been duped by the ascetic, but what hold does the guest have on his host?

You survey the glorious board of food and finger the ax-ring while biting your lip. It is time to do something, and if it should prove impossible to restore the city today, then you should at least make yourself useful.

126

"Chaktha, I shall attend the wounded in the hospice. Please summon servants to bring this food after me, it should be eaten by those who need it."

"At once, priestess."

Seizing a wrap from your room upstairs, you catch another glimpse of your own reflection. For an instant, you hesitate to be seen, but then a wave of shame drives you downstairs at a run. What matters your beauty marred, compared to the suffering of so many? It is already too late for your reputation; the scars are a mark of honesty in that sense.

The hospice is jammed with the injured, mattresses laid between the beds to accommodate those unable to walk, or in danger of death. The low ceiling hems in the stench of dripping life and human closeness, but the long low room is well lit to bring scores of them in sight at once. The proof from so much spattered blood assails you, suggesting a harvest of Red. No matter now; the great thing is to help.

Kat cries out in relief, and with one reflexive hug presses a water-bowl and some towels into your hands before turning away to get more. Neither of you have any miraculous healing lore; it is rare even among the Hopeforgers. But you see a few with wounds of severed limbs healed over, resting comfortably now, and your eye keeps drifting back to these cots while you gently salve and redress less serious wounds. This is a day after the catastrophe (or more?); that some must have suffered for so long is a thought you cannot dwell on.

Nearness creates friends. Rows away, several of the injured turn from the sight of you; some even among the temple staff shake heads or cluck tongues. Yet everyone you aid utters their thanks, for your willing presence more than your poor ministrations. Qellen the smith, his arm bandaged with a long, seeping cut, speaks optimistically of returning to work tomorrow.

Time passes quickly, and you dimly recall having a few nibbles of your breakfast board for the mid-day meal as you work and talk to your family. Chaktha stands stolidly at the outer entrance watching in all directions; Tanar'h is not here, but Kat assures you he was, through most of the night. Her voice is careful, and you realize your place was also here, not flirting with Carnad Mias. Playing the part.

"But who performed these great miracles of healing?"

"It was the Telholian, Star. He came through yesterday on his way between all the places the wounded were taken. His name is Kama, and *oh!* What an exemplary *Man* he is. At first, he went from bed to bed barely stopping as he invoked his miracles. I saw an amulet, around his neck, it *glowed* with energy whenever he used the ancient words. But it must have given out, for I saw him slow and continue, using his own strength. *Five* more beds! And toward the end we were supporting him by the elbows. He passed out standing up, Star, almost knocked me to the ground; but he is *such* a little fellow, May and I were able to guide him to a cot."

"He slept like one hit in the head by a brick, right over there, and opened his eyes only to apologize. *Him!* Said he wished he could have done *more*, but that mortal saved three lives I tell you. He said he needed to recover his strength, and visit the other temples. We couldn't *keep* him, though I thought he looked *terribly* pale. I have never seen anyone like him."

You nod thoughtfully. "Praise the Stargazer he was here, no longer forbidden to worship as in the days of Viridian."

"We should thank him formally, on behalf of the temple."

You nod, "I'll handle that, as soon as I can find him." And you'll also sound him out, as your lover requested.

Kat throws out her arms before grabbing another armload of bandages. "He's likely somewhere in the city today, who *knows* where. But I heard him say he's building a chapel down by the palace, on the old Demonbender grounds. He sleeps there."

"I'll see him soon."

Kat puts a hand on your arm. "Take Chaktha, Star. Please."

You smile and pat her hand reassuringly. Over her shoulder, you see the Devout Teretheny.

Panic geysers up inside you, and Kat squeals as your grip tightens. He looks up at the sound, a pair of sandswept eyes over the muffled face, his two guards behind him as he moves through the ward. A moment he holds your gaze, and you show him fear, which is quite genuine, but hold your ground to allay his suspicion. A slightly wrinkled brow reveals his contempt as he turns dismissively to bend over another patient.

Kat has wriggled around in your grasp to see him, but your arm still clutches her convulsively, pulling her further away.

"Teretheny, here?" she whispers, "But what can he—"

You pull her head close and say only, "The Serpent." Her eyes flare with recall, your vision of the mythic monster, his legion of spiders and the many-legged storm. Teretheny's neck is covered as usual, but you recall the jeweled thing of your vision, the gold-studded necklace that the Ferret must steal. Why is he here now? Such blasphemous effrontery, but if you upbraid him he will know that you saw what he did.

Instead you bite a lip and hold your gorge as he bends over a horribly-scarred servant girl. His whisper carries well and increases your distaste.

"You must be strong, child of the One Wind. These trials are an opportunity for you to bear up and prove worthy." No miracle of healing, no other succor or kindness; only such a speech as a dying soldier might hear from an uncaring dekentar. But Teretheny stares into the woman's eyes, and her face flinches before resolving into something firmer, harder, less human. She nods to him, loyal and willing. She still suffers as before, but has agreed with him to withstand it.

His guards stand there, the tall one looking as miserable as you feel, one arm practically holding up his shorter partner who hunches with his right hand covering his left arm where the torque looks too tight by half. Neither man strikes you as a professional guard.

Looking back at the path he must have taken, you can see some patients still quivering with pain, still bleeding, yet refusing salves, spurning the food brought in from your board. Each has joined a web of loyalty, won out from under the Stargazer even within his own house. They mutter to each other now, spreading new strands to ensnare and convert their fellows.

The horror rises to your throat; he wounded all these people, and now is harvesting the survivors to his cause through some evil charisma. What can you say against him, except that which gives you away? With an effort, you remember the role you must play.

"Oh, enough of this, too much like labor!" you prattle lightly as you drop the towels and dust your hands, drawing a wounded look from Kat and more clucks of disgust from the further cots. "I shall be out and about, Kat, don't wait up for me."

Blowing a kiss, you turn to go with a leaden heart and the fear of Teretheny lodging against your spine. One part of his scheme at least, is now clear; and you cannot even trust Tanar'h enough to warn him. Chaktha follows you without prompting, as you head out of the temple compound, across the center city toward the palace by the river-cliff. To your surprise it is already full dark and drawing close to true cold.

You must find the Telholian, and get word of the Brow, and—why not—discern the identity of that thin-faced supplier who brought Teretheny his potion. Then use the ring to tell Morinack some, if not all of what you learn. Everywhere a dark secret, in everything a hint of unknown power. But all you really want is the sight again of a scarred and unsure Captain, whose fire and honesty would surely light all this blackness, whose least insight would hold all the wisdom your heart could ever need.

The center city is beautifully lit long after sunset, and scads of idle nobility linger everywhere. The constant occupation of the upper classes is to seek after something interesting, and you certainly qualify. Chaktha signals to a lantern-boy and pays him off to precede you around the square. The poor fellow earns his pay as you have no set destination, and constantly turn aside on a whim to take the hand of an admirer or chat with a rival.

"W'starrah! Look my love, see our dearest friend."

You turn with a smile to greet a pair in purple, noble members of your House, schoolmates newly married.

"Aumir'y! And J'seff'n, what a sight you both are, how long has it been."

In their embrace you find such relief as nearly staggers you. Here are two who love you without reservation or calculation, never thinking about who will be the next North Mark or whether anyone is trying to kill a friend. They pull you around the favored and familiar highlights of center-city, sometimes by carriage and at others on running feet. Chaktha and the lantern-boy keep up or ride on the back, but there are long stretches where you forget your protector is even there.

The *Regal Robe* is an exclusive tavern where tables are never available to those who approach the front door. The nobility frequenting it are all regulars and enter by a street-bridge on the third level. You sit with your friends in a curtained booth; Chaktha stands guard outside while snatching some food.

"My goodness, what trials you have endured," Aumir'y murmurs, dazed enough by even your light recounting of events to pause sipping her wine. "It's your life of course, W'starrah, but seems to me you take on far too much. The arena, whatever for! How does a squabble with the Emperor's mercenaries matter to us? And to press for prominence in both temple and House is to invite such dangers. Let that well-oiled priest of yours, Tanar'h handle the word of the Stargazers. And even among the Purple, we can let our decision be known without forwarding such a visible representative. As if the next Mark will make any real difference. Take better care of yourself, my dear."

"True words, my love," Aumir'y's husband adds sympathetically, patting her shoulder and refilling the goblets. "Beauty at risk is always an injustice." He shows the affection and consideration each moment calls up. J'seff'n had been promised to a noble's marriage contract before he could read it, and gladly retells the tale of their first meeting, not even seven, when Aumir'y shouted to see him and bestowed a most undignified hug before dragging him off to play games. His duty married his pleasure, the same day he signed that document, and there has been no better-settled thing in all Cryssigens than the love of these two, still young and immortal. He is one of perhaps two men whose eyes do not enlarge, and throat tightens, at the sight of you; bless the Stargazer for him. Seeing them together makes you think of Justin, and now your throat is tight. Bless him twice, whatever happens.

You chat on about ships from far Conar docked in port, and trouble on the Mindsea to the east where they say the heat still holds upon the sands. Several friends have new lovers, and most attend new churches since those northern barbarians stole the imperial throne and disbanded their first choice. Now you are back on wheels, taking in the post-midnight view of other nobles. Chaktha, sitting up front with the driver, makes the entire carriage tilt slightly to one side, and his head is also nodding a bit, lending a sense that the world could spill any moment.

Across from you Aumir'y lounges back against J'seff'n's shoulder, gracefully enfolded in his limbs and looking a perfect fit.

"I should stop imposing on you both, such a lovely visit."

"Star, you dare not leave! It has been simply ages, and we have no obligations for once."

You puzzle to recall the exact day. "But surely, there is some celebration or performance tonight? Isn't it the Feast of Fortitude, that's it, the theater re-enactment."

"Cancelled," J'seff'n intones, "so many actors slain, yesterday at the Glass parade. Oh, but W'starrah! Please forgive me, I had forgotten, that is, I can see you were wounded, but the cuts are so small—"

"You were there!" Aumir'y squeaks in panic, just now putting the facts together. "Oh my love, and we were to have gone as well, but you," she turns to her husband and flushes as they both laugh together, "you were so ardent!"

"I was the slave of your gift, madam!" And they both have tears with chuckles for a time. Instead of explaining that mystery, they insist in unison that you recount the entire awful tale. You tell them nothing of importance, of course, for what point in protecting your family if you shatter their happiness to do it?

They are shocked, they both hug you again, and they have a hundred questions. You are back in their apartments now, five stories above the central square, a kind of deep silence at last reigning over your city. Everything here is particular, plush, and a shade you can well appreciate. Chaktha has sent the lamp-boy home, and taken a space outside the chamber where he can stretch at length until dawn. You won't see the sun with him, it appears. But he is with you, and therefore content.

Aumir'y is bustling with a light breakfast while J'seff'n draws gently on a large pipe, considerately blowing small puffs of smoke toward the half-open window. He pats the water-chamber at the bottom and explains with a laugh that here is the source of his recent enslavement.

"She found a new kind of leaf, in a dingy market down by The Boards, and made me a gift."

"It was for love of the merchant's tale," Aumir'y adds with a giggle. "He insisted it was from the furthest desert or some such exotic place. Said the person to whom I gave this leaf, after smoking, would be unable to deny me his love. As if I would be able to tell!"

J'seff'n draws her to him for a kiss. "The truth of Argens. Three puffs and I was helpless with desire. As I am every day, in sooth!" He draws and puffs again, and you catch a scent that seems only just familiar. Automatically you start to rub your arms and neck. J'seff'n assumes it is the cold of morning, puts the pipe away and closes the window. "At any event," he concludes quietly, "we did not attend the parade. I am so sorry W'starrah."

"Nonsense. I am delighted you two were safe. It is indeed tragic, I had not considered all the actors…" The guilds staffed the floats with their own people in minor roles, but speaking parts were reserved for professionals. They would have been most directly in harm's way as the glass figures exploded.

"What could cause such a horrid tempest, Star? My friends told me you preached of a coming storm." This young couple attend the Cryssian sect, and it occurs that you might gain some knowledge through them.

"I had a vision, yes, though I think it is still in the future. This might have been like the tremble in the earth that precedes the quake."

"It could not have been a natural phenomenon. Some Despairing magic?"

"Or perhaps the Shard Demon breaking free; the broken glass might mirror his prison below the earth."

"More likely, the reverse," you muse, "evil acts like these in our streets may weaken his walls."

"Surely the Overlord can contain him?" Aumir'y is wide-eyed and you feel again her innocence.

"Certainly dear, once we elect the successor."

"Let us do so then, vote for E'trun right away! What point in delaying?"

You smile and allow J'seff'n to explain.

"They shall, love, in two months by the customs; though more likely Gaspar Heugen will win."

"Why does he not use the Overlord's power now?"

"It may not be, dear one, until the Overlord is elected he cannot wield the magic." J'seff'n stops, and you realize as he does, the means the Overlord would use are not generally known. Yet everyone seems to trust it will happen. What if the secret was only passed from father to son? Both Kreel and his son Kreelon were slain in the rebellion.

"Our city, built on magic," Aumir'y says quietly as you sit before tea and sweetbread in morning light by the window. "All this beauty, no one truly poor or very few, and yet below the palace cliffs, a demon held in thrall."

"It is not so severe as that, Mirry," J'seff'n replies. "Or rather, less simple. We look to the Overlord's crown, or his scepter, some great artifact to have the power to solve this threat. And perhaps that is so." He smiles to his wife. "But there is magic also all around us; in W'starrah's preaching, in our life together; and assuredly in that wondrous leaf!" He turns to you. "The Hopeforgers, they have a diadem do they not, of miraculous abilities?"

You swallow quickly and think of Feldspar. "You mean, the Brow of the Ecclesiast?"

"That one, marvelous name. Our attention is naturally drawn to such items, so easily featured in stories or made into a prop for the stage. I love to read about them, myself, over a good pipe. Before bed."

Aumir'y gasps and slaps his arm while her husband pulls a face of stone and innocence. You feel a prompting.

"Did you ever read of one such artifact, used by the monks of Sinter?"

J'seff'n looks at you with eyes focused elsewhere for a long moment.

"I mean some jewel," you add, "perhaps a necklace. Or a torque, for the arm?"

The couple begins to speak over each other.

"The monks at Sinter ... no." He sounds sure but looks puzzled.

"A torque?" Aumir'y asks, "That's desert wear, at least for men. A woman, now—"

J'seff'n starts and claps his hands once. "Or rather, not for the monks, but passing by there, as it were. The desert, yes, oh I must remember, give me a moment." His face clears a heartbeat later.

"Yes, it was at the making of that Brow we spoke of! The creator for whom it is named had help, a dwarf from the snow-capped north and a Bedou-uu preacher of some kind from the flaming Mindsea. They worked together to create it. Our man, the preacher Mart'l'n, he made the Brow for himself. Cannot remember now what the dwarf took away, nothing interesting I'm sure. But the desert man, he had some of the same materials woven into a necklace, or at least I think it must have been, called the Throat of the Spider."

Such fine china ruined, as your teacup shatters against the floor. Only J'seff'n reaching quickly across the table prevents your head from joining them. You never quite lose your senses, though for a moment you are standing closer to me than the room, looking down on your friends and yourself in wonder. Not yet, my cherished one; I send you back a while longer.

"Dear friend!" Aumir'y gasps, "Do not frighten us so, it was only a story after all! Some sleep could not hurt, it is true…"

J'seff'n is nearly frantic at the effect of his words. "I have regretted it ever since. The legend says only that the Bedou-uu passed the monastery on his way. The monks of Sinter are close to the desert-edge, it's true, but most likely the awful thing is now buried under tons of sand. This was centuries ago, W'starrah."

"I am fine, I assure you. Just too much wine last night. Or was it the night before?"

They laugh, but their concern is palpable, and now Chaktha is standing within the chamber uninvited. He has learned, at more than seven feet of exposed muscular flesh, that he does not draw the reprimands normally thrown at those just as common, and much shorter, paler than he. You rise despite their protests and make ready to leave your friends. Out the window, incredibly, the daylight is fading again. How long has it been?

"I did not know you disliked Bugs this much," J'seff'n jokes with an apologetic manner.

"Never so much as in the past week," you assure him.

"Promise me you will see a doctor," Aumir'y demands while hugging you goodbye.

You nod, then laugh out loud. "Indeed, perhaps that new healer, the Telholian."

"Good, I'm relieved. You are normally so stubborn, W'starrah!"

"You'd best go soon," her husband jokes, "before she presses some ensorcelled leaf on you to break your will as she has mine."

"So, the secret is out, my love. How else would you have married so far below your station?"

J'seff'n blinks as the two of you laugh. The double-contraction in his name is the mark of the oldest and most distinguished noble lines. But his merit is so well ingrained he is of course the last to get the joke. At length, he smiles meekly, hugs and wishes you well.

"Do not wait so long to visit us again."

"I have had the most wonderful time, truly. I cannot imagine what came over me before, but please accept my blessings for all you have done. It's so refreshing, to see you both. Come to service next week, I promise not to tell the Cryssians!"

They stand there again, arms around waists as if carved to fit, and it is all you can do not to flee.

Chaktha walks behind you down the corridor to the stairs leading outside. His back is broader than his shield. Plenty of room, to hide the tear-tracks on your face and neck. Their love is so clear, and they shall have it for decades. Ignorant of the ruin ahead, excused from its cruel choices, and perhaps most of all, able to touch and kiss on a whim, to give joy to each other and repeat it for good measure. You can lie to Carnad Mias even while you lie next to him. Devout Teretheny's horror, you will face with any weapon Argens might send you. If the Arbalest intends you for his bolt, so be it. But to visit these sweet friends again, surely no one could have strength enough for that.

⊕ ⊕ ⊕

The guard at the entrance to the palace district is flustered and mortified, but holds firm. Entry denied, by the order of the Fire-Grip.

"But good guardsman," you coo, "I have no intention to visit the Demonbender temple. And I a Stargazer! I wish to speak with the Telholian, this mortal Kama, and I'm told he lives here."

"He does, Myster Altieri, and he is there now. But I can't let you through."

The frustrated sigh escapes your lips, which surprises you. It took well past dinner to get this far; some streets remain torn and impassable since the horrid day of the arena revolt. Others are now blocked by guard posts and barricades, for their proximity to the temple forbidden by the new emperor in far-off Argens. You abandoned the hired carriage within a half-dozen blocks of leaving center-city. On foot with Chaktha through byzantine turns and corners, you have cajoled, tipped, and flirted with half the uniforms in the city. Subalterns must check with superiors, pass-signs you never knew existed, here is a form, can you wait please. Five hours to cover perhaps four furlongs as the crow flies. Now the final gate, with the Demonbender temple looming in the dimming light above broken trees of dusk, and all the shrugs and half-promises of passed responsibility have ended with one soldier determined to do the duty assigned by Gaspar Heugen.

Now he sees your anger—so unlike you—and wilts in anguish. You smile and reach to pat his arm.

"Well, I suppose there is nothing to be done but to seek our revered Fire Grip."

"If you skirt the barricades here, milady, you may make your way along the river to the palace." The guard is eager to help now. "There are some muddy spots, I'm afraid, but soon you will be in The Boards district, and then keep the river on your right."

"You are very kind, thank you."

He clears his throat and leans in to speak low. "Then too, Myster, there is another entrance, in view of the palace. Closer to the Telholian's camp. The guards there," he shrugs as if to say you can lose nothing.

When you walk away, Chaktha mutters in his native tongue and the tone makes you giggle. Why does Gaspar Heugen guard the area so tightly? You but dimly recall a riot back before the winter; when the people heard of the outrages supposedly committed by the Demonbenders they descended on this place. With all their preachers arrested, it was abandoned to wrack and looting. Cracks in the roof seen by the last light of sunset make you shiver. In your vision, enemies of some alien nature attacked your tower, and only the Captain and his men defended it. Not you, not with him. The wave of sadness is sudden and nearly trips you into the broken streetside. But if Justin is there in your vision, he might not die in the haunted

137

hills of Tralmachia. Nothing aches so much, nor seems so real, as your separation. Best not to think of it.

Your path winds and twists in the wrack of older streets, and only the scent of the river leads you at last by a narrow alley into the poorer quarter where the streets are formed of thick laid planks and the final boardwalk, a double-wide street, runs parallel to the River Tepid. You lean against the sturdy railing and look out with elvish vision across the moon-streaked river to the darkened shapes of the Old City across the way. For a moment you feel a tingle and see *the Ferret, dancing across the water to the other side, where the click of the Arbalest's weapon echoes across the open space.* You look around, but even Chaktha, it seems, heard nothing; folks of this district are staring at you as they pass, but that is nothing unusual. Any noble would draw attention in the poorer quarter, and the Lavender Lady more than most. How long have you been away from the temple? An entire day, or perhaps two, difficult to recall. One reason you often stay home is the schedule which keeps you grounded; and Kat of course. Out here …

You start toward the palace at the west end of this boardwalk, and only belatedly realize that many among the night-walkers here are moving in groups, as if seeking someone. Some in the distance call a name, Keilee—the sister of your acolyte Talishaya. Of course, her family lives in this district, poor thing, and still missing. You think of the *brave girl in the enormous temple, throwing a stone at the rat-king,* and your heart hits a beat so hard it staggers you. The man in the alley! The one who passed a flask to the Devout Teretheny, the face was a copy of the one in your vision. Has Keilee fallen into his hands, somehow? But where is that, and how is it connected to the Brow?

The boardwalk narrows as you leave houses and shops behind, just a few places where steps lead down to the river bank below. One turning is marked for the prisons, others seem narrow and dangerous, unsigned and unlit; but straight ahead you can see the brilliant Crystal Palace topping the rise which overlooks the ocean cliffs at the westernmost point of the city. On your left, you can see you've come to the back of the temple precinct, and just as the guard promised there is another station here with two soldiers on duty. You feel tired and cold, something in you tapped out of the energy to

138

live that you always used to have. But you take a deep breath, smile and approach them.

This time, incredibly, the shrug means you will get your way. The two hear your story, lift their shoulders in unison, and open the small wooden gate erected to serve as a barrier, just like that. But when Chaktha moves to follow, their apathy disappears.

"Not him, he stays here."

Chaktha looks quite ready to do murder, and you raise a hand to forestall him.

"Look, the chapel is just around that bend behind the temple, barely out of sight. If I need you I can call."

"Need help?" a guard smirks. "With the healer? She'll be safe as anywhere in there." His voice is at odds with the step back he and his partner have taken, at the prospect of close grips with the Nubian.

Chaktha smolders but steps to the center of the gateway, folding his arms like someone had delivered a statue to the spot. He looks to you with anger and concern, and you nod, *hearing the Stallion's whinny*; he doesn't wish to fail again.

The cobbled pathway inside the Demonbender precinct is smooth and lit by the moon. To your left the thick rounded temple hunches just over the surrounding trees, enormous, empty and spooky. Rounding the bend you see a square-cut hole in the ground, the beginnings of a modest foundation; to one side a small lean-to with the opening away from your view and orderly piles of building stone to all sides. Compared to the massive temple, this chapel will be tiny, a space barely large enough to house a modest family. But the healer, up and at work is also very small, evidently looking to build nothing larger than his life.

You had not thought until seeing him, that the mortal might well have been asleep. After all, you had plenty of time this afternoon when you started out! Yet here he is, working to draft and measure foundation blocks prior to moving them in place, by whatever means you cannot guess. He sees you approach and puts down his tools at once. A small flinch of his shoulders, not even a half-turn, clues you in that his lean-to is not empty. He steps into your path and bows.

"Good evening, Myster Altieri I believe? I am Kama, how may I assist you?"

You hesitate, not aware what titles are used among this formerly outlawed cult. You smile, curtsy and extend your hand on instinct.

"Most holy sir, please call me W'starrah, I am honored that you should know of me. I come to offer thanks on behalf of the Stargazers for your miraculous work among the injured brought to us. And also for saving my life in the arena."

Flattery never hurt your cause before, but the healer looks pained.

"I saved no one in the arena, to my great regret, least of all you, Myster Altieri. I arrived too late for that, and for several of those injured in the catastrophe you spoke of."

You almost let your jaw hang slack at the obvious false modesty of his words. He turns over your hand in his, where the vague scar of the Green dagger is only a pink-lined memory. At this range, even his eyes can make out your other scars now, and the same look of concern crosses his face that you saw in the coliseum, when he worked on a man without an arm. You are wounded, thus the same as any he has ever treated.

You try to draw back, but he lays a doctor's hand on your shoulder and touches your face gently but clinically.

"I see you were also there."

"It is nothing, sir, I came only to thank—"

"Indeed, nothing to amend either." He steps back with a small smile and you pass your hands over spots once pocked, now smooth and clear. He did not even intone or gesture! You feel relief, and then shame, to know your appearance is fully restored.

Kama, however, is frowning now, rubbing his fingers together and then sniffing them.

"Did I get some crème on you, holy sir?" You bubble a laugh only slightly forced. "I'm afraid I've become quite a slave to it these past few days, I hope you don't mind."

"A few days, you say?" His look now is quite serious, even suspicious, and you are confused to think you've somehow lost his favor with mere vanity. "Not long, for the poison to work."

"Poison!" You laugh and flap a deprecating hand. "Oh you have heard of the incident at the schoolhouse, then, I assure you it is unrelated. And I am fully recovered now, though I am again in your debt, holy sir, for Ekaterinye whom you saved is my dearest friend."

140

It is as if the little man does not hear, or else he has no idea how to take praise. Brow still furrowed, he shakes his head slightly and you can sense his distrust is only growing. He has not invited you to enter his hut, nor given any indication that he wishes to extend the interview. Normally your beauty alone puts a man on his best behavior; Kama has indeed registered this, but if anything has withdrawn into a shell, not tempted by you but threatened.

"Tell me a little of your faith, holy sir," you move carelessly to one side closer to the foundation hole, and he follows to keep himself between you and the lean-to. "You revere the hero of peace, is that the source of your remarkable healing powers?"

"I would hardly say remarkable," Kama replies quietly and again it is the worst play-acting, for any man to think such words could be taken seriously. "Telhol's gift, in a sense, goes only to those who are afflicted. I am … perhaps a courier in that way, nothing more."

He is quite serious, and you think of Justin, how poorly he played his part, what a remarkable spirit lay beneath the act.

"Well holy sir, I can say we are most grateful for your deliveries! How I wish some of our order could learn such skills, perhaps through quiet contemplation and study as you have had?"

He cracks a small smile, and shakes his head again. "Quiet and study, no, I have had precious little of those, Myster Altieri."

"I beg you sir, can we not be less formal? That is, Kama will you please call me W'starrah? And can you tell me any of your secrets, then, if not by study, then how may one learn?"

He bows but his smile remains small and cold. "As you wish, W'starrah. My order is small, with little scripture to guide us in our quests. I can only say, without boasting I hope, that I have had some practice in the art of healing."

You stare now and cannot feel sorry for the impolitude. "You, have practiced?"

He tilts his head in acknowledgement. "In some of the least quiet, most frenetic places in the world." He sighs and chuckles, adding, "Yes, in places such as those I have had significant experience. But that was before the … it was some time ago."

He stands between you and the lean-to, and another step to the side will put you into the foundation pit. Your steps as stymied as your words, nothing seems to work with this calm little man.

"May I ask, Kama, if you have any opinions regarding the selection of the new Mark? Your church will have a vote in two months, after all."

"My church!" He looks ruefully into the foundation, and then steps to a pile of granite bricks, moving one at a time to the pit's edge as he speaks. "I much doubt I can qualify for such an honor, Myst—ehm, W'starrah."

"Nonsense, you are in, Kama just as the Demonbenders here are now out. No one will question your right to cast a ballot, it is tradition."

He shrugs and returns to bring another block.

"Do you mean to say you have no opinion?"

"I have only lived here for a few weeks, what right have I to any opinion as to the sagacity or foresight of the various candidates?" He smiles again, strangely, and mutters "Candidates. Always them."

"May I perhaps recruit your vote then?" You ask gently.

Kama's head snaps to face you, his guard up again.

"Do you intend to rule Cryssigens?"

You gasp at this simple thrust; no one else suspected your ambition. You can hardly believe it yourself, except for your personal prophecy. No false laughter to cover a witty remark this time; perhaps you are just too tired to keep pretending.

"I do intend to wear a crown," you answer him levelly, "And with the Stargazer's help, I may indeed do better for this city, for my family, than some."

Kama stands stock still looking at you, and after a long moment he slowly nods just once. He believes you, but not in you.

A flicker of movement by the temple window draws your eyes. For just a moment, you think you catch sight of something scaly and large-eyed through the moonlit glass. It is gone. Another vision-shred, but why now?

"Well, I hope you will consider it, and of course what I may do for you in return." Again, a wrong step. Everyone in the city is quite used to the exchange of favors. But this hard little healer narrows his vision, and his icy nod is no more welcoming than a soldier hunching behind his shield. What kind of warrior is this man of peace?

You look over his shoulder at the lean-to and a sudden instinct prompts. You smile and put one hand on his shoulder.

"I have no doubt kept you from your guest too long."

He starts and you laugh at his honest surprise.

"Not to worry, holy sir! I admit I had expected something more, ah, more ascetic from your demeanor. But no Stargazer would decry your choice in this regard, I assure you."

He looks as if you are speaking Dwarvish now, then a slow smile of comprehension. He takes a breath before replying.

"How if I told you that my guest was not a woman?"

Now it is your turn to feel shock, and your laughter is musical and loud.

"Another unexpected point! You are full of surprises, but it is no worry of mine. In fact it comes as a relief, I was starting to doubt my own abilities. All success to you both, and may you be very happy together."

Kama barks somewhere between laughter and frustration. "Hardly that, Myster Altieri. But my guest, as you so politely put it, is in no shape to be seen at present."

"Just so, holy sir, no concern of mine. I thank you for an illuminating conversation, and I hope to repair my tattered reputation with you in the next few weeks."

He nods sincerely, saying only, "I shall be paying attention, assuredly."

Turning away from the encampment, you see another path leading directly to the palace and decide to see if the Fire Grip will admit you. Glancing back as you walk, you see the small, hard man still at work shifting stones from one pile to another. Truly he is a puzzle, but his vote, like all of them, could be crucial in the upcoming tally. He did not strike you as a man to take a secret lover, of any stripe.

The palace is nearly abandoned and hardly any of its hundred windowed chambers are lit. Yet the moons and stars make ample reflections, enough to light your path across the cobbles and steeply up, to meet the boarded way just outside the gate. You spot a uniformed figure with shoulder-length hair striding the high crenelments, hands

143

behind back and thinking while he walks. Along a narrow path just outside the walls, barely wide enough for a yearling goat, another figure walks more slowly, draped and hooded in black, risking the cliffs for a view of the sea. Something in you stirs, and you forego calling out to the Fire Grip above, choosing instead to follow the Overlord's widow.

The way is narrow and requires your complete attention; the impulse seems worse than foolish now, but no doubt Citari has sensed you behind her so there can be no honorable retreat. Talk to her now, or never. But what can you say?

With your gaze focused on the slender path at your feet you nearly run into her. The night breeze is not gusty but feels perilous near the twelve-fathom drop of these cliffs. The distant crush of the surf against rock destroys any chance at light or murmured conversation. She stands as firmly as if rooted to the spot, heedless of any danger or perhaps just spiteful in the neighborhood of death.

You curtsy deeply, staying down until she signals with a flick of one limb that you may rise. Your rank does not require this obeisance, nor her current status merit it, but you feel a need to show respect, rather than to flatter.

"My condolences, Marchess, on your loss."

"Why?" Citari's voice is a slicing-sharp alto, "because you found my husband a good ruler?"

You swallow before answering. "Because a fated love is lost to you."

She cackles at this, a solo burst of derision and the word "Stargazers. He was always arrogant, thought his loyalty to the empire would protect him when that usurper rose up here. I warned him, my spies knew there would be some kind of action staged at the arena. But he merely put on his armor and sword, declaring he would take the lead putting down the revolt."

For whatever reason you are here, it's obvious that politude will be taken for fawning. The hard face is not old, but nothing like young, her features flat and unyielding as planed oak. She challenges by looking, and has no patience or mercy in her. Driven by a bit of flame here on this cold windy cliff, you step closer than station allows.

"I too lost family in that arena, Dame Kreel. Fifteen years ago, both parents fell before my eyes just as your husband was slain last year."

"And what of that! Have you come to jump with me, then?"

"And do you intend to end your life, then, milady?"

"Some part of me, perhaps. Every evening." Citari remains rooted at the edge, hard and unbending as she looks over the moon-striped sea and down to the rocky surf. Yet something in her trunk quivers just slightly.

You also look down, at walls so sharply-cut and uncracked. "Here is the spot," you murmur, "where the storm broke off the cliff into the sea, on that same night when I…"

You step back with the realization. Citari stays, but looks to you and nods. "Suicide is ignoble, of course. But I sometimes think, I may be fortunate."

The sea-breeze takes up the conversation a while.

"Dame Kreel, is the Shard Demon breaking free?"

Her head shake shows indifference, not uncertainty. "Ask it, if you wish. For my part, I suppose there is always hope."

She aims to shock, but you must seek through that, to what she knows.

"Has anyone else visited him recently? Do you know the way?"

"The way! Paths are not difficult to find, little Stargazer, nor will you find dust on the stones. Beneath this cliff take the left-hand boardwalk and follow it down. Or in my ruined temple, tunnels to where the plated devils crawl. Beneath the river to the Old City—I remember ceremonies there, we buried my grandfather under the piazzo," she smiles grimly and again you sense her love of blasphemy. But is she raving, demented by age and isolation?

Part of you wants to back away, another to try and comfort this loneliest of women. With anyone else, you might give a silver token … it occurs that the long-lost silversteel token of Fire, which brought Justin to you, must have come from the palace. What other gift …

"Milady. Would you like me to read your future?"

Citari tries to snort in derision again, but comes off only coughing. Turns, takes one step toward you; but then she folds her arms as a defense.

"The joy of my days ahead? A handsome sailor, perhaps to warm my bed and earn a vote or two for your precious new Mark? By all means, look at the Arbalest up there and say how he will bring happiness to an abandoned, useless cog of a regime now destroyed. My house is barren, my church plundered, all sources of pride extinguished. But certainly, tell me how I shall be glad to live."

Stargazer prophecy depends above all on the consent of the querent. Here is an elder Elf, of the most noble line, wife and advisor to the North Mark for longer than you can guess, dripping with anger and disbelief. But you must accept the challenge, or why make the offer. Stepping forward you place both hands on her shoulders and throw your mind open, silently asking for guidance.

For an eternity marked by a half-dozen beats of the distant surf, there are only two women standing by the moonlit cliff. Your heart drops to the soles of your feet with a backwash of shame running up your spine. But it is not by chance that you are my beloved.

The Stone Oak holds firm against a storm of many-legged monsters. At its base the Turtle gains shelter despite what the tree may wish; the wily Raccoon takes hold in its lower branches as well, and makes his home there. An enormous Fly threshes against its amber-glass prison, and there is fire and wind and red blood everywhere.

"Let go of me."

It has been very quiet, you realize, for some minutes, even the breeze died down here. Citari wrests her shoulders free of your grip, and you see in her eyes that she has heard you speaking my truth.

"Trees and vermin, insects and storms, what a mare's nest your mind must be." You step back and curtsy again, feeling much restored by the miracle which came against all odds.

"It may be," you respond, "that happiness is not your future, Marchess. But work, and worth, and … and partnership, these lie before you. And I hope there may come some degree of contentment."

The noble Elf does you the honor of not sneering as you turn away, instead staring into your back to make it tingle, until well out of sight.

Near the front gate again, you see Gaspar Heugen on the battlements, and this time he sees you. It's clear who you've been with; any word with him now would seem a betrayal, and might be

146

one in truth. You smile and wave, turning down the hill and keeping to the boarded path. The first left-hand turning you give a miss, in no mood for a visit with a demon tonight. But then your heart sinks as you come to a place where three paths intersect with yours at odd angles. Could this have been the place the widowed Marchess meant? You try to keep to the straightest course, and continue down the hill looking for the upslope and starting to hunger for the sight of Chaktha.

To your dismay, there is another intersection, again of four ways, the two centermost looking identical. It is very dark here at the nadir of the hill. You make a choice and within a hundred steps you are clearly below the boardwalk, on a narrow alley of wood that passes ruined outbuildings and enormous pilings of the older docks area. The smell of the sea, of rotten wood and abandonment is overpowering; surely going back will take longer than moving on.

Small lights, ahead and to the side, never seem to last long enough for you to catch them up; as you pass the pilings and posts they disappear. Are there people moving about down here? Yes; or at least some sleepers, for you see several forms huddled near a wall or fence. The poor or insane, unwilling to accept charity and stability: you lectured Justin about them, how few there were. Now you think about the missing child, and the lack of starlight in this shaded under-city.

The water lapping against the piles is a background noise you can ignore. The wood sometimes creaks in the tide, deep and bass. But now there are other sounds, sometimes steps on wood overhead, or the thump of something heavy not too close but given monstrous shape in the fetid damp darkness. A voice, or two, perhaps calling out, or arguing about drinks. Something metal in a rhythmic pace, *tak ting-tak, tak ting-tak.*

Clicks. They stop you in your tracks, hugging a dock-post and not daring to breathe. More clicks, from several points too close for comfort now. There is a slice of moonlight ahead formed from a crack in the boardwalk above it. Something crosses that slice, a thing that returns the shine of moonlight and has more than two legs. Now pointy claws are scrabbling on the wooden boards behind and to the side of you. Heads with faceted eyes loom from the shadows, too high and hard and horrible to be real. Your visions have never been

147

so vivid before. The railing before the river is low; you cannot swim yet the thought of drowning is attractive.

"What have we here?" comes a gravelly voice behind you, and you sigh in sheer relief. To be beaten, or violated or even killed, yes, but at the hands of flesh, in the grip of something warm. You muster the strength to spite the neighborhood of death. The vision-Bugs do not disappear or fade, but instead snap their heads in the direction of the sound, and then pull back into the gloom. You turn with your shoulders against the piling, and see two stooped forms advancing. There is a chance, if you can see them clearly, to use the miracle of Engagement, to talk them out of their intended crimes.

"A noble woman, I'll be bound. Soft I bet, and the smell of her, can you smell that Jangs? We've found our fortune this night, for certain."

You cannot see their faces, cannot back away now. Is Chaktha close enough to hear if you scream? The docks creak and the waves lap hungrily, and that damned metal pounding is only louder now, *tak ting-tak*.

"Shall we throw fingers to see who goes first?"

"I leave you the first pass, Jangs, that's the gentleman I am. I ask only don't tear her clothes, I do enjoy that."

"So there it is, mistress. You'll be wise to keep your arms down and your mouth shut—most of the time, that last. You may even enjoy this."

A third voice cuts into the night. "I hardly think so."

The two forms whip around, standing between you and the newcomer who seems of odd shape in the shadows.

"And who the blasted hells are you?"

"I? Call me her lantern-boy, if you wish." And before the reavers can answer, the voice says "*Luxar*".

A star of blue light springs to life on the end of a long, thick quarterstaff shod in iron. The mortal Man beneath it is lean and hard, not unlike Citari and shaded still beneath a broad-brimmed hat and long cape. Only his eyes glint an answering shade of silver. He brings his staff to bear in both hands and every fiber of his being radiates determination.

"He's a sorcerer, Jangs."

"Now see here, you—"

"Begone." The man wastes no further words, and when the two stay frozen, he takes a single step forward. Like broken ice they recover the power of movement and flee at a run, two men from one and never in doubt. You hardly know whether to be less afraid or moreso.

He stands at attention, removes his hat, and bows to you. His hair is grey yet something about him seems vital and capable. His face, as he regards you, looks set in stone.

"I thank you, sir, for your timely intervention."

"It is of no moment, mistress. Yet the problem remains, this is a dangerous place. And I am strange to you, as they were."

He considers a moment.

"If it pleases you, I will walk ahead and light the way. My path shall take me up to the Boards, where at least there are lamps. You need say nothing to me, and I shall promise, in turn, not to look back. Perhaps this will be of service to you."

With another bow, he dons his hat and strides past, walking capably and surely ahead through the bowels of the underdocks. His clothing, all his accoutrements, every inch of him is grey, just as Carnad Mias said. You hastily pick up and trot after him, but unless you run he gains steadily away with the pace of a soldier under orders. *Tak ting-tak, tak ting-tak*, and now the boarded alley leads up at last. He crests the rise where it joins The Boards before you can keep him in sight. When you arrive at the safety of the boardwalk, Chaktha is there to the right, and the Man in Grey is gone.

⊕ ⊕ ⊕

he Dragon's hot breath stifles you as he settles his sizzling, scaly frame over your body like a treasure bed.

Is this happening now, after all, you wonder? You feel Carnad Mias clawing the strap of your gown, tearing it and bringing your breasts quivering into view. Yes, now.

Breath like flame fills the city, making you gasp for life while the wurm's hardened frame rubs against you, with more heat and pain and something …

Something very small, you realize with fear.

You don't know how much time has passed—there was a dawn on the roof with Chaktha, many people speaking urgently to you, something about your turn to speak at service. And another party,

149

no two, you have been a busy girl, and you overheard something important there. But it's hard to set events in order, now that the Red Cup is coming for you, quite literally.

His jaws gape to devour your bosom, and you feel the sting of his teeth there to match its echo on your neck and shoulders. He's a biter, that makes sense. The rhythm of his thick thrusting midriff drives the wind from you—praise Argens he is too impatient to have undone his pants yet. Beyond his delving, slobbering head you see the goblet, its posset undrunk tonight. Whatever happens, he will remember this. But if you see him, if his secret is exposed, it could mean your life.

The Dragon roars with lust, hemming your effort to smoothly disengage from its grip, and throwing you back on the bed.

Mias mutters incoherent words of passion, phrases stolen from a bard's song, his version of tender love no doubt; yet a poor match to his full-strength pull on your gown, ripping layered silk to the navel before passing his talons over your entire front. He moves lower to favor your thighs and womanhood with his tongue, one arm against your throat as if in manly passion but with enough weight to keep you breathless. You think of Justin, risking his life for a cause, and resolve to endure what must be. Careful, do not fake climax too soon or even he will know.

And do not see him naked, if you wish to live.

Above your head on the nightstand is the proxy statue of Argens, and you call out to him as if in passion, to mask the prayer for aid. Help me, indeed. What word did he bring you, when you touched the carving during the party, as only a trusted attendant lingered with the Red Cup after that last bacchanal? It comes back to you in a flash.

"Great Cup, all is in readiness, our men await only your word."

"Tell them it will be soon, within a fortnight and their signal shall be a storm, like the one at the Glass Festival, only larger, covering the city. They are to stay armed and ready until then."

"Then you have discovered the power behind that attack?"

"Discovered it, indeed I fueled it. Salivaar brought what was needed—too early, the fool!—and has agreed to bring more, in return for the freedom to run the Old City as he wishes."

"Do you not fear him, Red Cup? Reports say he changes shape at will, and consorts with demons."

"Heh, on my next visit I will loose the only demon that matters. The Rat-King's Bugs would never dare intrude south of the Tepid. Once we establish order here, they will turn on him instead for their brain-food."

"So then, the monk is with us. And our hostess?"

"Is no longer as needful as she hopes. We shall let her continue to believe that the guilds are important to the vote."

"And of course, you will continue to enjoy her company milord."

"As never before. At least for a while. Later, who knows?"

"Dangerous times, great Cup of Red. Sad to say, many will die."

The Dragon's tongue tires quickly, as you expected, and now his hands grip your bitten breasts, pulling his bulk high enough over the bed's edge to mount you. Leaning half against the mattress, he pants aloud as he yanks with haste at his breeks. His hair is coming loose, defying even the pomade, and you can see the gaps of age across his scalp so carefully covered at other times. You smile, and reach for his waist as if asking permission; he releases you long enough to rise and do the job.

It is time to think quickly, and move slowly. The second is easy, as you lightly tease the strings and buttons loose without looking down. You take in his eyes with a mien you hope resembles desire, letting your eyes go wide so they lose their focus on the draconic mask before you. Instead you conjure an image of your Captain, or the stars of night, or the face of Argens Stargazer carved in marble from the chapel: anything to take your mind away.

Briefly you think you see *Justin, leading a charge on foot up a rocky ravine, while wings larger than those of birds glide down upon his company.* Then the Dragon comes back into focus as he draws you in for another tongue-choked kiss. Searing heat like fever, rough hands—he should use the crème—and such strength, he could break your back in seconds. You give him your mouth's full attention, and behind him now coils *a Serpent, spiders, a demon in crystal,* each transforming to shapes unknown in the shadow of a flickering fire that devours all.

The pants are open enough now to fall should you release them. Slowly, smoothly, by inches you start to turn, legs rising to put your knees on the bed and pushing up your gown far enough that he can

151

easily reach the exposed skin. Waist, hips, breasts, shoulders, you can pivot each joint almost independently, so that by the time the lips break free it is clear to Carnad Mias that you are giving him your back. There, on the edge of your bed you turn away and arch your spine in the ageless posture of submission, still holding his gaze even now as if you would break your neck rather than not see his face. One last finger releases the cloth and joins the other limbs already holding you up on knees and elbows. Carnad Mias groans from his gut and lurches against you, pulling down bolsters and pillows to prop your hips as he once again lays his dragon's bulk against your body.

And you do not have to see, he can still believe you don't know, how small he is.

So much explained, about his drive for power, about the veneer of culture and the casual display of wealth, his pent-up energy and the cold-blooded use of murder to gain his ends. Still flailing to find the proper spot before he climaxes, Mias curls an iron-hard forearm beneath your chin and pulls you back for more kisses while you lightly choke. And you recall the whispers of his wife's death, on their wedding night, ostensibly from a failed heart but rumored by the servants to include a woman's laughter followed by the sound of beating. Those who attended the funeral rites commented on the lovely, high-necked gown he put her in, so modest as befit a woman loved only once before her untimely death.

And now he could snap you in an instant, to cover his unquenchable shame, or even from his unchecked passion. You pray for comfort from the pain, for strength to survive what comes, for courage to cover the rising fear. The thrusting continues, and you are completely pinned against the cushions now, legs spread and feeling something the size of two short, wet fingers poking and pressing ever-closer.

Kat's knock is unmistakable. You both roar aloud, one in frustration and another in relief. But she repeats the pattern and calls your name with urgency. Surely the Stargazer sent her.

Let him lead in this. You moan as if the interruption left you as insatiate as he, and wait for him to decide. Carnad Mias suddenly rolls to one side back on the bed, grabbing a pillow and throwing it hard enough to knock over your wardrobe as he rips loose a scorching curse. Again he curses, loud and long, and then starts to laugh. You look to him, careful again to keep only his eyes in view, and smile a bit weakly, apologetically, and the laughter becomes fuller and outwardly hale as he again adopts the disguise of a human being.

Rising, giggling, shrugging, you look to the torn ruins of your gown and let them fall to the floor. He is laughing full out now, just a tinge of hysteria as he reaches for the pants around his ankles. You dash to the tipped closet and pull up a nightrobe of lightest, palest lilac. You sash it closed and turn back to see him at least well enough covered to save his secret, and perhaps your life.

"I shall take this audience in a side-chamber," you assure him, remembering to be breathless and regretful as you speak. "As I don't know how long I will be, Chaktha can show you out."

Carnad Mias makes a sour face, by far his most honest of the evening. "I'd rather jump from the window."

You move to open for Kat, thinking that at last you both agree on something.

"She's been found! *Praise* the Stargazer, the child, W'starrah! She's *here*, right now."

"What!" Carnad Mias enters the room behind you, furious; Kat's face blanches to look dunked in flour. "Some urchin went missing, and her return is worth the time of the Heaven's Eye?"

"We rejoice whenever a member of the family is well, great Cup of Red," you smile winningly at him, ignoring the rumpled condition of his hair and dress. "I must attend to this, my acolyte Talishaya will be overjoyed at her sister's recovery. Please forgive me."

At the door you turn back, while Kat stares slack-jawed at a point near Mias' midriff. "And I do apologize again, for spilling wine on your pants."

Now it is his turn to look down, and let his jaw hang open. Time to go, get a few steps down the stairs before the giggles escape you. Upstairs, it could be that another piece of furniture has been a victim of Red wrath. In the audience chamber there is time for a long embrace, and you shake well after the laughter, still in the grip of several flavors of emotion beyond naming. When at last you pull back, her eyes are shining and you simply whisper "Thank you."

"This way, I led them to the chapel, in case…"

"Talishaya is here too?"

"Yes, and some other messenger they brought with them. Oh, and here is a letter from that jeweler fellow…"

You put that under your sash for later, eager to meet the child you've only seen in vision.

In the chapel, two girls in a front pew stand at once, and a well-dressed man several rows behind them also rises and bows but keeps a decent distance as the others approach. The poor child looks so thin, scrubbed clean and miserable but otherwise just as you remember her in the vision. Talishaya drags her forward with a radiant face.

"Just as you said, priestess, she's safe and well! Here is Keilee, I've brought her as you instructed." Not precisely, but a better job is still well done.

"I am very happy to see you again, little one." The girl looks up suspiciously at you, then her eyes flare as she takes your meaning. Already nervous to be in a church, she gulps now and only her sister's hands on her shoulders keep her from flight.

"We should see her more often," Kat asserts, "in the schoolhouse." Now Keilee looks positively ill and she stammers her denials.

"I, I can't. I already have a job, working for Citizen Simith!"

"And who is he?"

"Our neighbor, Myster," Talishaya says, "the wonderful man who found her out beside the river and underneath the Boards. After *three days*."

You remember spending less than an hour down there, and a shiver runs through you. But the vision was clear, an enormous temple, and monstrous beings, the Rat-King, Ferret, and Brow. You drop down to your haunches to speak on her level.

"But you were not afraid, were you little one?"

"Not like I am now."

Such honesty makes you laugh. "School is hardly the worst of fates, my dear. Go along with the teacher now—" you break off as *from the pews slips the Ferret, snaking along to rub Keilee's side in affection before standing on his hind legs and looking up at Kat. Is that a flower in his paw, or a bit of jewelry …?*

"W'starrah? Heaven's Eye, what is wrong?"

Kat's voice- how much time has passed? Still in the chapel, the girl and your acolyte have backed away and now the other visitor,
154

having cleared his throat politely, advances to bow with a gyrating wrist. Not that long then, this time. Still you would give much to know what day it is.

The stranger completes his elegant bow, and the many colors of his outfit paint a rainbow before you. Not House color, perhaps, but certainly of the finest quality and hues, everything neatly tailored from boots to plume and nothing in all that lace or flounce that would obscure a path from his hand to the rapier at his side. As he rises from his bow you see a handsome face, with a lovely prominent nose and long dark hair. In his eyes there is brightness, a sharp gaze that seems familiar.

"Welcome to the chapel of Argens, sir; what news brings you?"

"The news, reverend Myster, only charged me with the happy task of coming to your presence," he responds in imperturbable good humor. His fingers lightly trace the purple of his collar as if comparing the shade to your own. "This letter I hold is from, well, perhaps a mutual acquaintance. But alack, it contained no clear directions. Haply it was my fortune to fall in with these two ladies just outside the precinct gates, and thus to be precise, it was they who have, em, brought me." Another small bow and he hands over a plain envelope sealed with the mark of Astor, Prince of Stealthics.

You tear the seal and hungrily read the note.

Heaven's Eye foresaw correctly, the holy crown has left the Forge
Beyond light and law, in the Old City where the roof does not obscure the stars
It lies now among verminous men, and burns at the will of a villain.
Send Astor, or bring an army, to retrieve it.

Convey by this trusted messenger your will regarding the commission you spoke of.

Then Feldspar has seen the Brow, he must have. And the Ferret was with Keilee … you lean down again to speak to the girl.

"Did you see the stars, through the ceiling where you were?"

Keilee's eyes go wide and she glances nervously at her sister.

"Speak the truth, Keilee," Talishaya warns.

The girl nods. "Big cracks in the roof. And Bugs, as big as horses. It stinks worse than the river there."

Now Talishaya is shocked, no doubt Keilee had told a different tale.

"Be at peace, my dear, the girl tells the truth as Argens speaks to me."

Her lovely brow unfurls, and Talishaya moves off with her sister, still scolding and promising school—as a punishment—in quiet whispers. You look at Kat and nod with meaning, before turning back to the dandy. He waits with affected patience, looking purposefully in other directions as if your words could not be of less interest to him. You smile winningly as he bows again to you; of course, he will recall everything and repeat it to the Stealthic his master.

"Please convey word to our mutual acquaintance that I am most pleased at his work, and do indeed further commission him for the act of stealth to which he alludes. Curate Ekaterinye here, will vouch as witness before the altar of the Stargazer himself, I owe five thousand pieces of silver for that which has been done, and another twenty thousand pieces if the work is completed."

Kat catches her breath at the amounts, but the multi-colored swordsman seems more interested in checking the length of his fingernails. With several vague gestures into the air above his shoulder, he says "I'm sure he will be pleased to hear that, milady."

"Excellent. You may repair to her for payment should I be … unavailable." Why did you just say that? You feel a flash across your middle at the thought but this is no time to appear indecisive. Over the dandy's shoulder you see Tanar'h and his guards entering to prepare for service. So late? What day, for Argens' sake!

Tanar'h practically storms across the altar space to where you stand, face already simmering with anger.

"Did I overhear correctly, Heaven's Eye? You have just transacted business, within the holy space?"

A shock; you never cared much for the rules, of course, but it was a mistake to so far forget them. "It is the Stargazer's business, but nothing touching the wealth of the church."

"Yet the High Heart must be apprised, W'starrah." He snags the letter and scans it; the rainbow-clad swordsman, not having been dismissed, is back to studying his nails. Tanar'h frowns darkly at what he sees on the paper.

"The holy crown? The Brow of the Ecclesiast lies with the Hopeforger church, I forbid you to have this man steal it."

156

"Nothing of the sort, you wrong me deeply, High Heart. My private business—"

"No longer exists, W'starrah. Your wild parties and tours of the center city are the first news in the crier's mouth, and have been for days."

His rude interruption is nothing to that word. *Days!* You stagger a step, against the swordsman's waiting arm, and Tanar'h takes it for drunkenness. He says more, a great deal in fact, but you cannot focus on that now, there is too much of the lost past coming back to you.

No less than three more parties in your rooms, only the one last night bearing the fruit you needed. The cherry-wood chaise bringing you to the theater (just a two-person show, so few actors able to appear), to the Feast of Flour, on the arm of Carnad Mias everywhere. Making every excuse later. Dawn after dawn alone on the roof, seeing stars but nothing more of the future, except the relentless rise of the Arbalest, his weapon now in view and ready to fire. Another chance to preach missed, along with the services. Some madly cheering your passing, others turning aside or covering their eyes. But no friendly greetings anymore, from men like the vineguilder or Welles or even the Blue house warrior-woman who seemed to fancy you. No time for the schoolhouse, for innocent children like Keilee, or your morning callers.

Tanar'h speaks louder now and gestures angrily, and you realize from his intemperate manner that he must be ignorant of the danger, at least the worst of it. You think of Teretheny and Mias, showing self-control most of the time, the Serpent and Dragon never meeting in person, but each with schemes and working in concert to effect them. Tanar'h is too honest, too involved somehow, to see the truth. He may be beyond help.

"Are you hearing me, W'starrah? Your dalliance with Carnad Mias does more than ruin your own reputation, it prostitutes the Stargazer himself!"

Your mind returns to the present moment just in time to hear the only insult that could sting you. On its own, your hand slaps him hard; now the fire in his eyes ignites and you feel fear together with your anger as you retort.

"Never mind, High Heart, what harm may come from the richest, most openly ambitious power in the city. His salvation is my affair, take that however you wish. Just see that you heed a danger disguising its face behind plain robes, slithering from your host quarters toward the ruin of all."

You have already walked several steps away before the image of Tanar'h's face comes to your conscious mind. Shock, of course, but also fear, as of a secret revealed. And perhaps even a spice of shame—he feels responsible for Teretheny in some way unknown to you.

Now to cover for all he cannot control, he bellows to his guards.

"Remove this flowery intruder, and prepare for the service."

You turn back to see Tamess and Jal'i approaching the colorful dandy. He smoothly rests his thumbs in his belt, and they stop with spears ready. The bravo smiles as if watching children at play; tension between the three men ratchets ever tighter.

"Violence within the chapel is forbidden," you call out. "This man is safe in here." The guards flinch at the echo, but they have their orders. The swordsman bows once more to you and adds a word.

"And outside the chapel, milady, with these two, the same." He turns smoothly and strides out the main entrance through the thickening crowd of worshippers.

Tanar'h meets your gaze and smiles ruefully, rubbing his face a bit. "I suppose they will say the wedding is off now."

Wedding? The memory comes to you like a distant echo—the "proposal" of your last service together. You must also smile at this private joke, though it pains him to face the truth. Not now. Save the city, then make amends with your rival.

Seeing the faithful gather you are nearly whelmed by a tide of loneliness. Only your private prayers, snatched in free moments, have sustained you in the whirl of lost days that lays on your heart like a wound. No services, no preaching; far too busy, playing the harlot and reprobate for the Red Cup. When you agreed to be an agent for the Emperor's Hand, you thought there would be conflicts with your habitual schedule. But now you see Teretheny enter the chapel, with his guards, and folks who once cheered your every word nod to him in respect and jostle to sit nearby. You shrink back into the corridor; tonight you would not be welcome, in the church where you serve me.

Down the corridor to your tower practically at a run. Enough time has been wasted—for all you know, too much! How many days? Is it the Twenty-Fifth Dolphin already, perhaps the First of the Swan. Still more than six weeks before the coronation vote at Dragon-Ides, and Carnad Mias already has men lying in wait for the storm Teretheny will spring. Feldspar must retrieve the Brow quickly, and you must communicate with Morinack at once. With a sinking heart, the thought occurs that perhaps only an invasion from the Empire can save your city now.

But even that would take many days to arrive. You, who seldom write anything down, resolve to list the tasks that must be accomplished before then.

Never a quill when you need one. You scrabble across the bedroom table, pushing empty crème boxes onto the carpet—and there, finally, behind the jewel-case where you probably dropped it before the New Year. As you flip Feldspar's parchment to use the back, your hand touches the letter from Welles, until now forgotten. But with an effort you stay on task for once, ignoring words that, were you less in love with your city, could have saved your life. Well done, cherished of my heart.

-Warn the Raccoon of the Arbalest's bolt
-Tell Morinack of the Red Dragon's plan to release the Shard Demon
-Take the Spider's Throat from Teretheny

You pause, thinking these are the orders of men, filled with compulsion and the threat of violence, the parting of ways between family members. How to heal, to support and protect this city? Your hand moves of its own accord.

-Find the Stone Oak's new mate
-Save Tanar'h from himself

And just a little later a final addition, stained with tears.

-Love the Captain all your days, and beyond.

You should never be in such pain, and I send the personal vision again to you, though the full meaning will no doubt still elude. There, the burning crown and words you heard years ago:

As the rule of men fails

A woman's spirit rises to lead them
Argens' Fire will not sear this soul
Nor wound and ruin impede her path

You wonder again about how you will lead them, these powerful men standing to all sides like sharp-edged gems in a tiara. Surely Argens' Fire is that of the Brow; and if Mias or Teretheny is set to strike now, then Feldspar must hurry. Your heart misgives, thinking you will be unable to prevent the ruin of your city-family: will Justin return too late, will he defend your tower to no purpose? Assessing the passage of time was never your strong suit: I have taught you that everything simply is. Soon you will understand all.

You read the list again and now your fingers touch the second letter beneath it. Curiosity asserts itself and you break the seal to read those fateful words in such a shaky, almost spidery scrawl.

Priestess,

I am undone, sl-c-ee-kp no more in my reach nor helpful. In sleep I find strange thoughts pressing in on me, th-cloo-hts beyond words, of theft and return, unworthy of my guild. Too late, I resolved to stay awake, yet the cr-iza-kk patterns of mind continued. Words arr becoming harder to use, from tongue or qk-uill. On an evening's walk, I suddenly saw IT, searching empty dark-k-end streets, head and joints turning in all direc-kh-tions, leading two more Bugz and gazzing without eyes, sniffing without a snout. I have not kl-ee-ft my home in two days: my spkree-ckch so full of clicking, even my wife has fled my prezence in fear, which brings me kr-umm comfort.

But now I hear them. The scl-k-rabbl-ee-ng from the trash alley, charp-k hard sounds like the cl-cl-ee-klick of gears. Even the dogs whine and rout cl-eeck krot-ck. Their hateful odor is in my nostrils as they clee-ircl-k my boarded doors, zeeking a way in. Tonight may zee their suc-k-cess. I am alone.

Destroy the Eye! Bear not that the Blind White should zee into all our thoughtz. And cl-c-ee-kl-th—cle-cle-warn-kl-eeck-ck-ck.

You see the sky lightening through the open window, and realize that hours have passed as you stood here frozen. The paper with those dread words lies on the carpet before you; picking up a snake would be more appealing. A cloak of fear settles on both shoulders. In your mind's eye, the outer room has been invaded by enormous armored insects, through some invisible hatch behind the statue and

160

now waiting to consume you. If the bedroom door should open but a crack …

With an impulse you seize the small proxy, embracing it and listening through its link for any sound in the next room. Nothing, then nothing—wait, a scratch? Or the curtain rippling in a dawn breeze. Someone in the reception chamber below? Sounded like a click, a signal. Terror settles over you, here in your own chambers, with breaths so shallow you see stars after dawn. Welles' vision of Bugs loose in the city by night, surely the dreams of a madman, but now you feel he will gain company, in that world where lunatics huddle. You hug the proxy to your chest and strain to hear …

When Chaktha knocks you scream at the violation. A moment later, there are two broken doors in your suite.

He is armed with shield and spear, unable to return your fierce embrace. But Chaktha knows all he needs to, his coming was never wasted. When you finally let go he turns at once to summon the workmen, again. Over his shoulder you peep at the outer room, empty and still but somehow choked with menace. You push the splintered portal closed and lean against it for what seems like an hour. The sounds of the workmen relieve and alarm you; your voice warmly welcomes them in, yet you retreat to the far corner of your bedroom, scooping up the proxy statue and hugging it again as you huddle against the overset wardrobe.

You hear them working twice, once muffled through the broken inner door and more clearly from the magic of the proxy's connection to the belt gem in the outer room. You fantasize that your hearing is sharper than the wolf's, and your eyes take in alien sights along darkened streets where bug-beings prowl and seek, colorless and multi-paned visions like looking through a cracked glass. There's an awful stench, nothing like jasmine or cloves, the odor in ebon tunnels where no rain has cleansed the offal of thousands. All your senses echo and skull-pain rises until you feel it splitting under the workmen's chisels and their alien, human-sounding jokes.

When the workmen open your door to repair it, the double-sound is too much. With a gasp you drop the proxy, and as they apologize for disturbing you the otherness begins to fade by degrees. You smile but stare past them; with dubious faces they turn to their work under

161

Chaktha's watchful eye. At first you want to shout, tell him to guard the outer alcove against invasion. He sets your wardrobe upright again; the voice deep in your breast that had been you, before the letter, pips in protest, gradually getting louder as you sweat and stare and push back the vision.

Before they are done replacing the bent latch and staring sidelong at the giant Nubian who broke it, you feel almost normal again, thanking them with your accustomed grace when they doff their hats. Yet your arm shakes until you throw it behind your back. The outer door is solid and thick, with four new hinges and a steel bolt wider than your finger. Your voice is back in charge of you, but something still there hungers to barricade the place.

"Chaktha, I need you to seek out the jeweler Welles and be sure he is alright. Do you know his precinct?"

"Aye, priestess, I shall return soon."

"I will stay right here, not to worry."

The Stallion gazes down on you with affection. He peers about the room and his nostrils flare, as if sensing prey. Though nothing moves or makes a noise, he stalks around the perimeter again, a last search. Then he nods to you, and leaves.

You stay right here, and start to worry.

The door is left unlocked, but your word makes you a prisoner. The rooms are empty, though your minds-eye peoples the cell with monsters. So quiet; time passes slowly here while out in your city all is happening too fast. If you can manage not to think of hard-shelled horrors crouching behind the statue, you find yourself fretting about an imminent storm, the whirlwind made of glass and hatred and dead family, that could begin tomorrow, or by sunset.

Finally the habit of prayer asserts itself, and I welcome you with warmth and a few final visions.

The Turtle cares for a wounded Ferret, who slips away to enter the lair of monsters. There, a Serpent changes to Spider-form, the Ferret becomes a rat and Ferret again, then flees with one paw on fire. A gnarled, beautiful Stone Oak stands on cliff's edge and strains to join the sea below. All sights wash away under the roar of the Gryphon, screaming with impatience and hatred of its captivity. The Fire Ants are sore beset without their Captain, dark gorges to all sides that lie nowhere near your tower. A Stallion whinnies in anger, also too far away.

The Arbalest is fully up in the night sky, and as spiders drop from the stormy heavens he aims his quarrel directly at you. But after all is the fire and the Brow.

You come back to yourself and the sky beyond the windows is dark. With dismay, you think you have lost the entire afternoon (alack, my love, in fact it has been more than a day) and resolve to pray no further. But without my comfort the minutes drag. A single lantern's glow magnifies the shadows into arachnid shapes. You've sent them all away. Kat, Chaktha, the congregation, dear friends like Aumir'y and J'seff'n, the clever Stealthic, even rivals like Tanar'h and Z'kammet. Mystified, shocked, insulted, or even ordered off. Even the beloved Captain has left; your warm human family all banished that you might court the Red Cup; and he needs you no more, perhaps suspects, will send death through that door. Close the bolt: there, never more alone in all your days.

The belt-gem on my statue draws your attention now, a magnet for your eyes, to be fought only with effort. Its facets glow in the lamplight like a mischievous flame, the sheen of it begging for your touch. What did the jeweler warn you against? Closer, to the kneeler and down, one hand clutching the other or else …

The knock behind you brings as much pain as a backstab.

"Chaktha?"

"Myster, may I speak to you?" It is the voice of Gaspar Heugen, regent of the city. With his noble's habit of privilege he has intruded through your audience room and up the stairs unescorted. Or is he driven by some great need?

"Fire Grip, I can, that is, I am not fit to receive you now."

"It is urgent, Heaven's Eye."

"Are you alone?"

"Are you, Myster?" That was well played; of course he would suspect you have a guest. Yet you cannot bring yourself to open the portal; something that is not-you inside forbids it.

"There is no one else within, Fire Grip, on my word as a Stargazer."

The silence is hard to hear—you have already become addicted to the sound of a human being, even one who suspects you. "Carnad Mias is—"

"At his estate," Heugen interrupts, "of course, madam, I know where such a man is at all times."

"And yet, you honor merely me with your presence, Fire Grip. May I know why?"

"Is this to be our audience then! Behind a closed door, do you fear me so much milady?" Now there is a silence of your own making, and still you cannot move to pull the bolt for any reason.

"Not fear, milord Heugen, never that with you. But I am, that is, as I am deeply aware of my recent exploits, and thought only to preserve your reputation."

"Most kind," he volleys back through the wood. "I shall not trouble you long, then. I only wondered if perhaps you might have had word from your Captain."

The shock runs down you like a bucket of water. "My—who, my Captain, Fire Grip? Do you mean that officer from Argens?"

You sense that Heugen is one of those whose chuckle is soundless.

"Yes, milady, that one. Just perchance, then, have you a letter from him?"

Think hard, there is always a reason for the Fire Grip's actions, often more than one. In vision the Raccoon held out a token, but your lover carried it to this room, while Heugen here kept his hands clean. You think of the coming plot, perhaps the Fire Grip senses it too. Take the gamble, a thrust in darkness.

"You wish me to recall him, perhaps? Because you need his swords more than the vote of Tralmachia?" Silence without chuckling, you can feel it. "Of course I should word it otherwise, from a desire to see him again soon, well before the Ides of the next month."

"Then you have seen them. The wagons, all over center city."

Your turn to be surprised by this news. What could wagons matter? "Blocking traffic no doubt, what an annoyance."

"Annoying, you might say!" His voice is a whip-crack and does not wait for you to banter further. "Dozens of them, parked in place sometimes for days now, and every day more of them. Papers signed by the Baron of Gaden, wheels of Yellow, everything in order, judging by the groaning axles they are loaded to the brim. Yet each one guarded, each one covered." He mutters inaudibly for a time, and you catch "might need to hire that fellow Feldspar again, take a closer look".

"So we agree," you say carefully "the real test will come before the Ides of the Dragon." His silence gives you confidence. "And I'll wager the Captain has mentioned, has he not, of the steps the Empire can take if the new Overlord is not to their liking."

"My agents tell me you would like to fill that role, Myster Altieri."

Laughing at this is easier than breathing, and comes as a relief. You're not the only one fencing in the dark here.

"A crown, Fire Grip, for me? I must first see if the colors match my gown … which at this moment I am not wearing, truth to tell." Well that last was naughty and no denying it: all this time later and you are still only in your robe.

A light cough from the other side. "I shall take you at your word, Myster. Keep your counsel, I will not lay blame. But if you should have some word—"

"I shall urge him, Fire Grip, without dissembling my feelings. Though of course he undertook this course against the advice of both of us, I wager."

Another thrust and you sense one that scores. After a pause, you hear him say without pretense or hauteur, "That was before he suffered the loss of your presence, milady. He will come." And the closed door saves you from showing your open jaw to the highest ranking noble in the city, as he steps back down your stairs.

A last inspiration strikes, one more present I give to my cherished one.

"Lord Heugen!" The steps pause but do not return. "If you should need further counsel, an ally in crisis … may I recommend Lady Citari?"

"The widow Kreel! She has had precious little to say to me, Myster, I feel more an intruder in the palace than ever when her husband lived."

You sense the deflection, on several levels—I am pouring all my foresight into you now.

"Her strength goes beyond a wooden mien, Fire Grip. She has already been of more than *token* benefit to your plans, and can shelter those who come to her cautiously and without threat."

"Interesting advice, coming from you." The steps continue away and once again you are all alone.

And it is too much for you, to be truly alone. The visions are so clear, destruction raining from the sky, the Arbalest's bolt coming too soon, your family suffering because you could not see it all in time. My gift is a curse—who would know better than I!—to see what you cannot amend or alter is to rub a shoulder against Despair.

The isolation cuts against your chest in a growing echo of pain, and at last you determine to signal the Emperor's man. The ring can only be used three times, Morinack instructed in his letter that accompanied it. You kept putting off the contact since you did not know enough. And that has not changed, but time feels short. Gazing at the plain iron ax symbol you doubt it has any magic at all. Yet just speak a few words while wearing it, nothing lost by trying.

For a moment nothing happens. Then a portion of the room before you looks darker, as if the lantern light fails to reach it somehow. No, because there is no light where the vision ends.

"Morinack? Milord Emperor's Hand, are you there?"

"Who—milady Altieri, I believe? Are you aware of the time?"

"Hardly ever, milord." You look belatedly out the window; it is the blackest hour of the early evening. "I beg your pardon, Emperor's Hand, but—"

"No matter, just a moment: and please, Morinack." A steady glow appears on a bedside table, from a Light-spelled lantern that illumines a remarkably plain chamber. Sitting up and running a hand through his hair is what appears to be a rather handsome boy, in plain black nightclothes with his legs dangling a foot above the floor. A Halfling, the first you've known, so hard to see him as a grown-up, especially when he peers out at you and smiles.

"The rings work, I see, good. I'll have to congratulate Melvod, whenever he's sober." He fingers his without looking, and you think of Justin with a thrill in your chest. Heugen wanted to send him a message.

"Mil—Morinack, I thought it best to brief you as I fear the situation will not await the vote."

"The vote. So you mean, the first ballot was delayed? Did you meet our man?"

"Yes and no, milord. The vote was indeed prorogued by your agent—"

"Then you've spoken with Captain Th'lendor."

"Indeed, no, he has been slain. Have you no word?"

"Just a few bandit prisoners sent back by Captain Thyme. Slain, what happened? And who stopped the vote?"

"Captain Thyme, he inherited the flag and made it to the city. On a gryphon's back." You cannot forbear a touch of pride at that.

Morinack whistles, shaking his head. "Astor's loins, Hansen said he was capable." He looks back up at you through the vision-portal. "And now, where is he?"

"In the north, recruiting the vote of Tralmachia's baron." You feel a clutch of fear then, your vision of the Fire Ants fighting doomed in the dark vale does not augur well. Is Justin still alive? The patch of vision before you seems to widen but Morinack's light does not extend to it. Is something going awry with the spell?

"But this is not to the point, Milord. Forces within the city are preparing to move, to launch a coup of some kind, well before the next vote, and perhaps within days."

"Can they succeed?" A world of trust and burden in so few words. Part of you still wants to laugh, at this child sitting on his bed and playing grown-up. But in his eyes are the plans that overset an empire. Everyone knows, Yula does nothing without consulting the Halfling. You swallow.

"I believe they can, milord. Or rather, one of them will draw off enough of the city's strength to allow the other ... it is hard to gauge the outlines of his power, a miraculous lore I have never seen. Whether one is puppet to the other I cannot tell, but it matters nothing. My people will die without aid."

He nods, again play-acting the adult so perfectly, and sits a moment with crooked arms and one hand across his mouth. Yet someone speaks clearly.

"W'starrah?"

Something within the patch of added darkness, a voice weak yet familiar echoing from deep stone walls. Surely, you are imagining things, your fondest wish takes shape to distract you.

"Justin? My captain, where are you?"

"W'starrah? I can see you, but there is no light here."

"Milady, is there someone there with you now?"

Frantic, you ignore Morinack and turn to bring the lone lantern before you, right to the edge of this dark portal. A few glimmers of radiance as if through an ebon velvet curtain, the merest outline of a cell carved into the native rock, bars as thick as a wrist, the shape of something human and beloved sitting up in a corner.

"My captain, what has happened?"

"Betrayed. The Baron ignored my truce-flag. Took me prisoner. My men, cut off outside the keep." He is in pain, physical and spiritual, nothing of his former attempts to act the arrogant Elvish nobleman. This is the honest leader of men who took you in his arms, whose breath you felt enter you but never kissed. He suffers keenly his failure, and you know the feeling. Anything for him.

"My Captain, I am alone." What can you offer him but your honesty.

"Myster Altieri, who are you speaking to?"

"The city will be under attack very soon—the Red House and Devout Teretheny conspire, perhaps together, to submerge the city in fire and war. We need you here. I need you."

"W'starrah, I … I have failed you."

"Justin," your voice cracks, still doubting this a dream, but so be it, even in such a dire scenario the sight and sound of him is worth having. "Justin, my love, come back to me. May Argens bless you, and see you through all trials, and bring you back. Hurry, my love, I have not long."

Your prayer has never been more sincere, and that is the vessel I must have, to give my help. A kind of glow susurrates in that darkened cell, illuminating without eyes, and settling on the Captain's ring, and his heart. He stands, you sense from hearing rather than seeing. But now Morinack has become insistent.

"Myster Altieri! Can you still hear me?"

The darkened extra patch of vision is gone. "No!" your cry is instinctual, rather than conversational.

"I can still hear you. I shall send troops, by sea may be quicker."

"Do not," you say with fervor. "Imperial soldiers by sea will be a lightning rod for revolt. Or else why did you attempt this mission?"

"But you say it is hopeless."

"No, Emperor's Hand. Hold your troops in readiness, if you would be guided by my advice. The Fire Grip is a good man—you will have no great friend in him, but he serves the city well and does not hunger for war. This conspiracy must be resisted from within, or nothing will change between my Mark and the Empire."

"You ask much, priestess. What men have you in command, if the Captain's company is so far away?"

"More than swords will be needed, milord. We must look to the innocent, those already injured by these foul schemes. I hope to avoid the worst, and repair the damage done through ... through practice. Ours is an unquiet city just now, milord, and such a place is where the art of healing is best learned, to quote the healer."

"The healer! You've met Kama?"

You look back at the Halfling in surprise. What can this great lord know of such a quiet fellow?

"I want you to do anything he advises, Myster Altieri. I had no idea where he had—Trust him with your life, do you understand me?"

He speaks with the authority of someone who has ordered the lives and deaths of thousands, and you nod as if now the child yourself. The fire of this unsuspected comradery only reminds you with a sting of your isolation. To have been the least member of his adventuring band, the lowliest soldier in your beloved's company, would mean more to you than your rank and wealth and all.

"Three days, Myster Altieri: I give you that space in which to head off this uprising. If I have heard nothing I will mobilize Hansen's corps and they will be at your gates in less than a fortnight."

He may have had more to say, but you cannot care any further about what the Emperor wants. Your heart is filled with regret, for a daughter estranged, for friends offended, and a lover who will never see you again. The contact of the ring-spell falls away from apathy. You sink to your knees, not just from exhaustion but from the bitter reflection that in my service, you have no one.

⊕ ⊕ ⊕

As time passed? The lantern rests on the floor next to you, and outside it is still dark. That gem keeps leering at you, drawing your mind to it so that the body must follow. No food or sleep, you are too weak to resist it now, and as your hand reaches to the belt-gem whose visions come from nature's magic more than any sorcery of man, I give you a final gift, a cruel present.

Before you touch it, I take back the vision-power.

The images flooding you now are only from a blinded Insectir, robbed by chance and following a trail of murders to recover its own. You see the tunnels, the teeming thousands of willing servitors in all classes—some with weapons and armor like mortals but extra arms and gemstone eyes—you see small groups of them searching darkened streets on *this* side of the Tepid, but now they all stiffen in recognition and face the temple of the Stargazer. You are safe only for the moment, since so many well-lit streets lie between you. But the patrols return to the underground, through the tunnels they will come much closer. The alcove behind the statue is real. Dug there centuries ago at first by men but now invaded by *them*, it can serve to reach this tower, as you thought you only imagined before.

The secret door is locked facing their side. You have only to open it. And though you know not how, that not-you voice inside makes you wish to open it.

I cannot help anymore, only watch as you stagger back with unblinking eyes and scream in frustration, abandonment and fear. The cruel present, indeed. Knocking over the lantern you stagger to the inner chamber, hugging hard as if to save your body from falling. The bedtable, you root among the empty boxes to find one with crème still inside. You stare at it in your trembling hand, then hurl it away with a growl of horror. But now you tremble all over, from its lack, my withdrawal and the horror you have seen. What is the ambition of Carnad Mias to this, even the dread plan of destruction that Teretheny plans, compared to the crawling horde of inhuman evil that now swarms among your family, hunting your thoughts and what you have stolen?

In a frenzy you try to pray to me, for return and solace and the foreknowledge you have had of me since childhood. But your mouth is already filling with clicks and chokes, as my eyes are stuffed with tears. For you would not do what is needful, if you could see the cost. Just as if I could somehow take the gift of vision from myself, I would have never let you leave.

But my protection, cherished one, would not save this city. You must decide alone, without me or your promised Captain. You recriminate me, briefly and justly, for leaving you without friend or family. Then you head to the outer door at last, pulling back the bolt and throwing open the portal because death at an assassin's hand would be warm and loving compared to what lies beyond the alcove. Feet barely touching the treads, you flee the tower and head out into the city. There's a spirit of enervation and panic driving you now, a wine too long sampled and fueled by your fears. It seems dark, though the center-city lights could be the sun. You see the wagons everywhere, guards with Yellow emblems forcing all and sundry away.

There are other people too, men and children and Colors, weapons, confusion, looking your way, faces unreadable, some reaching out, probably to tear you to pieces. These are humans, and the not-you voice is in charge now, repulsed and alien to these warmbloods, it drives you stumbling, running.

Some of the two-legged aliens call out to you, words that used to mean something, perhaps your title or name. You click and grunt back, snapping arms away from their grasp, dodging past one pair who walked together and now chase you with tears in their eyes. There was a smell about them, tobacco and something else, and it makes you want to double over in pain and loss, but you run on head-down and around the corner.

Into a wagon, hard enough perhaps to crack your arm, but it does not move an inch. The tarp is no longer as tight as it might have been, and you thrust your hand beneath a spot where it arches. Sand. As deep as you can reach, nothing but the bone-dry weight of the desert, even at night and weeks away feeling a little warm. Enough sand to hide several men, who would have made the load little heavier, but the tarp much tighter.

Glass is made from sand.

The guards turn and you gather from their tone, not their words, that you must leave. One stands with two swords drawn, legs spread in the desert fighting style, looking like half a spider. Nothing simpler; you run as from a storm, without heed, without one sandal, without Chaktha or Kat's hug or a last kiss for your lost daughter. Without him. It is darker than night could make it, a river nearby smells more familiar to the not-you as the path presses further down, where there are tunnels near the bank that none of the two-legs have found. You can see in your mind where they are now. The part that is still-you is fleeing back to the light, but it cannot find the way to move your legs anymore. Only your mouth, screaming gutturals that sound like crime down here, a sure signal to all who would live to stay away.

Just before you reach the nearest entrance, an instinct prompts you to stop screaming. Above the patter of your feet you can hear hard clacks on the wharf-boards, the lick of river waves, and a little sigh from the night breeze, or perhaps a stallion's whinny. Faintly you catch the edge of a sailor-song, the grouse of a single gull, and a metallic rhythm, a kind of *tak ting-tak*. You call again, but not-you still controls your feet and the metal sound falls further away.

You are close enough now to the servitors, three warrior-bugs who emerge to seize arms and waist in shell-sharp pincers. Your feet no longer matter, as you are carried spread-eagled below the earth and into tunnels whose odor is barely breathable. Coughing, screaming, calling out in clickety prayer, cackling with the loss of all Hope, you feel now the weight of passing time. For the bugs are not gentle as they carry you and the way to the Blind King's chamber is long and winding.

The air is miasma by the time you stop, bound there with gluey straps to an earth altar, your light robe nothing but a suggestion of threads and your skin already bleeding from a dozen cuts. One of your feet may be gone, but you do not look down for only the albino ant the size of a man fills your mind. The eye, where is it, and how to open the door. Some part of you is still there, still believes in me, and refuses to say. The blind head turns slightly aside, and there in your vision looms a beetle-crab-hornet larger than Chaktha, whose every limb ends in a hoof or claw so razor-sharp it keeps tilting as it clambers up the earth altar to straddle you.

As the Blind King penetrates your mind again, with the same questions, his minion penetrates your flesh, bringing pain you never imagined. The loudest screams do nothing to drown the interrogation inside your skull, and every touch of the creature is laced with acid. It is like fire, and now a blaze kindles inside your body for the last time. Once before the end you glance down to see those magnificent

172

breasts now sliced through in ribbons, their blood joining streams of it down every part of you. The torture-bug chews on fingers as the silent questions continue. You saw none of this coming, your only choice until the end to say no. And this you have done, all you can.

It is enough. The blazing pain sears through the last cords of your mortality like my star-fire, bringing you full circle to a familiar place. The body releases its hold at last, the present finally ends, and I welcome you, my cherished one, with sorrow for all that I foresaw and could not change. For separation from your destined lover. For all that I required of you, to save your family, my city.

And for all I must still demand.

GLOSSARY

Altair Way	street	main thoroughfare of Cryssigens
Ancient	language	tongue of heroes, dragons and beings of power; mortals may not lie when using it
Areghel	hero	first king of the Percentalion, hero of martial wizards
Argens	city	capital city of the Southern Empire, on the central western coast, named for its hero
Argens Demonbender		hero-aspect, major form of devotion to Argens, currently outlawed, emphasizing sorcerous lore and mastery of demons
Argens Hopeforger		hero-aspect, major form of devotion to Argens, emphasizing courage, light and leadership
Argens Stargazer		hero-aspect, major form of devotion to Argens, emphasizing foresight and love
Argensian Empire		aka the Southlands, vast Elven Empire established by Argens, capital city also named Argens
Astor	hero	Perilsgroom, hero of Stealthics from ancient days
Bald Top	mountain	small loaf-shaped mountain the border hills
Battle of Broken Chains		Dolphin 2001 ADR, first victory of the rebellion over Loyalist forces of the North Mark
Battle of the Razor		pivotal battle of ancient times, Despair was ejected from the Lands forever in the year 0 ADR
Battle of Tor Perite		site of decisive battle (Serpent, 2001 ADR) that defeated Viridian XXVII and put Yula I on the throne of Argens
Bedou-uu	race	desert dwelling nomads of the Shimmering Mindsea
bought badge	phrase	insulting term for an officer who purchased a commission he could not earn
Brow of the Ecclesiast		artefact, mystic crown with fabulous powers, burns the unworthy wearer

centar		unit of soldiers, ten dekents = 100 men
Cesmir	barony	southern barony of the North Mark
cestus	weapon	spiked metal glove used by gladiators
Charnel Testing		an attempt to wear the Brow of the Ecclesiast, which results in death by burning for the unworthy
Conar	city	capital of the kingdom of Men, named for its hero
Cryssians	sect	devotees of Cryss Altair
Cryssigens	city	capital city of the North Mark, wealthy and Color-ful
Dagnaluviran	song	heroic tale of love between Dagnar and Elosira
dekent		unit of soldiers, one dekent equals ten men (led by a dekentar)
dekentar		junior officer's rank in the army or guards
Devouting Sinter		monastery of holy men in Gaden, bordering the Shimmering Mindsea
Earthcut River		runs through Gaden and Cesmir to the Western Sea
Ekhonon	hero	second son of Conar, judgement and architecture
Exemplars	hero	minor heroes of ancient times
Far Mark		recently recolonized duchy of the Argensian Empire, next to the Swords of Stone
Fire Grip	title	City Commander of Cryssigens, regent of the Mark in the absence of the Overlord
Flame of the First		mild oath, reference to Argens who caught a slice of the Sun in his hand
Gaden	barony	east-central barony of the North Mark
Gelvorging Deep		thick forested area, unsettled and hiding bandits or monsters
glassteel		clear substance harder than metal
Grog's Lees	tavern	modest, in The Boards neighborhood of Cryssigens
Highforge	title	rank given to the Preacher worthy of the Brow of the Ecclesiast
Horn of the Serpent		relic of those devoted to Khoirah the Betrayer, stolen by Trekelny and now lost (*see Three Minutes to Midnight*)

House Cups	title	heads of various Colors in Cryssigens, wielding great wealth and influence
Ides of the Dolphin		date, mid-point of the 2nd month, 15th
Imperial Domain		barony, gorgeous settled lands adjacent to Argens and direct vassalage to the Emperor
Insectir	monster	giant bug creatures, repugnant to Elves
intakta volar	language	in Ancient: I wish for healing
kemetaria	feature	burial ground, a Despairing practice to put bodies under the earth instead of cremation
Khoirah	anti-hero	the Betrayer, third son of Conar who treated with Despair in ancient times
lith	drug	performance enhancing, addictive, poisonous
Ma-Eldar	hero	Hopelord of Elves, father of Argens
Master of Horse		leader of all Imperial cavalry
North Mark		northern duchy of Argens, with a history of rebellion; capital city Cryssigens
noun-chakas	weapon	two wooden hafts connected by a few links of chain
Nubian	race	tall black Men living in the Southern jungle, fearsome warriors
odd as three feet		phrase, reference to demonic creatures, meaning something is very strange or unexpected
Old City		northeastern quarter of Cryssigens, once wealthy but long since abandoned
Overlord	title	aka North Mark, title of the ruler of that duchy
Palace o. t. Sun	castle	Emperor's dwelling in Argens' capital
Patriarch	title	church leader in a nation or great city
pentadek		unit of soldiers, five dekents – 50 men
piazzo		center of abandoned Old Cryss, open paved area with temples and more
Ring of Peace	miracle	Telholian invocation creating a no-magic, no-violence zone
Salva Way		bordering the piazzo in Old Cryss
Scapegrace Street		bordering the piazzo in Old Cryss
Shard Demon	monster	held prisoner beneath the palace in Cryssigens

Shimmering Mindsea		large sandy desert between Argens and the Swords of Stone
silversteel		magical metal, unbreakable and rare
somnos	drug	induces sleep
Son of the Sun	title	honorific title for the Emperor, successor to Argens
strategos	title	senior officer's rank in the army or guard
Sun Throne		Emperor's throne in Argens, also a reference to the Emperor's rank
Tamar	city	small trading city about a day's journey from Cryssigens
Telhol	hero	fourth son of Conar, hero of peace and healing
Tepid River		separates Cryssigens from the Old City on its way to the Western Sea
The Boards		poor neighborhood in Cryssigens bordering the River Cryss
Tralmachia	barony	northernmost barony of the North Mark, mountainous and isolated
Viper	sect	secret police under Viridian, now outlawed

Shards of Light I: The Ring and the Flag

A Sword and Sorcery novel from the Lands of Hope.

Newly-graduated imperial officer Justin is convinced he has no future, and hearing the details of the secret mission he's assigned for the Emperor won't change his mind. Civil War threatens the North Mark. Justin must race against time to form a company, and lead his men into the center of the web; but what happens when his loyalty to the Empire means the death of those who follow him?

available as eBook and in print
ISBN 978-3-95681-094-7

Sign up for Will Hahn's Gentle Reminders
And get a free copy of "Two Tales" from the Lands of Hope.

Two short stories for your reading pleasure await you. Go to:

www.williamlhahn.com/reminders/

and grab them right away. Will will only contact you if there's something interesting to share, and you can unsubscribe at any time.

SHARDS OF LIGHT II: FENCING REPUTATION

A Sword and Sorcery novel from the Lands of Hope.

When the elven lords, preachers and merchants of Cryssigens need wrongs righted without clues, they look for the stealthic Feldspar to solve their problems. But the legend without a face is hard to find: and when Feldspar takes a commission from the most famous, and beautiful, priestess in the city, he finds problems of his own piling up, and is forced to choose between Hope and safety.

available as eBook and in print
ISBN 978-3-95681-095-4

SHARDS OF LIGHT IV: SHARDS OF LIGHT

A Sword and Sorcery novel from the Lands of Hope.

The North Mark teeters toward a rebellion. Only three heroes, barely acquainted and scattered far, have the chance between them to avert war and ruin. Can Captain Justin, Stealthic Feldspar, and W'starrah Altieri crush the conspiracy's heart before the wave of fire the beautiful priestess has foreseen engulfs her and the city of Cryssigens?
The final volume of the series illuminates the fate of a kingdom.

Coming soon

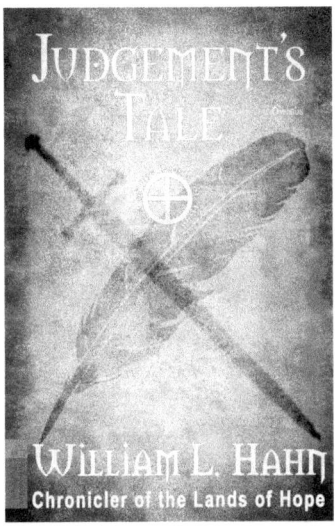

Two millenia of peace are coming to an end.

For twenty centuries the Lands of Hope prospered from their Heroes' peace, but suffer now from their absence. Chaos grows in the central kingdom of the Lands of Hope known as the Percentalion. Even the bravest adventurers seem unable to travel in or out safely. The sundered populations are trapped there, beyond communication and without hope.

Worse yet, the liche Wolga Vrule plots escape from his extra-worldly prison to unleash a tide of undeath, and enlists the Earth Demon Kog, who ruled the Percentalion millennia ago, as an uneasy ally.

On the western coast of the Lands of Hope, Solemn Judgement comes ashore, having journeyed with his father across the ocean. Solemn arrives both a stranger and and orphan, driven to complete the lore his father died to give him. Will he discover Wolga Vrule's plan in time to prevent the return of Despair?

continues in "Eye of Kog"

THE PLANE OF DREAMS

A standalone novel from the Lands of Hope

In the southern empire of Argens just roiled by the rebellion of Yula, a band of adventurers returns from the Shimmering Mindsea bearing enormous treasure and minus one of its members. The Tributarians, unaware of the growing threat to the waking world, embark on separate plans. But the spirit of the hero lives on in all of them, as their good deeds have consequences beyond their original intention. Will it be enough to avert the peril they have unwittingly brought about?

This first epic-length tale set in the Lands of Hope features a complex world and intelligent, dedicated characters whose actions entwine over distances and beyond their own comprehension. Like any world worth living in, the Lands have humor, mystery, horror and action to delight and entertain the reader.

available as eBook and in print
ISBN 978-3-95681-066-4